FLIGHT INTO DARKNESS

The FLIGHT TRILOGY

BOOK ONE
Flight to Paradise

BOOK TWO
Flight into Darkness

BOOK THREE
Flight to Freedom

Please visit author's website for current and future works.
www.coebooks.com

DEDICATION

To commercial airline employees, air traffic controllers, fire and rescue, air marshals, security officers, inspectors, law enforcement, medical personnel, and all those who dedicate their lives to the common goal of ensuring that when we fly on a commercial airline, we are flying on the safest and most efficient form of transportation.

FLIGHT INTO

Darkness

A novel by
Mike Coe

ISBN-13: 978-0-61556-211-7

PRINTED IN THE UNITED STATES OF AMERICA

CoeBooks.com

PART I

"The Lord is my shepherd; I shall not want. He makes me to lie down in green pastures; he leads me beside the still waters. He restores my soul; He leads me in the paths of righteousness for His name sake." Psalm 23:1-3

CHAPTER 1

Thursday, July 11, 2002

Captain Ryan Mitchell waited patiently in the left seat on the flight deck of the Boeing 767. He checked the time—10:59 p.m. The checklists were complete, passengers briefed, and flight attendants seated. All that remained was a takeoff clearance from the control tower. His mind instinctively rehearsed the litany of emergency steps committed to memory in the event of a problem during takeoff: a blown tire; an engine fire or failure; a bird strike.

He breathed deep and exhaled slowly to relieve the stress as he anticipated the most critical part of the flight. Despite the tens of thousands of takeoffs he'd made during his airline career, physiological forces beyond his control always sensed when takeoff was imminent. Twin adrenal glands stood ready to meter adrenaline into his bloodstream, just as multiple fuel pumps would soon supply the combustion chambers of the two turbofan jet engines bolted under the wings of the B-767 with a metered supply of jet fuel. Man and machine as one working in unison to lift hundreds of thousands of pounds of metal safely into the air.

Amid the anxious anticipation of flight, thoughts of his

wife and family brought a subliminal wave of calm. The past fifteen years with Keri—the wife of his dreams—had slipped by in the blink of an eye. Their love for each other had matured over the years as their family had grown. His son, David, now fifteen, was a small-scale replica of his dad. When describing David, Keri would jokingly say, "The nut didn't fall far from the tree."

Born on Mother's Day 1993, their daughter, Martha—named after Ryan's mother—had Keri's beauty and Ryan's determined will. He longed to return to them; to hold Keri in his arms and never let go.

Countless separations from his family weighed on his heart. He'd grown weary from the numbing routine of an airline pilot: drive to the airport; spend two to three days traveling to remote locations; sleep in strange hotel beds; return home for a couple of days—repeating the cycle, week after week, year after year. Was it worth it?

This trip was especially painful. Today was his and Keri's fifteenth wedding anniversary—another anniversary they were forced to spend alone.

The unusually lengthy delay from the control tower tempered his anxiety. The background sounds of air blowing from cooling fans and hissing through vents in the cockpit engulfed him in a protective white noise.

He gazed out beyond the windscreen and into the still night. His pre-takeoff anxiety was suddenly replaced by a wave of amnesia. He had no memory of traveling to the airport. No memory of conducting the pre-flight planning. No memory of how he arrived at the end of the runway ready for takeoff. It was as if he'd been beamed from beneath the covers of his bed, transported to the Los Angeles International Airport (LAX), and dropped into the cockpit of a commercial jet waiting for takeoff—another routine red-eye to New York (JFK).

Before he had time to unravel his confused thoughts and

any fascination he might have with mind paralysis or time travel, the voice of the tower controller crackled in his left ear.

"Angel eleven heavy maintain three thousand, runway two five right, cleared for takeoff."

A sudden jolt of fresh adrenalin charged through his veins vaporizing his reflective state. His heart rate quickened. His muscles tensed. His pupils dilated for extra sight.

Ryan's copilot, responsible for handling the radio calls, repeated the clearance through the small boom-mike resting against his lip, "Maintain three, cleared for takeoff on two five right. What are the winds?"

"Wind two five zero at five."

"Thank you, Angel eleven heavy."

Ryan reached up to the overhead panel, flipped on the landing lights, eased the throttles forward, and maneuvered the B-767 onto the runway. After aligning the jet's nose wheel with the centerline, he advanced the throttles to 50%, checked the engine gauges, and then commanded, "Arm autothrottle. Engage N1/EPR."

The copilot flipped the Auto/Throttle Arm Switch to ARM and pressed the N1/EPR button. The throttles automatically advanced to computed, takeoff power.

The jet rumbled and shook as the large turbofans underneath each wing whirled to life, sucking in air like two, giant vacuums. The compressed air moving at hundreds of miles per hour blended with a perfectly metered mist of kerosene deep within the chambers of the jet's engines. Passing through rings of igniters, the gaseous mixture exploded. The newly generated energy from the high pressure air and volatile vapors converted into thrust, pushing the monstrous machine down the runway, slowly at first, then faster and faster until the big jet broke free of Earth's hold and *into the darkness*.

The tower controller said, "Angel eleven heavy contact departure."

"Roger, Angel eleven heavy switching to departure."

Hanging motionless in the smooth air above a moving Earth of twinkling lights, an uncontrollable eeriness washed over Ryan—a déjà vu of a familiar place filled with strange and unrecognizable sensations. A sluggish disconnect isolated him from reality. Something was terribly wrong.

His copilot checked in with the new controller. "Departure, good evening. Angel eleven heavy with you passing through two thousand for three thousand."

Ryan struggled to remember the copilot's name.

Nothing.

"Angel eleven heavy, Los Angeles departure radar contact. Good evening. Climb and maintain ten thousand."

The nameless copilot responded, "Roger, ten thousand Angel eleven heavy."

Ryan glanced over at the stranger. Why couldn't he remember the man's name? Why couldn't he remember *anything*?

He knew for certain it was his fifteenth anniversary. He and Keri had planned a quiet, romantic dinner at the Village Mediterranean Rim on Del Mar; a charming, cozy, and eclectic restaurant in San Clemente. His good friend and co-worker, Rex Dean, had offered to trade trips with him so Ryan could be off for his anniversary—or at least he thought he had.

Why am I here?

With each clearance to a new altitude, the copilot dialed the digits into the flight control panel on the glareshield, ensuring the autopilot would not exceed the clearance limit. Standard procedures required that Ryan verbally confirm any changes made to the altitude setting, which he did.

Passing through five thousand feet, Ryan selected the autopilot ON as the big jet powered its way higher into the black sky.

He tried to recall any conversations he'd had with his copilot. He tried to remember details of getting to the airport.

Nothing.

It was as if the events leading up to takeoff had been erased from his memory.

What's going on? Did I tell Keri goodbye before leaving home? Why can't I remember?

His mind waffled back-and-forth between his pilot duties and his apparent lapse of memory. The dialogue between the air traffic controller and the copilot continued as the jet stair-stepped higher into the night.

"Angel eleven heavy turn left heading one eight zero."

"One eighty, Angel eleven heavy," the copilot replied.

Instinctively, Ryan reached up to the glareshield and dialed in one eight zero on the heading-selector knob, commanding the autopilot to bank the jet to the selected heading.

The silky-smooth air beneath the jet's wings masked the sensation of being hurled through the black of night at more than two hundred miles per hour. Every event prior to takeoff remained an enigma, including his nameless copilot.

That's odd. The radios are too quiet.

His eyes locked on the altimeter spinning past ten thousand feet. He turned to the copilot, expecting to see him alarmed by the jet's unmonitored flight, but, instead, the copilot had one foot propped up, reading a novel, seemingly enjoying himself.

"You must read this," the copilot said. "Very inspiring."

What's that dimwit doing? We can't just blast through the sky without a clearance!

Ryan's uneasiness morphed into fear. He tried to speak but couldn't find his voice. Suddenly, he was no longer in command of the airliner, but a spectator, suspended, floating at the top of the cockpit.

I'm dreaming.

While consciously aware yet still deep asleep, the absurdities—floating in the air, a nameless disinterested, novel-reading copilot, and the jet blasting through the night sky—

were now acceptable conundrums within his unconscious mind. As long as he stayed lucid, he was in control. He could invite characters—imagined or real—to join him. In the safety of his dream he could release his frustrations, rehearse a conversation, or experience a pleasurable fantasy.

The copilot turned and looked up at Ryan. The fact that Ryan was floating like a helium balloon against the ceiling of the cockpit did not concern the nameless, novel-reading copilot. "This book is awesome!"

Ryan tried to speak. His mouth moved, but his words were muted. He was unable to engage the copilot in conversation. He was trapped in his dream as a spectator.

The copilot marked his place in the book with a two-dollar bill, and then he closed it, and admired the cover. "So inspiring. You must read this."

Ryan strained, hoping the book's title might provide a clue to why his subconscious had propelled him into such a crazy dream. The copilot's hand blocked all but one word of the title: *Freedom.*

The book had something to do with freedom. It meant nothing to Ryan.

The copilot locked eyes with Ryan. In an out of character tone, the novel-reading pilot stated boldly in a voice much deeper than he had previously used, "Freedom is found in hope. You must not forget that. Everyone is depending on you. If you don't find the answers, we will all die. It's up to you. Everything is up to you. You must find freedom! Time is running out!"

In the blink of an eye, the novel-reading copilot was no longer dressed casually and was no longer reading his novel. He had returned to his piloting duties appearing to be in complete control of the jet.

Ryan watched as the two pilots seated beneath him conducted their routine duties.

Then, the captain turned, looked up at him and smiled.

You've got to be kidding—Rex?

"How's it going, Dude?" Rex said.

Why is Rex in my dream? He trip traded with me and is flying my LAX to JFK red-eye. He is probably half-way to New York by now. Sure. That's why he is in my dream.

Ryan played along, knowing he was not actually talking to Rex. "Thanks for flying my trip tonight. See you when you get home."

I think I'll leave now and float away to something more interesting.

Before he willed his dream to another setting, Rex said, "Are you ready?"

"Ready for what?"

Silence.

"Rex! Ready for what?"

My voice is still muted.

Rex turned back to his piloting duties. Ryan urged his subconscious to find another fantasy—a different location—but, lucid or not, he was unable to will his dream in another direction. He was trapped in a familiar recurring nightmare, unable to escape the horror he knew was imminent—paralyzed on the wrong side of Death's door.

Oh no! Not again. I'm so sick of this.

Fear returned. His heart pumped wildly in his chest.

His recurring nightmare was, no doubt, the result of months of reflection on the brutal execution of the innocent pilots—just like himself—during the tragedy of 9/11. Until now, the pilots in his dream had been nameless. This time the dream was different. Rex was his friend.

He called out to warn Rex of what Ryan knew was coming, but, again, his attempt was muted by the dreammaker. Rex sat calmly at the controls.

Ryan turned to the copilot. He was no longer in his white pilot shirt, but, instead, now dressed in a monk's hooded cowl. The hooded man looked up at him. The shadowed face of an albino man stared back, his blue eyeballs twitching back and forth like two pendulums on a metronome rocking at 300 beats per minute.

This is too weird. Remember, it's all a dream. It's not real. I'll wake up and it will all be over. Get ready! Here it comes!

BAM! BAM! BAM!

The cockpit door burst open and slammed against the wall. In a blur of bodies and flailing arms, two men charged through the opened door, screaming wildly. Within seconds, in one swift motion, the first man yanked Rex's head to the side and sliced a sharp blade across his exposed neck. The razor-sharp weapon quickly parted the protective layers of skin and muscles and ripped open his carotid artery and jugular vein spewing life-giving blood destined for his brain throughout the cockpit. Rex's body fell limp in his blood-soaked seat.

NO!

He attempted to reach for the attacker, but the fury that raged within his muscles was met with an unyielding resistance.

Please! Stop!

It was too late. Rex's head, severed to the fifth and sixth vertebra of his spine, hung limp. The side cockpit window was opaque with bright, red blood.

The jet continued its climb into the tranquil sky undisturbed under the precise control of the autopilot.

The first man, his eyes dilated and crazed, turned and met Ryan's panicked stare. In his right hand, the killer clinched a blood-soaked black ceramic knife. His hands and arms were red up to his elbows. Dream or no dream, it felt real…it looked real.

Rex's voice yelled out, "Act, don't think!"

How is that possible? Rex is dead.

Unexplainably, as if the act of violence had never happened, Rex peered from behind the lunatic, his head still attached to his body; no sight of blood anywhere. "Ryan, don't be blinded by your fear, act! Act now!"

"What do you mean?"

"Everything you need is here. You'll find answers in the here."

"What, 'find answers in the here'. That makes no sense! Answers to what?"

"Don't let your fear blind you, get busy!"

Rex opened a small, compartment door in the ceiling of the cockpit and pulled out a rope that uncoiled onto the floor. One end of the rope remained attached to an anchor point in the ceiling. It was the emergency rope used by pilots to egress from the cockpit in the event normal exits are blocked. The rope had sufficient length to allow the pilot to repel down the exterior of the fuselage to the ground, but the rope was useless in flight.

Rex gathered the rope, crouched in the captain's seat, and then dove through the cockpit's thick, multi-layered, side window, as though it did not exist. He was gone, swept away into the dark of night.

Ryan's attention returned to the crazed killer only seconds before the man jabbed the ceramic knife deep into Ryan's chest. Ryan's body lurched. His eyes fluttered open in a frightened panic. Soaked in sweat, he jerked up on his elbow.

Where am I?

Tangible realities streamed into his mind: home, bed, my dream—a nightmare. His heart slowed to a normal rhythm. His muscles relaxed. He checked the clock on the nightstand—1:46 a.m.

He glanced over at Keri. She was sound asleep.

He remembered. He and Keri *had* gone to dinner. Rex *was* flying his trip. No one had died. He lay back in bed and took a deep, cleansing breath and exhaled, hoping to purge his mind of the horrid nightmare.

When will the pain stop?

His weekly flights to the East Coast—especially to New York and Boston—reinforced the visual images of horror choreographed by his evil dreammaker—images used to torment him for the past ten months.

On Ryan's descents for arrival at New York's Kennedy or La Guardia airports, he would often gaze out the cockpit window at the location where the Twin Towers had once pierced the Manhattan skyline. At the mercy of demon-possessed men on a mission of death, thoughts of the panicked passengers and crewmembers aboard United Flight 175 riveted to his core.

On Ryan's morning departures from Boston's Logan International Airport headed for LAX, he retraced the steps of the doomed pilots on American Airlines Flight 11.

Nothing would ever be the same. The tragedy of 9/11 changed everything, acting as the catalyst that ignited much deeper struggles in Ryan's life. His life-long love for flying had ebbed years earlier, replaced by a much greater passion—his family. The massive amounts of time he spent away from home weighed heavy on his heart. His children were growing up fast and he didn't want to miss it—he'd already missed too much.

Perhaps the upheavals in the airline industry—fighting for survival—were simply a divine sign that it was time for a change. The onslaught of cost cuts, layoffs, and bankruptcies had put many pilots on the street; others saw their pay slashed by as much as half.

Every passenger was the next terrorist. Every flight was the next target of some lunatic on a personal mission of death. Ryan had been unable to tell Keri how he *really* felt about his job, afraid she might worry more than she already did.

He wanted to quit flying, find a normal job, and stay home with his family. Possibly move back to the South and raise their children in the same, safe surroundings he and Keri had known growing up. The thought of it brought a sweet relief from the fear of knowing that—it was not *if* but *when*—something as horrid as 9/11 would be repeated.

He closed his eyes, praying that, somehow, his subconscious mind would let him rest for a few hours.

Please God, help me find a way out.

CHAPTER 2

Ryan opened his eyes and checked the time as he'd done at 1:46…2:20…3:15…3:50…and 4:10 a.m., hoping it would be near enough to daylight that he could terminate his nightly dance with Mr. Sandman. The clock on the nightstand glowed—4:59.

Good enough.

His doctor called it "sleep performance anxiety" or the difficulty in returning to sleep after awakening. He'd said, "Simply put, when you wake during the night, you're trying too hard to go back to sleep. You need to relax."

Ryan was cursed with an overactive mind. When asleep, much like the power-saving feature of a computer, his mind compromised a complete shutdown by entering standby, suspend, idle, or sleep mode. If awakened, his neurotransmitters immediately commenced firing data files across the hundreds of trillions of synaptic clefts to waiting neuroreceptors. The endless files of sleep-stopping thoughts whirled through his cerebral analyzer at "thought speed" (six to seven times faster than real time) much like a dead, tree branch might whistle through a wood chipper.

It might be the thought of tasks he needed to do, had done, or had promised to help someone else do. Perhaps a schedule change he needed to submit to flight planning in the morning; or ways to silence the neighbor's annoying, barking dog without doing something he might regret; or the details of a project his fifteen-year-old son, David, needed help with. Each thought led to a new thought, then another, until he tired. Many nights, he wandered the house, a hopeless insomniac, returning to the battleground beneath his sheets, hoping things might be different. They never were. Scorned by the sandman and cursed by Morpheus (the Greek god of dreams), sleep was not his friend.

The many years of irregular flight schedules and relentless disruptions of his circadian rhythm sentenced him to a life of fatigue. He'd slept so little in the past ten months that his fatigue now kept him awake. Sunrises and sunsets were met with the same cold indifference; the horizon merely the thin line dividing fatigue from insomnia.

Beside him, Keri breathed softly, oblivious to the demons of the night. Sleep always found her within a minute of putting her head on the pillow and closing her eyes. She seldom stirred during the night; after eight hours, she woke in the same position in which she had gone to sleep—rested and invigorated. Ryan attributed such perfect sleep to her ability to live in the moment and her peace that was the result of great faith. To her, the far future was next week, and she trusted God completely to take her there whether or not she planned the journey.

Ryan's strong mainspring was wound tight. He dwelled as much in the future as in the present, envisioning where he wished to go, relentlessly mapping the path that ought to lead him to his high goals. Although he, too, trusted in God's divine guidance, he struggled with control issues.

Considering their contrasting natures, they shared a love that seemed unlikely. Yet love was the cord that bound them together, the sinewy fiber that gave them strength to weather disappointment, trials, and even tragedy.

Weary from brooding over another night of broken sleep, he lifted his tired body from the bed, careful not to wake Keri. Pausing, he stared out the open window into the black of morning. A familiar, low, mellow call of a morning dove broke the silence, "coo-ah, coo-coo-coo." It was a mournful, yet pleasing sound that reminded him of the warm country evenings as a young boy growing up in Georgia.

A cool breeze brushed across his face. He drew in a breath then moved quietly around the end of the bed and into his dressing room, pulling the door closed before flipping on the light.

The walk-in closet was large enough to accommodate a "his" and "hers" side. On the "his" side, collared shirts hung on racks, evenly spaced, fronts facing to the right, and systematically ordered: work shirts to the left and casual shirts to the right. On a lower rack, pants hung evenly spaced and ordered. Pull-over shirts were stacked and perfectly folded on shelves. His watch, ID tags, wallet, and keys all in their dedicated place and orientation. His bills were folded and arranged; twenties in the back, ones in the front. Coins were neatly stacked; quarters always on the bottom, then nickels, then pennies, then dimes.

He'd always approached his professional life head-on with a plan; always in control; always expecting to succeed. Every event was handled the same way: understand the situation; develop a plan; execute the plan. His disciplined approach to life had yielded him many trophies. He'd graduated top in his class, both in high school and at the U.S. Naval Academy. He finished first in his pilot training class. He landed an airline job with his top pick of companies.

However, his personal life had not been so perfect. He was blindsided in his first marriage when his California bride, Emily Anderson, abandoned him after two tumultuous years. But the bittersweet circumstances surrounding her departure birthed the miracle that brought him back to Keri, his first love.

His early years of heartache had long been buried in the distant past, replaced by fifteen, wonderful years married to his best friend and soul mate. Their two, beautiful children filled their lives with purpose.

After slipping into a pair of shorts and throwing on a T-shirt, he flipped off the closet light and opened the door. The house was quiet. The children were asleep. He paused beside the bed and gazed down at Keri, still fast asleep. Soon enough she would be called upon to resume her busy duties as a mother and a wife, but for now, she was free to dream.

In many ways, he and Keri were complete opposites, and, though she was as beautiful as the day he met her, it was her charm, her intelligence, her spontaneity, her sense of humor, her laid back, relaxed way of looking at the world that continued to captivate him. His calculated, orderly existence was balanced by her spirited, loving nature and positive outlook on life, something he needed now, more than ever.

He gently eased the covers up over her. She turned, smiling, as she extended a hand for him to join her in bed. He leaned down and kissed her. "Go back to sleep," he whispered. "I'm going downstairs."

"Just for a minute," she pleaded, then threw the covers back and scooted over to make room. She smiled.

As the skilled archer, Cupid, might propel one of his gold-headed arrows, her invitation zeroed in on the soft spot in his heart: the spot she owned and controlled. Contemplating her request, his body tingled with desire to embrace her. He eased in beside her, pulling the covers over his legs. She snuggled up close, her warm hand slipping under his shirt and gently roaming across his chest and stomach. A surge of blood rushed through his body.

"Did you sleep?" she said in a soft voice.

"I don't know if you call it sleep. I had the dream again."

She put her head on his shoulder and pulled him tight.

"What can we do?"

"But this time it was different."

"How?"

"The pilots were more than foggy aberrations…I mean I could see their faces…and guess who the captain was?"

"Who?"

"Rex."

"Weird. Why was Rex in your dream?"

"I guess he was on my mind. It could be because he flew my trip last night. It was as if I was in the cockpit with him while he was flying to New York…until things got ugly. This time the details were more vivid and in color. Instead of some no-name, dream pilots, I had to watch the attackers butcher Rex—"

"Sick!"

"Yeah, it was bad. I had to keep telling myself it was only a dream, but, boy, did it feel real."

As she listened, her hand continued its soothing exploration of his body. Her touch eased his weary mind and comforted his soul like nothing else could.

"After waking up in a cold sweat, I tried to go back to sleep, but, as always, it was a futile effort. I just wish I could get *one* good night of sleep—just one."

"Poor Baby." She kissed him on the chest. Her hand slipped below his waist. Her rubbing had aroused him.

"I'm just sick of it all—the company, the job—always waiting for some wacko terrorist to slip through security and pick my plane to transport him into the afterlife."

"I wish you didn't have to fly anymore."

"I really don't have a choice."

"When I think back on what happened, it all seems like a dream," Keri said. "None of this would be happening to us if my dad had been smarter."

"Don't blame your dad. Remember, if it hadn't been for him, we might not be together today. He couldn't help it that

Gold Street Capital was run by a bunch of crooks. The SEC (Securities and Exchange Commission) should have caught them long before their little Ponzi scheme blew up."

"But really…a hundred million dollars? How could he lose all of it?"

"In hindsight, your dad's big heart was his downfall. He wanted to make everything easy for you—us. Once he learned that he only had a few months to live, he had to act fast. That's when he consolidated his entire estate with Gold Street. At the time, they were one of the few firms able to handle such a large portfolio of real estate, securities, and cash. He just happened to get trapped on the tail end before everything imploded. As far as Ponzi schemes go, that's the worst possible time to get on board. The guys on the front end can make out okay. The poor suckers pulling up the rear get crushed. I'm sure he did his homework and, like I said, he only wanted to make it easy on us."

Keri sniffled.

"Are you okay?" He brushed his hand over her head, pulling her hair back.

"Yeah."

"We need to forget it and move on. Every time we bring it up, it only makes us hurt.

"You're right. It's only money."

He turned and looked into her eyes. "As long as I have you, I don't care if I live in a refrigerator box under the pier." He kissed her.

She smiled and hugged him tight, then kissed him with passion. Engulfed in the warmth of her body, a fresh charge of currents rippled from head to toe. As if she knew, she rolled over on top of him, sat up straddling his hips, and slipped her nightgown off. She encouraged him to lift up while she pulled off his shirt.

As she kissed his neck and ear, she whispered, "Thank you for last night. The meal was wonderful. And afterwards…well…let's just say…the dessert was absolutely scrumdiddlyumptious."

"But you didn't have dessert."

"I'm talking about after we got home…the bath…the massage…and…well, you know. All I can say is that you were amazing!"

He smiled. "No, you are the amazing one. If you'd let me, I would spend the rest of my life bathing you and rubbing lotion all over your body every night."

"I think I like your plan," she said. "You're hired."

"Why, thank you, ma'am," he said playfully in a poor Southern dialect. "Jest you rang yo' silver bell when you is ready for me to come put a good scrubbin' and a rubbin' on you followed by some of my good ol' lovin'."

She smiled then continued to kiss him on the neck, cheek, and lips. In her seductive voice, she said, "You need to relax. It's my turn."

CHAPTER 3

Ryan descended the stairs and proceeded to the kitchen following the sweet and clean aroma of freshly brewed, Costa Rican coffee; a blend he had picked up on a recent trip to San José. After retrieving his favorite mug, he quietly closed the cabinet door then filled his cup. Steam rose from the dark, caffeine-rich liquid as it swirled around years of brown stains.

He sauntered over to the sliding glass door, stood, and gazed out. The black of night, yielding to twilight, releasing the once colorless world from its prison of darkness. He sipped his coffee, taking a moment to admire the garden. Calmer shades of green from elephant ears, pygmy date palms, and creeping ivy showcased the eye-popping effect of delicate roses of various hues, lavender, lilac, climbing bougainvillea, hibiscus, geraniums, hummingbird trumpets, baby blue eyes, bird of paradise, and more. All the credit went to Keri. Amidst her busy schedule, she'd still found time to design a garden that was aesthetically pleasing and inviting; a sanctuary of peace in the middle of a chaotic world.

Keri was *his* sanctuary; his anchor in life. The sight of her smile or the sound of her laughter never failed to cast a light on the dark path he journeyed. Without her, his robotic life would surely remain imprisoned in a colorless existence, adrift in a tumultuous sea.

He studied a cluster of five potted pineapple plants on the near side of the patio. He and Keri had started the small, backyard pineapple "plantation" after learning of the idea on one of his trips to Kauai. New leaf growth had appeared within a couple of months, but after almost two years the plants remained fruitless. It was a depressing example of the relationship between time and reward—if the reward ever comes at all.

The continued ingestion of caffeine ignited his sleep-deprived mind into frenzy, snatching his thoughts from the tranquility of the garden, spiraling them into darkness.

I'm trapped. I need a break from my crazy flying schedule. How can I keep going if I can't sleep? The fatigue is killing me. I'm always irritable and disinterested. I wish I could quit my job. I have to provide for the family. I can't stand to see Keri worry. The kids deserve more. What is happening to my life? Sometimes I think it would be better if I were dead, then they could move on with life.

His dear mother had suffered a slow death after being struck with mind-debilitating Alzheimer's—a disease that slowly robbed her of her memory, thinking, and behavior. St. Peter had denied her the blessing of a swift passage through the pearly gates, but instead cursed her to wander for many years in the chasm that exists between life and death.

This must be what it's like: living in the middle between life and death. Why has God cursed me? He has put me in this darkness. Even when I cry for help, he shuts out my prayers.

The word *God* ricocheted through his subconscious, searching countless subliminal files of positively charged images and phrases, perhaps seeking balance to the onslaught of negative thoughts.

"In this world you will have tribulation. Fear not. I leave

you peace." The words of the Almighty Son of God offered no magical powers regarding his struggle. To the contrary, they burdened him even more.

Fear, I command you—be gone! Nope, didn't work.

When all hope seemed to have taken wings and flown away, he recalled the old adage his mother would often repeat: "It's always darkest before the dawn."

His mind snapped back.

Please! How could it get much darker? Where is the proverbial "dawn" you always clung to, mom? I don't see it!

He chuckled at the thought of his mother's smile. She would surely be smiling at his thoughts. It was not just any smile; it was a particular smile. During his many attempts to rebut his mother's wise advice, telling her she was old fashioned or didn't understand, she often remained silent and simply smiled. It was *that* smile. It was a smile of quiet confidence in her belief that one day her son would understand the source of her faith and trust. He smiled, wishing for one last conversation with her; to hear her encouraging words reflecting her unwavering peace and strength.

Martha Mitchell was a woman of great faith. After her death, the remembrance of the many pragmatic applications of her convictions had inspired Keri and Ryan to consider a broader view of God's divine guidance in everyday situations. It was as if, somehow, every effort to exercise their young faith connected them to Martha.

One such opportunity came with the birth of their daughter. After three years and three miscarriages, Keri had been diagnosed with endometriosis and told that her chances of a full-term pregnancy were infinitesimal. Praying for a miracle while trusting in God's ultimate decision, one year after her diagnosis, Keri delivered a healthy baby girl. They named her Martha.

Even as Ryan reflected—on the miracle of little Martha's birth, the great faith of his mother, and the outstretched hand of support from his beloved Keri—his misery and self pity continued unabated. There was no match for the darkness that engulfed him.

Another sip of coffee fired up the cranial machine. Random images and words from his nightmare popped into his thoughts:

Freedom. Freedom is found in hope. Everyone is depending on you. If you don't find the answers, we will all die. It's up to you. You must find freedom. Time is running out!

Was it that his family would not be free as long as he remained in the chasm between life and death? Life—a normal life—seemed so far away while death seemed so near. He quickly tired of the strain of recounting the details of his dream. It was a puzzle with no answers. He needed more caffeine.

Before turning away he tugged on the sliding glass door, not surprised to find it unlocked.

Why can't she learn to lock the door? I should have checked it last night.

These were the little things that kept him awake at night, especially when he traveled. He attributed many lost hours of sleep to his never ending worries. The simple worry of the door being unlocked—during one of his late-night arousals— would lead to a multitude of 'what ifs'. As a multichannel worrier, cursed with an overactive mind, he always considered the worst case scenario for practically every possibility. After all, it only took one doped-up crackhead roaming the neighborhood in search of something to pawn to enter their house and murder his family in exchange for a trinket of jewelry.

He closed the door, flipped the latch, and then headed for the coffee pot.

After filling his cup, he made his way into the adjacent den, picked up the TV remote, and pressed the ON button. He was instantly drawn to the KTLA news reporter's somber voice. The reporter was on location. A beautiful shot of the

Pacific Ocean filled the background.

Probably another distressed whale...maybe it's a shark attack...or a drowning.

Ryan looked closer. The TV cameras scanned what appeared to be a tragic accident at sea. Rescue boats, rocked by ocean swells, searched through floating debris while helicopters circled above. The camera slowly panned the hopeless scene, occasionally zooming in on pieces of wreckage as the news reporter recapped:

> *"Late last night at approximately eleven thirty, a commercial airliner departing Los Angeles International Airport bound for New York's JFK was shot down by U.S. fighter jets. We have been told that authorization to destroy the airliner was given after officials learned the plane was headed for a target in northern California. Numerous unsuccessful attempts to contact the pilots left officials with little doubt that the plane was under the control of terrorist hijackers."*

"Shot down!"

Impossible! How could that happen?

Ryan focused on the chunks of wreckage, looking for anything that might give him a clue as to which airline: aircraft type; paint scheme; or logo.

The tail. God, no! It's one of ours!

His heart raced. A wave of dizziness ambushed him. His overactive mind scrambled the possibilities like a mixer.

The crew? Are they L.A.-based? Do I know them?

Although he had access to the flight information through the Internet, the company would have it locked out before he could fire up his computer. His mental synapses, faster than any computer, raced to process the known facts.

Last night...LAX to JFK...after eleven...it had to be a widebody...a 767 or 757.

The sound of Keri's bedroom slippers shuffled across the hardwood floor. Ryan turned from the TV and met her gaze. Before he could speak, she had eased up beside him, slipped her arm around his waist, and turned toward the TV. "What's going on?" she asked.

"One of our planes crashed last night."

Keri pulled back. "What?!"

"It crashed off the coast of California just south of San Francisco."

She turned back to the TV. "How do you know it's one of ours?"

"Look at the tail." Ryan pointed to a piece of the vertical stabilizer floating in the water. "See the paint? It's definitely one of ours."

She looked up at Ryan. "Why? What happened?"

"They're saying U.S. fighters shot it down because it had been hijacked and was headed towards a target in San Francisco."

"Why would they shoot down a commercial airliner with hundreds of innocent people on board?"

"If they think a plane is a threat to a protected asset, that's what they say they'll do. I just can't believe they actually did it!"

"That's insane! Have they released the names of the crew?"

"We won't know anything until after they notify the families."

It was just a matter of time—not *if* but—*when* terrorists would strike again. The thought had haunted him every day since 9/11—especially on the days he flew. Even with the new security enhancements, it was impossible to seal up every crack, especially when the current administration, Congress, and the private sector had failed to act meaningfully on almost half of the recommendations set forth by the *National Commission on Terrorists Attacks Upon the United States* (9/11 commission). And thanks to airline executives whining about costs, airports still didn't have the equipment needed to detect for bombs in carry-on luggage or in cargo.

Keri wrapped her arms around him, both of them continuing to stare at the TV in disbelief. The news reporter had said the pilots did not respond to the air traffic controllers nor did they acknowledge the fighter jet's signals to follow them. This left Ryan with only one logical conclusion: the plane must have been in the hands of the terrorists—but how?

With enhanced classified onboard security protocols, reinforced cockpit doors, and with many pilots now armed with handguns, how could these multiple layers of defense be penetrated? In addition, it had been proven that, since 9/11, passengers would meet any attempted hijacking with potentially lethal resistance.

There was one far-fetched possibility—one that even security experts couldn't dismiss: A terrorist might avoid detection—almost entirely—by infiltrating the ranks of commercial airline pilots. It would only take one person who is associated with a terrorist group—appearing to be a legitimate employee in good standing with the airline—to slip through the cracks.

He had another thought. With the number of airline pilots entering alcohol and drug rehabilitation programs at an all time high, and bankruptcies and divorces among airline employees raging, ruling out a pilot-assisted suicide was not completely out of the question.

Without warning, his mind buzzed in a completely different direction.

Oh my God!

He glanced down at Keri, her eyes still glued to the TV

screen. Beads of sweat popped from the pores on his forehead and underarms. Clamminess washed over him.

He eased away from Keri. "I need to take a shower."

"Okay." She paused, apparently alarmed by his sudden move. "Are you okay?"

"Yeah, I just need to get away from this." He left the den and hurried to the bathroom, pushing back the urge to vomit. Closing the door, he braced himself on the vanity. Covered in a clammy sweat, his legs collapsed beneath him. He eased over to the toilet, closed the lid and sat.

Details from his nightmare ambushed him: Rex; the creepy-hooded, novel-reading copilot; the attackers; the blood. Dizziness danced in his head to the ringing of a chorus of cicadas spinning him to the horrid conclusion.

It was Rex. He was flying that trip—my trip. If he had not trip traded with me, I would be dead...not Rex.

CHAPTER 4

Istanbul, Turkey
Ten months later—Sunday, May 25, 2003

Samael Janus, a tall, broad-shouldered albino man, stepped onto the balcony of his third-story, four-star, boutique hotel, the Hotel Daphnis, and peered down at the shimmering, blue waters of the Golden Horn River. The afternoon sun mirrored sharp flashes of light off the water's surface causing him to squint. His prescription, transition lenses were worthless shields against the dancing diamonds of light. He quickly pulled his wrappers from his pocket and placed them over the prescription lenses.

Much better.

The geriatric-looking wrappers shielded his sensitive eyes and were excellent for hiding the uncontrollable and embarrassing rhythmic movement of his eyeballs. In addition to his heightened sensitivity to light, he'd been plagued since birth with nystagmus (a pendular quivering of the eyes) and a mild case of achromatopsia (inability to see color).

With his bald head shielded beneath a hooded cloak, the moon-faced albino gripped the balcony railing with both hands, closed his eyes, and lifted his head toward the heavens.

His mind journeyed into the distant past—*his* past. As he remembered, a smile spread across his face.

On that glorious day in 1453, under the blood-red moon of a partial eclipse, the words of the prophets rang true when Constantinople—along with its allegiance to Christendom—fell under the ruthless hand of the Ottoman warrior, Mehmet the Conqueror. It marked the beginning of the greatest period of growth for the Ottoman Empire.

A rush of adrenalin burst through his veins. His chest tightened and his white skin tingled with excitement as his time-traveling mind visualized the siege of the city. The screams of slaughtered and tortured Christians echoed in the darkness as blood ran through the streets of the city. Ottoman soldiers and Janissaries massacred men and women, young and old, by the blade of the scimitar. No one was spared. Married women and girls committed suicide to avoid being savagely raped. Men chose to die defending their families to avoid being taken as slaves.

After the killing came the gathering of slaves. The most beautiful women would be added to the harems of sultans. The strongest, young boys would be trained as Janissary warriors. The less fortunate, fair and delicate lads were given over to the soldiers to appease their sexual appetites. The adult men would be sold in the slave markets or chained to the oars of Muslim warships.

From his lofty perch over the Golden Horn, Samael took in the panoramic view and the activities along the quiet river's shores. Couples strolled along her banks. Children played. People sat and read or basked in the sun.

He was drawn to a woman walking alongside a bearded man. The woman's head was covered by a white shawl. The man wore a woolen hat. A young boy, about ten, ran up to the woman and hugged her. As the woman leaned down and embraced the boy in her arms, Samael felt an ache in his heart. His eyes grew watery.

At the age of fifteen, Samael learned from his adopted parents of his abandonment as a newborn in an alley-way dumpster in downtown Chicago. The news clipping read:

> *May 29, 1970: While taking the trash out, a local merchant noticed what appeared to be the head of a small doll protruding above the pile of rubbish. The man said, "When I got closer, I saw the hands moving."*

The first nine of Samael's thirty-three years he'd spent warehoused at St. Mary's Asylum for Boys, a Catholic institution for emotionally troubled adolescents, located on the outskirts of Chicago.

By the early 1970s, the Illinois Department of Children and Family Services had forced almost every orphanage still operating to shut down, allowing only the most emotionally troubled adolescents to live in institutions. With nowhere to go, St. Mary's Asylum had agreed to care for the freakishly abnormal infant until he could be placed in a home.

Samael's horrid appearance resulted in merciless name calling and abuse from the other children. They tagged him with names such as whitey, freak, monster, spot face, and demon-boy.

During the frequent, adoptive viewings, prospective parents would poke and prod the children, testing for strengths and weaknesses. The head nun, Sister Bertha, would push little Samael to the back of the line, hoping not to startle the prospective parents or cause a disruptive outburst from the children as they eagerly competed to point out the freak as a "must see" attraction for the unsuspecting guests. A mere glimpse of Samael—a large red birthmark on his right cheek, oscillating eyes, and ghost-like skin—would always unleash recoiled gasps and impulsive outbursts: "Oh my! That poor child!" The mere sight of the child often sent prospective parents scurrying for the door.

Rejected, ridiculed, and depleted of all hope, refusing to be further humiliated by the embarrassing, adoption interviews, Samael resorted to whatever means possible to avoid the fruitless and painful examinations. He hid in closets, under beds, in trash cans, laundry baskets—or wherever— until the guests had departed.

One day, while hiding in a utility closet, he overheard Sister Bertha and Sister Mary talking. They'd stopped by the water fountain located in the hallway beside the utility closet. The deep, raspy voice of Sister Bertha said, "The train is our only option."

"But if we put him on the train," said Sister Mary, in her sweet, almost angelic voice, "you *know* what will become of him."

"Well, we can't keep him here any longer. No one wants him, and it won't be long before we have serious problems with the other children. God forgive me, but they should have left the poor child in the dumpster. He will never make it in this world."

At the time, Samael thought the train sounded like a good idea. He liked trains. But he soon learned that "the train", referred to by the sisters, was merely a code name originating from a social experiment conducted from 1854 to 1929 where Orphan Trains were used to transport orphaned, abandoned, or homeless, city children into the arms of loving families throughout the country. The modern-day "train" the sisters were referring to was not a train at all, but, instead, an underground child sex service operated, surprisingly, by top government officials, bureaucrats, and diplomats. The orphaned children were flown around the country to engage in child, sex orgies with American's ruling elite. The sisters had previously used the "train" to rid themselves of problem orphans.

The day before the train people were due to arrive, a

Muslim couple phoned St. Mary's requesting to adopt a handicapped child. Their only requirements were that the child be disabled, under the age of ten, and of sound mind. Without question, Samael met the first two requirements.

Forced from his room by the sisters, eager to rid themselves of the little white freak, Samael stood reluctantly in the viewing room waiting to be scorned and humiliated. When the Muslim couple saw the frail, little, white boy, instead of the usual scrunched-up faces and ghastly comments, they smiled. "He's perfect!" they said.

At the age of nine, Samael had found a home.

Samael grew up in Bridgeview, Illinois, a suburb located fifteen miles southwest of Chicago's downtown Loop, in the heart of one of the U.S.'s largest Arab communities. He attended an Islamic private school until the 12th grade. Although ostracized by his brown-skinned classmates, his massive size ensured that he was no longer picked on.

Unlike the other children who had been brainwashed in the ways of Islam since birth, the doctrines of Christianity had been hammered into Samael's mind by the nuns during his formative years at the asylum. But since his days in the asylum, those he'd come in contact with that claimed loyalty to Christianity lived their lives in apathy, indifference, materialism, and godlessness. He saw no unity among the nations who aligned themselves with the Christian faith. Most had sold their souls to the ideologies of political correctness, anti-nationalism, and multiculturalism. The teachings of the Koran were emphatic that apart from being a Muslim, there is no hope for a person. Though Samael favored the religion of Islam over Christianity, his life grew evermore twisted and confused, finding no satisfaction from either.

During his last year of high school, unexplainable paranormal experiences began to torment him day and night: telepathic encounters with disembodied spirits presented themselves in the form of spatially extended systems of energy; apparitional experiences with unrecognizable human figures; dreams of war and death. But most disturbing were the visions of what he believed to be his beloved natural mother.

His adoptive parents had emigrated from Turkey allowing them a dual citizenship. As their legal child, Samael had the same privileges. After graduation, with the blessings of his adoptive parents, he followed a strong inner prompting and headed for Istanbul, Turkey, to discover the city as it was gloriously portrayed by his parents. He stayed with relatives while he traveled and explored. Because of his massive size and strength, manual labor jobs were easily obtainable. He opted to work in the factories, rather than outdoors, due to his sensitivity to light.

Since he first arrived in Istanbul, fourteen years ago, he had searched for answers. He'd found a partial peace within the religion of Islam, but, as with all religions, there was constant strife and confusion: Sunnis and Shiites at war since the birth of the religion in the 7th century; ridiculous traditions and rituals created by power-hungry, religious zealots.

In his pursuit to make sense of a senseless world, Samael became a student of the 13th century Persian mystic Jalal al-Din Muhammad Rumi whose teachings were neither secular nor religious, but most certainly spiritual.

Rumi's mystical poetry offered a metaphysical approach to the physical world's interaction with the intangible—something Samael desperately needed as he struggled to unravel the chaos in his head. Coming to terms with the existence of a nonphysical reality had opened the window to his soul. No longer did he *have* a soul; he *was* a soul. Rumi led him to Sufism—Muslim mysticism—considered by some Muslims to be outside the sphere of Islam.

In February 2002, he'd read an article titled, *Understanding Your Dreams – The Secret to Your Past.* The article claimed that through past life regression (PLR) a person could find healing, purpose, and peace by unlocking the secrets of their hidden past lives. The article was written by Usman Ali.

Usman, a computer geek claiming to be a PLR therapist experienced in the use of hypnotherapy to unlock the journey of the soul, had spent most of his young professional life as a tour guide at Topkapi Palace.

In great need of "unlocking" his tormented soul, Samael followed a website link he'd found in the article (www.freedomthroughplr.com), paid the $499 lifetime fee, and signed up for Usman's online PLR program. After several months of guided online regression therapy with Usman, Samael began to learn of the multiple journeys of his soul into this world—exercises in spiritual purification—each with specific tasks.

Usman's teachings had opened up for Samael a fresh new love for his past, finally allowing him to explain his strange love for the glorious city of Istanbul: the ruins of the original city walls and their gates; the topography of the land; the salty smell of the sea.

Samael hoped *this* life would be his last, but everything hinged on one remaining task. Success would guarantee him freedom from his tormented and lonely life—including the cursed white body riddled with humiliating flaws. Failure guaranteed him yet another earthly life and the continued recycling of his soul in search of a higher sphere before his ultimate release into the afterlife.

With the direct rays of the sun now hidden behind the hills to the east, he left the balcony and returned to his room. Staring into the mirror, the horrid image of his face angered him. Twisted and tangled, his soul cried out to be released to a higher consciousness. He needed to whirl.

He quickly readied the room by pushing the furniture as close to the walls of the small room as possible. He effortlessly turned the twin beds on their sides and pushed them close against the wall with their mattresses facing out. The small, round, antique, wooden table in the middle of the room, covered with a laced tablecloth and potted plant, were stacked in the recess of the bay window.

Looking around the room, the narrow wardrobe and waist-high dresser were already against the wall. He smiled happily seeing that there would be adequate space to whirl freely without worry of hitting something.

The hard, wooden floors would be perfect against the slick, leather bottom of his boot to allow for a near frictionless spin. But, first, he needed to move the area rug. He rolled it tight and placed it across the tops of the beds standing on their sides against the wall.

Excellent.

He paused when he noticed the light fixture hanging from the ceiling. Standing beneath it, he raised his hands to check the clearance. He could touch the fixture if he extended his hands straight up, but he doubted he would extend them directly above his head at any time during his whirling meditation. The ten-foot ceilings of the old building proved to be adequate to keep the light fixture clear of his whirling hands as long as they stayed at the normal forty-five degree angle, or less.

The last thing was to close the drapes. Everything looked ready. He didn't want anything to interfere once he started whirling.

He had learned about the practice of whirling while attending an Islamic prayer service. When he first tried it, within the first five turns, he became dizzily sick. He was encouraged to keep trying and reminded that success with the ritual would only be realized when he learned how to release his mind from his body; stop thinking.

"Quiet the mind, and relocate your center," he was told. "The dizziness will disappear once you reach a trance-like state." After much practice and persistence, he became quite good, hardly ever feeling dizzy.

With the room cleared and ready, he removed a small, cassette tape player from his suitcase and inserted a tape. Pressing the play button, he positioned the speaker of the player toward the center of the room. Traditional Turkish melodies, with hundreds of scales from instruments such as the end-blown flute, the trapezoidal, plucked zither, different types of lutes, and kettledrums, filled the room.

He then began to dress while the music set the mood. Each piece of clothing carried a significant, symbolic meaning. The tennure, with its long white skirt, represented the death shroud. He slipped this on first.

On top of the white skirt, he wore a voluminous, black cloak with long, large sleeves, symbolizing the tomb or grave.

The last item was a tall, cylinder-shaped hat made of camel's felt representing a tombstone. At first glance, it might resemble an oversized Shriner's fez, a brimless version of the tall, red and white striped hat worn by the cat in Dr. Seuss' *The Cat in the Hat*, or possibly an alternative look for Marge Simpson's tall, blue hair on *The Simpsons*.

The Turkish music played while he stood in his whirling costume in a prayerful state repeating, "Allah, Allah, Allah." His hands were crossed onto his shoulders with his erect posture representing the number one, testifying to Allah's unity.

Prior to starting, he removed his black robe revealing his white robe beneath, symbolizing a release of his soul that lives within and beyond this life.

With his left foot fixed, as a point of contact with the Earth through which divine blessings and understanding could flow, he was ready to begin. Using his right foot to spin his large, white body around, he began to turn slowly at first, in short twists, in an anticlockwise direction.

The fundamental condition of everything—every object, every being—is to revolve, from the smallest particles of matter to the incomprehensible vastness of the stars in the galaxies, everything takes part in revolving. Soon he knew he would unite with the universe that was always spinning around him, and in him; planets around their axis, planets around the sun, and the cloud of electron shells spinning around their atoms, always seeking balance.

The shared similarity of all created things is the revolution of the electrons, protons, and neutrons within the atoms that constitute their basic structure. By whirling, he would participate consciously in the shared revolution of all existence. He would become whole for as long as he whirled.

Like a bird taking flight, his white-sleeved arms unfolded and rose out and above his shoulders. The right hand opened to the skies in prayer, ready to receive Allah's beneficence. The left hand, turned toward the Earth in a gesture of bestowal.

"I take wing and fly, turning round and round, burning up my pride. Am I a moth in flight? Allah, Allah, Allah."

His eyes remained open but unfocused while staring into space, smiling peacefully. His head tilted back against his shoulder.

After a fifteen minute period of slow rotation, he gradually began to push harder with his right foot, building the speed up over the next thirty minutes. Spinning faster, the room blurred into a swirling whirlpool of colors. The rhythmic rotation and incessant music created a synthesis which induced a feeling of soaring, of ecstasy, of mystical flight, and of union—his soul with the universe.

Practice had taught him how to work through the dizziness much like a sailor learns to accommodate seasickness. His white skirt billowed and his soul soared. For a time when the world around him appeared to be fractured, he felt connected and freed from his white prison.

Soon he would be whirling so fast he would not be able to remain upright. His body would fall. The fall would not be made consciously nor would he attempt to arrange the landing in advance.

Knowing that the fall was inevitable, he had turned the beds up against the wall with the mattresses facing out toward the center of the room. This precaution had been made to avoid the possibility of striking his head against the pointed feet of the bed's metal frame. Other items in the room had also been placed in such a way that there were no sharp corners to hit in the fall. He knew the Earth would absorb his energy.

Less experienced whirlers might opt to end the whirling meditation by slowing down rather than falling. Having been whirling for an hour or so, he knew the slowing process could take ten minutes or more. In addition, choosing to slow rather than fall would spoil the second part of the meditation process—the unwhirling.

After the fall, he would roll onto his stomach immediately putting his navel in contact with the Earth, like a small child pressed to his mother's breasts. Keeping his eyes closed, he would then remain passive and silent for at least fifteen minutes letting his body blend into the Earth.

Spinning now at top speed within a vortex of peace, his face was flushed red. Sweat streamed from every pore in his body.

As expected, his body fell to the floor uncontrollably, like a massive skyscraper implodes within its footprint under the careful execution of a demolitionist. His large, white body lay spread out on the floor, face down and motionless.

As his soul slowly rejoined his body and the two blended back with the Earth, he felt the sobering reality of where he was, who he was, and what he had to do. Once his mission was complete, his soul would be rewarded with freedom and union with his beloved mother.

Rumi's teachings and Usman's PLR therapy had freed

Samael from the physical and released him into a dimension
not bound by time and space. Not only had he uncovered the
hidden riches within his internal confusion, he'd found a
structure of meaning and purpose for the existence of his
current life.

Tonight, for the first time, he would meet Usman Ali.

CHAPTER 5

Fort Rosecrans National Cemetery, San Diego
Sunday, May 25, 2003

Under a canopy of clear, blue sky, overlooking the San Diego Bay and the Pacific below, peaceful winds laced with the taste of salt, rushed up surrounding cliffs, whispering through the branches of easterly bent pines. Uniform white grave markers, glistening in the sun, dotted the carpet of rolling green lawns. The tranquil and somber setting was the shrine for thousands of brave men and women who fought to their deaths while attempting to rid the world of monsters.

With reverence and respect, Ryan and Keri approached two, four-foot polished marble markers. The world outside had quickly forgotten—like it never happened—but inside the boundaries of the cemetery, death, ironically, didn't seem so final. Like a sieve, death had graciously filtered out the many inadequacies and shortcomings of the deceased leaving only the good to be remembered.

Keri leaned down and placed fresh-cut flowers in the floral cone at the foot of the headstone, then stepped back. Two evenly-spaced granite markers, set flush with the grass, bore their names and the dates of their births and deaths:

REX T. DEAN: FEBRUARY 9, 1958 – JULY 11, 2002
EMILY A. DEAN: NOVEMBER 11, 1959 – JULY 11, 2002

"It's hard to believe they're gone," he said.

Keri said nothing.

He pondered the last date of their short lives chiseled in the stone: July 11, 2002.

Our anniversary was the day of the crash...July 11^(th)...Rex died on a Thursday.

He let the thought marinate.

When did I see him last?

It was the afternoon of July 4^(th). He and Rex had just returned from four days of recurrent training. They were standing in the employee parking lot at the LAX airport saying goodbye.

How could I forget? Keri and I took the kids down to the pier that night and watched fireworks. It was a Thursday night...the week before the crash.

He searched deeper.

I was telling him about our plans to watch the fireworks display.

Then, he remembered their last words together.

Are you sure you don't mind flying my trip on the 11^(th)?

Rex had replied, "No worries. I'm on it. You and Keri enjoy the night. Bro, remember, I've always got your back. See you on the other side." Then Rex said goodbye and drove away.

"I've always got your back"

They were the exact same words Rex had spoken in Atlanta, back in 1987, when he crawled out of Philip Darby's boardroom. Suddenly, everything good about Rex flooded into his thoughts. The sieve of death had done its job.

Without warning, grief wrenched Ryan's heart like a

sponge. His throat tightened. Surrendering to tears would be so easy. They would not only purge his heart of grief but wash out the need to care about anyone, anything. Blessed relief could be his if he simply admitted that the long struggle to understand wasn't worth the pain of experience. He wanted to scream out to God.

Why, why, why, why, WHY?!

Keri put her arm in his as though she could read his thoughts. "Rex would have done anything for you. He loved you like a brother."

In another life, Ryan and Rex had been best friends. They served six years together in the Navy prior to coming to the airline. Their final assignment, which began in 1981, was a three-year tour at the Fighter Weapons School at Naval Air Station (NAS) Miramar, San Diego, California, as TOPGUN instructors. It was then when he first met Emily.

His eyes shifted to Emily's marker: EMILY A. DEAN.

A crow cawed; a ship's horn sounded in the bay—both possible triggers propelling him through an imaginary portal; a crack in time—to a distant memory. The vivid details of December 22, 1983, replayed in his mind with the clarity of the present: the white, gift box containing a dozen, thornless roses he'd presented to Emily in celebration of their six months together; the sight of her standing in the doorway of her apartment, wrapped in a white bathrobe, no makeup, her hair up in a towel; her engaging eyes, excited playfulness, and loving affection; his anxious heart had filled with hope that she would accept his proposal for marriage.

During that carefully planned afternoon in December, he'd presented her with three visual images, hoping to send a coded message to her heart.

First: Rosecrans National Cemetery: *the brevity of life and the urgency to embrace the present.*

Second: the Old Point Loma Lighthouse: *the importance of relationships over places and things.*

Third: Cabrillo National Monument: *when faced with the unknown, willing to embrace the driving power of adventure and discovery.*

Knowing he would soon be leaving San Diego, he had feared she might not go with him. If forced to leave her behind, he would surely lose her to someone else. He had seen it as his last opportunity.

At the end of the day, although each hidden message had been clear and effective and his every hope fulfilled, December 22, 1983, would later be remembered, ironically, as the biggest mistake in his life—the day Emily became his wife.

I was too young to know...she was too beautiful for me to resist.

Suddenly, he couldn't think about anything but the pain. His choosing to love Emily had robbed him of many happy years and had nearly robbed him of the greatest treasure in life—Keri. For a long time, maybe even since that day, he'd known that being a victim was often a choice people made, but in this case, he'd been blindsided.

Akin to the man-eaters of all times, from Cleopatra to Jolie, she lured him into the rocks with the enchanted song of a skilled Siren.

I didn't have a chance.

Ryan's brief marriage to Emily ended suddenly when she was snared by her own narcissistic desires—much like the dog in Aesop's fable, *The Dog and the Bone.*

A parasite in search of a new host, she married again. But her second marriage ended abruptly and unexpectedly leaving her in search of a third male host. Fate quickly arranged her third rendezvous with, none other than, the *Rexter.*

Rex underestimated Emily's seductive powers and quickly found himself mesmerized by her enchanted song of the Siren. After they married, she kept Rex on a tight leash, forbidding him to have anything to do with the Mitchell family—for obvious reasons. From that point forward, Ryan's only social interaction with Rex had been at work.

Ryan stared deep into the face of the granite markers. "How can they get away with this?" He glanced at Keri and back at the stones.

Keri remained silent.

"Something stinks," he said. "The jet was off the coast over open water...they just blew it out of the sky! It's all wrong! The plane wasn't anywhere near a building!"

"Honey, calm down."

"Somebody screwed up and now they're trying to cover it up!"

"Why would the government want to lie about something like this?"

He ignored Keri's question. "They claimed that after multiple failed attempts by air traffic controllers and airborne F-16s to communicate with Rex and his copilot, the unprecedented decision was made by the Defense secretary to shoot the jet down. As they put it, 'To protect mass-populated areas and critical targets.' Without further explanation, the report concluded that there was substantial evidence the plane was headed towards a target in San Francisco. Over 200 innocent people were murdered, all because somebody had a hunch."

"Poor, Emily," Keri said. "We might never know the truth."

He turned toward her. "He didn't do it. Rex is innocent. He may have been a jerk, but he was *not* a murderer."

"We both know Rex would never kill Emily."

"I just don't understand. You would think the crime scene experts would have been able to find something—a fiber, a hair, a flake of skin—something!"

"I don't understand the blood-soaked footprints leading from the house to the garage where Rex parked his car."

"Easy. All the killer had to do was take a spare pair of

Rex's work shoes and make the prints."

"It's wrong."

"No, it's *impossible* that Rex murdered Emily prior to leaving for the airport. I'll never believe it. What I do believe is that they simply decided that it would save them a lot of time, money, and trouble to blame it on the dead husband. Neither of their parents are alive and there were no children. Rex was an only child and Emily's brother is in jail and her sister is a crackhead. Case closed."

"Let's go," Keri said. But before she took two steps, she collapsed to the ground. Ryan quickly caught her, breaking her fall.

"Keri! Are you okay?"

She rolled over and vomited on Ryan's shoe. "I'm sorry...I'm so sorry...." She wheezed and coughed, breathing deep.

"Are you okay?"

She quietly gained her composure. "I think so."

"Here, let me help you."

Back at the car, Keri said, "You and I both know Rex didn't do it, but do you think they'll ever find out who did? I mean—"

"I doubt it. As far as the authorities are concerned, it's over."

After learning of the acquisitions made against Rex—that he had murdered his wife—there had been talks of his crash being a suicide. Some believed Rex might have, not only killed his wife, but committed suicide by crashing the plane into the Pacific. Ryan found the idea incredulous. Commercial airline pilots were one of the most highly trained, disciplined, regulated, and conscientious work groups on the planet, and Rex was one of the best. But Ryan's curiosity led him on a search to see if there was any record of such a thing ever happening. Surprisingly, Ryan's research revealed numerous disturbing cases around the world where commercial airline crashes showed circumstantial evidence pointing to pilot suicide.

In 1982, a DC-8 flew into shallow water short of the runway after a struggle between a mentally ill captain and his copilot, killing twenty-four.

In 1991, a Boeing 737 crashed on short final at Colorado Springs, killing twenty-five. Although initially thought to be a rudder malfunction, the NTSB concluded the cause of the accident to be undetermined. Many pilots working for the airline believed the cause of the crash to be a murder/suicide involving the captain and his first-officer wife, who were known to be feuding.

In 1994, an ATR-42 entered into a steep dive and crashed ten minutes after takeoff, killing 44. Reports indicated that the pilot disconnected the autopilot and deliberately crashed, committing suicide.

In 1997, a Boeing 737 departed normal cruise flight and crashed at a high rate of speed, killing 104. The cockpit voice recorder had been deactivated before the dive was initiated. Reports indicated that the captain's career disappointments and financial stress may have led him to commit suicide.

In 1999, a Boeing 767 departed cruise altitude of 33,000 feet and entered several dives and recoveries before entering a final, diving descent at a rate of 24,000 feet per minute, plunging into the Atlantic Ocean. Reports confirmed that the first officer's flight control inputs had caused the airplane's departure from normal cruise and that both of the plane's engines had been shut down. Two hundred and seventeen people perished.

Ryan knew that the causes of many commercial aircraft accidents went unsolved, classified by the NTSB: "For Undetermined Reasons". Of those classed as "undetermined", many were tagged as pilot error.

With the average age of commercial airline pilots at an all time high, managers pushing them to work more hours for the same or less pay, and stress, fatigue, and depression widespread, he could see how the mental stability of pilots could be tested—but not Rex.

"So do you think there are a lot of pilots running around ready to snap?" Keri asked.

"No, but the facts certainly make it easier for them to pin this on Rex, as some people believe. We have more pilots in alcohol and drug treatment programs than ever before. Divorce rates and domestic disputes are rampant. At our airline alone, we have had two pilot suicides in the last year. One guy hung himself in his garage and another one shot himself in the head with his handgun while on a layover."

"How do you know all this?" Her voice elevated with a new sense of concern.

"It has become a HOT TOPIC during recurrent training. We have a two hour class dedicated to making sure we are aware of how serious this problem has become. I'm sure all of the airlines have similar programs. The union is constantly trying to assure pilots that they have a safe haven—some place to turn—where they can find help before it is too late."

"Why haven't you told me about this?"

"I didn't want you to worry more than you already do. I guess this situation with Rex brings things closer to home. I know Rex and Emily were deeply in debt and their marriage was not in the greatest shape, but I can't believe it was bad enough to push Rex over the edge. He's not the type to crack under pressure."

Her concern growing, Keri said, "You're not going to snap, are you?"

"No."

"I worry about you...I mean...you have that gun with you when you fly...you aren't sleeping...I know you are under a lot of stress...and now hearing this story about some pilot shooting himself on a layover, and another one hanging himself in his garage—"

"Don't worry. I'm *not* going to shoot myself."

I should have never told her.

He continued, "As little as I talked to Rex, I honestly had no way of knowing what he was going through. I do know that Emily can be a handful."

"Are *we* doing okay financially?"

"We've taken on a little debt, but it's nothing we can't handle…as long as the company holds together."

She took his hand. "Promise me you will never keep any secrets from me."

In a loving and serious tone he said, "You have nothing to worry about. I'm fine…we're fine. Everything is going to be alright."

"I don't want to lose you." Her voice trembled. Her face drooped with sadness. "I can't live without you."

"Look at me." He lifted her chin up. "Nothing is going to happen to me. We're going to be fine. If things get too bad, I'll quit…find another job. We can move back to Georgia. All I care about is you and the kids. A job is a job… even if we do have to live in a hut and forge for nuts and berries."

She smiled. His words seemed to ease her, but the reality of his words blanketed him with a new wave of stress. Leaving the airline and starting over—at his age—presented many concerns. He was not eligible for retirement for another two years. David would be starting college in less than three years, with Martha close behind.

Thoughts of living in a hut and forging for berries were pushed aside when Keri said, "I just can't stop thinking about it." Sounding anxious and fearful, she said, "Why would someone want to kill Emily?"

"Calm down." Ryan took her hand.

"Well, if Rex didn't do it—and you and I both know he didn't—then don't you think it's kind of strange that Emily was murdered on the same night Rex's flight crashed?"

I don't want to get into it with Keri. If the two events

were tied together, someone would have had to know that I traded trips with Rex the week before the flight. To know that, they would need access to the company computers, or know someone who did. And if Emily was murdered simply because she was the pilot's wife...that means if I had flown the trip, instead of Rex, Keri would have been killed—and possibly the kids too.

A dizzy wave washed over him. His chest tightened, pushing his heart into his throat. His skin tingled with currents of electrical impulses.

If I had flown that trip instead of Rex, there would be four, granite markers in the grass instead of two.

He looked at Keri. Her eyes searched his soul as though she knew something bothered him. "What's wrong?" she said.

He turned away, not wanting her to see the fear in his face. He gazed in the direction of Rex and Emily's gravesite. His good friend and ex-wife were dead. Rex had died in his place. Emily had been a substitute sacrifice for Keri and his children.

"Ryan, what is it?"

"Nothing," he lied. Beside him sat the most dedicated and loving wife a man could ever dream of having. He needed her more now than ever. If he told her what he was thinking, she would freak.

The silence weighed heavy as they drove away from the cemetery. "What are you thinking?" she said. "I can tell something is wrong."

He glanced at her, then back at the road. He sighed. She shifted more toward him as if she was preparing to catch the outpouring of his soul, but the mere thought of verbalizing what he was thinking made him want to vomit—he should be dead, not Rex Dean. Emily had been murdered on the same night of the crash. If the two events were connected, as he was beginning to suspect they were, and he had flown the trip that night instead of Rex—as it had been originally scheduled—there is a strong probability Keri and the kids would have been murdered, instead of Emily. This put an entirely new twist on the fear he battled daily.

His heart raced. Bile rose in his throat. He swallowed hard. "We just need to be thankful my life was spared."

"I'm scared," she said, her voice weak and trembling.

He took her hand and looked her in the eye. "Honey, it's over. We both need to put this behind us. It's been almost a year."

"No! It's not over! It will never be over until they find out who killed Emily." She burst out crying and buried her head against his shoulder.

"Keri, we can't let fear keep us from living." The words he regurgitated were cold—almost mechanical. How could he expect *her* to do something *he* couldn't do? Every flight he flew carried the risk that some lunatic with a death wish might board his plane, but it was not until now that he feared for the safety of Keri and his children. Fear was the driving force in his life that had nearly robbed him of his sanity.

Then, suddenly, Rex's words from the dream popped into his head. "Don't let your fear blind you, get busy!" It must have been his subconscious using the dominate thoughts from that day to bring life to his dream characters. After all, dreams are based on the past, not on the future. Everything in our dreams originates from people, places, and words from our past. "Get busy."

Doing what?

"You'll find answers in the here."

Where is "the here"?

Keri lifted her head and wiped the tears from her eyes and cheeks. "Ryan, don't you understand? Next time it could be you—us?"

He pushed his fears aside, reaching for words that might calm her. "There are always risks, but the government and the airlines are doing everything possible to keep these kinds of things from happening. We'll be fine." Again, he knew what he said was not true. The government and the airlines only did what they *had* to do, not always what they *should* do.

Keri did not respond. She appeared to be in a trance. Perhaps the visit to the cemetery had been too much—too soon. The silence weighed heavy as they drove away from the cemetery, leaving behind the bones of those who sleep eternal and their whispers of satisfying remembrances of life.

CHAPTER 6

Heading north on Interstate 5 toward San Clemente, Ryan sat quietly focused on the road ahead. Keri wanted to scream, but the constriction in her throat made it impossible; partly due to grief and partly due to fear.

Since the funeral, everything related to the crash had been pushed into the remotest corners of her memory. She should have left it that way—buried and forgotten—but her guilt had forced her to return to the grave site, hoping for closure—promising never to return again. Seeing Rex and Emily's names etched into the granite had removed every ounce of denial.

She would never mention it to Ryan, but there were things about Rex she would miss. He was funny, playful, and in his own way, caring and sensitive. Disregarding the fact that he had deceived her and broken her heart, she believed that deep down he was not all bad. Death had a way of bringing to surface his good traits.

Years ago, when she had lost Ryan to Emily, Rex had been there for her. Even in his twisted way, he had provided the companionship she needed to work through her heartbreak. Who better than Ryan's best friend. There were moments when she believed her marriage to Rex might last. If Emily had not left Ryan, who knows, she and Rex might have had a life together.

The idea of *her* name being chiseled in the granite marker next to Rex sent a cold chill up her spine. She pondered a flurry of *what ifs*. Every choice in life ignites a separate set of consequences propelling us down a particular path filled with unique life experiences. When she looked back, she thanked God that her life had been spared.

Her thoughts returned to the present, but held tight to the image of the grave markers. A fresh wave of grief ambushed her, but it could not compare to the chilling fear that wrapped her in a death squeeze.

Ryan would be dead if Rex had not flown that trip. Emily was murdered because she was the wife of the pilot. I would be dead, and possibly the children, too.

The freeway blurred as cars droned toward unknown destinations. Ryan sat quietly beside her. He was alive. She was alive. The children were alive.

I need to hold the children. We need to get home, fast!

They were safe. But that was today. What about tomorrow and the next day and the day after that?

She quickly raised her hands to her mouth to silence a scream.

The children!

"What's wrong?" Ryan asked. "What?"

She gasped in jerky breaths as tears streamed from her eyes uncontrollably. She couldn't respond.

"Keri! What is it?"

She shook her head.

"Are you okay?"

She nodded, wiping her eyes, looking for a tissue."

"What's going on?"

She sniffled, and then turned to meet his concerned stare. "It's all connected, I know it is."

"What?"

"Whoever hijacked the plane also murdered Emily. I just know it!"

"We don't know for sure."

"Ryan, it's the only possible explanation. It's too freaky."

"Why would someone want to kill the pilot's family? What would it prove?"

"How should I know? All I know is if you'd flown that flight...." She paused. Her words ignited an uncontrollable flurry of emotions. Her throat tightened. Her eyes filled with water. An icy chill riveted up her spine.

"Keri, you don't know this."

She looked at him with a glazed stare. She couldn't understand how he could be so sure. Even if he agreed with her, she knew he would hide his true thoughts—especially seeing how horrified she was of the thought of anyone harming the children. "Ryan, I'm scared."

He took her hand. "There's nothing to be afraid of. Everything is going to be fine. I've got a couple of days off before I fly again. We'll work through it."

His words, "fly again", jolted her. He might as well have said: "cheat death again" or "risk my life again" or "give the barrel another spin again", as if his life were a game of Russian roulette.

Ryan drove into their subdivision and slowly rolled by manicured lawns with children playing in front yards. The moment he wheeled into the driveway, David and Martha burst out the front door.

The sight of the children—healthy and alive—ignited a rush of emotions. Keri fought back fresh tears.

David, leading the way, a stocky blond-headed, blue-eyed, fifteen-year-old beamed a big smile, his five-year-old sister close behind. Although trailing her big brother, she was first to latch onto her daddy as he stepped out of the car. David headed for Keri.

"How's my little princess?" Ryan lifted her up into a big

hug.

"Fine," she said. "I missed you, Daddy."

"I missed you too, Sweetheart."

Pictures of Keri at age five could have easily passed for her daughter. Martha had even inherited her mother's tiny dimples.

David grabbed Keri's hand as she exited the car. David was deaf. "Hi, Mom. Missed you." When he spoke, his free hand signed the words. Though understandable, his words were clouded in a guttural tone.

"I missed you too," she said, smiling, signing as she spoke. Ryan, Keri, and even little Martha were fluent in Sign Language. Whenever David was present, whoever was talking would instinctively sign as they spoke, so as not to leave him out of the conversation.

A small, beige-colored plastic button, the size of a bottle cap was attached to David's scalp just behind his right ear. It was part of a hearing device called a cochlear implant. A wire from the plastic button (antenna) led to a mini computer located behind his ear called a sound processor. The sound processor digitized sounds, sending them through the tiny wire leading to the antenna. The antenna, appearing to be glued to the scalp, was actually held in place magnetically by a receptor which had been surgically implanted under the skin. The device converted the digital signals from the antenna into electrical signals. The electrical signals traveled down an electrical array into the part of the inner ear called the cochlea. The electrodes stimulated the auditory nerves sending sound information to David's brain, bypassing the damaged part of the inner ear. Although David's cochlear implant provided sound signals—some would say robotic sound sensations—it did not restore normal hearing.

Keri's heart warmed, watching Martha cling to her older brother as they returned to the front door and into the house. She knew how much Martha loved David. It was a relationship most siblings never experienced. David's deafness insulated him from many of the negative influences most kids his age were exposed to. She and Ryan also did everything possible to shield him from a world filled with evil.

Once inside, Keri felt safe. Her family was together and Ryan was off for a couple of days. Hopefully it would be enough time for her to regain her faith in the fact that everything would be alright. Maybe she had overreacted.

Before leaving the foyer, she pushed against the front door, ensuring it was closed, and engaged the bolt lock. Pausing briefly, she reflected on the framed, cross-stitched needlework that hung by the door in the foyer. Behind the glass was a late afternoon beach scene; the sun three-quarters below the horizon and the silhouette of a bird in flight headed toward the setting sun. Two empty Adirondack chairs, side by side, faced the ocean. Three phrases were stitched into the fabric:

One below the horizon:
LEARN FROM THE PAST
One on the horizon next to the sliver of orange sun:
EMBRACE THE PRESENT
The third above the horizon:
HOPE IN THE FUTURE

The needlework was a wedding gift from Ryan's mom. It was one of her many marvelous pieces. It had hung in the small foyer of her own home in Atlanta before her Alzheimer's disease had forced her to move to Dallas where Ryan could care for her. She had often said that the needlework was a reminder to her before facing the challenges of the outside world. The simple illustration always reminded Keri of Martha Mitchell's optimistic and hopeful outlook on life.

The message in the stitching, combined with thoughts of Martha's strong faith, brought a tear to Keri's eye. Martha was in Heaven now. Keri wanted to believe that Martha was looking down at them saying: *"Everything is gonna be fine."*

CHAPTER 7

Samael darted from the lobby of the Hotel Daphnis to a waiting taxi. As he entered the back seat, the driver turned and flinched. Samael ignored the man's rude behavior and said, "The Pierre Loti Café."

The driver made quick time, arriving at the café within twenty minutes. Samael paid the man, exited the taxi, pulled his hood over his head, and hurried through the café to the terrace, ignoring the gawking patrons. He expected his height and massive size to draw attention, but the curse of his whiteness made it impossible to escape the incessant stares and whispers of onlookers.

The tree-shaded terrace café sat high up on a hill, centrally located within Old Stamboul. The popular café offered a splendid view of the Istanbul skyline, the Golden Horn River, and the Bosphorus Strait in the distance, stretching from Kagithane (the working class district of the city) to the Marmara Sea.

Named after the famous, French novelist and naval officer, Pierre Loti, the cozy atmosphere and authentic 19th century style furnishings were reminiscent of a more relaxed time in Istanbul's history; a time when the Golden Horn was rich with tulip gardens and green parks, where upscale people came to relax and row their boats under romantic sunsets.

With waiters still serving in period costumes, the café provided the perfect place for escape and reflection. Although he had never met Usman Ali, pictures from his website, along with the description Usman provided made it easy to spot the little man.

Samael quickly crossed the patio to a table Usman had secured beneath the trees with an amazing view of the Golden Horn River; something Samael had requested.

Usman rose to greet him. "Good to see you my brother," Samael said.

"The pleasure is mine."

When they embraced, Samael was careful not to crush the bony, skeleton-like body beneath the man's tunic. Considering the fragility of the pitiful specimen, Samael found the curse of his white skin not so disgusting.

Shadowed beneath his towering six-nine frame, Samael eyed the little man up and down. His head was covered with a kufi (a short, rounded cap). His black beard added an unnatural thickness to his narrow face, and a mustache encircled his full lips. He wore thick glasses with dark rims and a white thobe hung loosely from his shoulders. The legs on his baggy pants stopped just above his ankles exposing his sandal-covered feet. The little man appeared nervous and jerky reminding Samael of a Chihuahua puppy needing to pee.

"I've eagerly waited for this day," Usman said. He motioned for Samael to sit.

"Yes, me too."

Samael turned toward the Golden Horn River. "Look at her. Isn't she beautiful?"

Usman adjusted his chair for a better view of the river, Seraglio Point, and Topkapi Palace. "Yes, it's beautiful."

Samael closed his eyes, breathed in deep, then slowly exhaled. When he opened his eyes, a smile spread across his ashen-colored face. A relaxed satisfaction filled his soul.

This time, I will not fail.

"As I have told you, I believe it is my destiny to help you," Usman said. "Everything you have in mind, technically, is well within my capabilities. I have prepared a list of what we will need to purchase once we arrive in the United States. Are there any financial limitations?"

"The finances have been arranged," Samael said. "I want the best equipment."

"Wonderful."

"This mission is my purpose in this life, and now that you have agreed to assist me, your technical skills will be invaluable to our success."

"When will I know the location of the target?"

"Once we arrive in San Francisco, I'll take you there."

A waiter, dressed in a 19th century period costume, approached the table. "May I...." At his first glimpse of Samael's face, the boy recoiled, releasing a faint gasp.

"Two black coffees," Samael said.

"Right away, sir." The boy scurried away.

Within ten minutes, he returned with two coffees in glass mugs. A head of froth crested the rim of each glass. "Will there be anything else?"

"No," Samael said. The waiter hurried away.

"How did you finally decide on the date for this mission?"

Samael hesitated, focused on watching the grounds of the coffee settle to the bottom of his glass. He took a small sip. Hot, strong, intense, yet sweet and pleasing to his tongue.

"We both know the significance of May 29, 1453."

Usman nodded. "The day commemorates the conquest of Constantinople by the Muslim Turks—specifically Mehmet the Conqueror. It is a day that will live in infamy."

"I felt it would be fitting for Sultan Mehmet and me to share in the celebration on May 29th. You might not be aware, but May 29th is also the day my soul took residence in the albino body—the day I was born. Could there be a more perfect day?"

"No." The little man squirmed with excitement. Without lifting his glass off the table, he leaned over and sipped his coffee. When he lifted his head, Samael noticed a foamy froth trapped in the frail man's mustache. His eyes were hidden behind fogged lenses.

"Your PLR program not only freed me from my prison by opening the door to my hidden past, with practice, using your meditation and self-hypnosis techniques, I have learned how to command myself into other lifetimes, at will." Samael wrapped his hands around his mug of coffee, relaxed by the heat radiating from the glass. He leaned back in his chair.

"I can't tell you how rewarding it is when one of my clients progresses to the level of independence that you have. Most of my work is with those who are merely curious."

Samael was obsessed with learning all he could about his newly found non-physical reality. The journeys of his soul had interconnected him with the realities of the universe and the afterlife. He was like a child who had been given a lifetime pass to Disney World; a fictionalized version of a perfect world where visitors are invited to escape their containment in physical reality so they are no longer limited by time, distance, size and physical laws; a place that offers the fictionalized realization of humanity's deepest dream: transcendence.

He had more questions for Usman. "Is it possible for a soul to choose when and where it wants to go on Earth before making a decision as to who it will be in their new life?"

"Most definitely," Usman said. "I've been told by clients undergoing hypnotherapy, that their souls, while in the spirit world, see themselves in the future playing different roles in various settings, previewing the life span of more than one human being within the same time cycle. In most cases, souls will quickly recognize one leading candidate for occupation."

He eased back from the table. "However, our spiritual advisors give us ample opportunity to reflect upon all we have seen in the future before making a final decision."

Samael nodded. "Keep going."

Usman continued, "While still in the spirit world, after a decision is made, souls enter into a significant period of preparation, much like cramming for a final exam. Then, just prior to embarkation, souls go before the Council of Elders where the significance of a soul's goals for the next life are reinforced. Embarkation to Earth is much like battle-hardened veterans girding themselves for combat. It is the last time the souls are able to enjoy the omniscience of knowing who they are before they must adapt to a new body."

"Are you saying my soul chose this hideous, white body?"

"Yes, just as my soul chose this." Usman gestured with both hands towards himself as he glanced down at his frail body. "The purpose of the human experience has everything to do with the growth of the soul—nothing else. We start as beginner souls and progress to intermediate and advanced souls, ending our incarnations on Earth when we reach full maturity."

"How do we know what level of maturity we have reached?"

"Beginner souls are influenced by an Earth curriculum and are inclined to surrender their will to the controlling aspects of human society. Intermediate souls are ready for more serious responsibilities and are seeking spiritual wholeness. Advanced souls are rare. They typically have no need to seek out Soul Regression Therapy. These souls go about doing their work quietly, always focused. An example of an advanced soul would be Mother Teresa."

"How long does it take to progress through the levels of maturity?"

"It's not about time; it's about purpose and growth. Once

you satisfy the purpose of your soul's incarnation, you will leave your physical body and journey home to your nonphysical place of reality. If, however, your earthly life is cut short and you leave behind any unresolved issues, after a period of rejuvenation and assessment, the soul will be required to leave the sanctuary of the Spirit World and return to Earth."

"When I leave this place, I hope I never return."

"Your present feelings of apprehension and fear only exist because you are bound by time and space. The soul does not experience such fears. Fear is of the personality, and therefore, of space and time. Trust me, once you no longer exist in dualism, your senses of sorrow, hate, and fear will evaporate."

"My sorrow and hate will only evaporate when I have fulfilled my purpose."

"I believe what drives you now, is the same thing that has driven your soul for thousands of years. The subconscious mind is a storehouse of all of our experiences and thoughts from all of our incarnations. Nothing is forgotten or lost by the subconscious. It often takes multiple lives to complete our purpose. This is why it is possible for a person to accomplish such great things at such a young age. I'm sure you have heard the term *old soul*."

"Yes. That explains why my past lives appear to have a common, life purpose."

"Exactly."

Samael sipped his, now, lukewarm coffee. From the teahouse on the hilltop, he gazed into the darkness toward the Golden Horn. The path of the river was easily distinguishable as it carved its way through the city lights of Istanbul to the Bosphorus.

He followed the lights of cars along the shoreline drive and across the Galata Bridge. Tiny lights bobbed on the surface of the black river below, marking the location of boats. Twinkling red, amber, and white lights carpeted the once barren hillside rising from the river's bank.

Where there were lights, there were people—a city crammed with millions of people—all caged for the night, performing their nightly rituals of trivial tasks, like animals fighting to satisfy the cravings of their flesh: food, sex, drugs, and sleep; brains and bodies rotting from their nightly gorging of countless hours of television propaganda and junk food—a progressive atrophy of freedom, health, and independence of thought.

At sunrise, the hopelessly lost souls would once again return to their pathetic jobs like hamsters spinning mindlessly on wheels going nowhere. Life without purpose was the ultimate example of a cold, void, useless reality.

If it were not for his purpose, he would hurl the wretched body that enslaved him over the cliff and to its demise, returning his soul to the Spirit World for much needed rejuvenation.

CHAPTER 8

Samael took a drink of his, now, cool coffee, and then placed the mug back on the table. The cover of darkness, sprinkled with stars, provided a comforting sense of protection. As he reflected on his three incarnations, Byzas, Mehmet, and Suleyman, his heart longed for Keroessa.

Although his soul had embodied Mehmet the Conquer and Suleyman the Magnificent, two of the greatest sultans of all times, it was in the body of Byzas that he longed to return, for that was when he and his mother were last together.

Usman asked, "Can you recall the physical features of Mehmet and Suleyman? I've seen renderings, but hearing it from you would mean much more."

"I'm aware of what history tells us about these great men and I am humbled by it. My regressions have only revealed fragments of their lives. In my research, I have uncovered much more. I must say that once I was certain of my incarnations in these men, the history books have come alive. The details of each regression have been easily confirmed with absolute accuracy. Both men were much alike, and interestingly, much like myself: tall, well muscled and strong with aquiline noses. Each had delicate complexions, their skin very pale; almost pallor."

"Were they albinos?"

"I don't think so. They each had sharp vision, which is not characteristic of albinos. Not only am I cursed with being a spectacle in my white skin, my vision suffers greatly."

"I'm sorry."

"That's fine. I've learned to live with it." Samael had not yet shared with Usman his theories about his albinism. Before his first regression and the discovery of Byzas, he viewed his albinism to be a curse. After learning of the unnatural paleness of both Mehmet and Suleyman, and Usman's explanation of how souls choose their bodies, he was certain *his* soul had specifically chosen the white-skin man for a reason.

As they sat silently in the darkness among the faint conversations of other guests and the rustling of leaves in the trees, Samael noticed Usman wincing, holding his stomach. "Are you alright?"

"Yes, I'll be fine," he groaned. "It's nothing, just a touch of IBS."

"IBS?" Samael cringed at Usman's contorted face, growing with agony. It reminded him of a pregnant woman in the midst of a violent contraction.

Once the pain subsided, Usman wiped the sweat from his brow and replied in a soft voice, "Irritable bowel syndrome. Probably the coffee or milk. I love good coffee, but I know it's not good for me. Really, I'm fine. Continue with what you were saying."

"My progression from Mehmet to Suleyman was indeed a great advance for my soul, but I know now why my soul chose to live in the body of Suleyman."

"Why?"

"It's more than his great military victories for the Ottomans. I learned in the history books that nearly 100 years after Caliph Umar bin al-Khattab took Jerusalem for Islam in the year 1537, Suleyman ordered the rebuilding of the Old

City walls in Jerusalem. Four years later, when the project was complete, I sealed the most important double-arched gate leading into the Old City. The gate that has many names—the East Gate; the Mercy Gate; the Shushan Gate—but most importantly, it is referred to as the Golden Gate. It remains closed today."

"Why was this Golden Gate so important?" Usman asked.

"As a student of history, you should know that the Golden Gate on the east wall of the Old City of Jerusalem is an extremely significant landmark in reference to history and to eschatology for all three of the major monotheistic religions: Judaism, Christianity, and Islam."

"I know this, but I don't understand the connection."

"The Jews link the Messiah's arrival with this gate. According to Jewish tradition, when the Messiah returns, He will enter the Temple Mount through this gate. Christians have for centuries associated this Golden Gate with Palm Sunday and the Second Advent of Christ.

Around A.D. 33, according to the book of Luke in the Christian's Bible, Jesus entered Jerusalem through the Golden Gate (East Gate) as he came down from the Mount of Olives to the temple. It is prophesied that upon His return, He will again enter through the Golden Gate.

"But you and I know this is the place of Allah's final judgment. That is why I believe, as Suleyman, I sealed this gate to prevent the Messiah's entrance." Samael noticed Usman begin to squirm. Suddenly, he jerked in pain, grabbing his stomach. "Are you okay?" The contractions appeared much stronger than before.

Usman pushed back from the table and stood quickly, doubled at the waist. "I'll be back...."

"Take your time."

Usman rushed off holding his stomach.

Samael wasn't sure if he needed to bother explaining to

Usman the real story behind the Golden Gates. For the same reason Mehmet had sealed the Golden Gate when he took Constantinople, Suleyman sealed the Golden Gate in Israel.

Although the greatness of Mehmet and Suleyman is known by many, and their accomplishments are well documented in the history books, the history books do not record the common thread that Samael knew tied these two men together—their soul's deep yearning for Keroessa.

For now, he enjoyed the silence. Usman's questions and unbridled excitement had tired him. His mind emptied every thought, but one: Keroessa. He continued to reflect on what he believed to be the real reason for his soul's journey into the skin of the tall, white albino.

There can only be one Golden Gate.

CHAPTER 9

With Usman busy dealing with his spastic colon, Samael lifted his gaze into the black sky, closed his eyes, and released his mind to explore his past.

Three lives, three journeys—all for the polishing and perfecting of his soul—had prepared him for his next mission on Earth. Stirred with stimulating currents of focused energy, he was more assured than ever that the multiple journeys of his soul had led him to this point.

His newly-found freedom through regression had connected him with his past and purpose for this life. Thoughts associated with his beloved mother lingered, filling him with warmth radiating throughout his body. The leaves seemed to rustle in harmony with his sense of satisfaction.

Usman returned, walking slowly, his face pale. He stood by his chair. "Sorry for taking so long. The caffeine must have set it off."

"I hope you can handle the long trip that is ahead of us."

"I've lived with this since I was a child. I'll be fine." Usman quickly diverted the conversation. "I'm packed and ready to go."

Samael stood and hugged the small, delicate man. "I will see you at the airport in the morning." Usman bid Samael farewell. Wasting no time, the little man scuffled off holding his stomach.

Their flight was scheduled to depart tomorrow from Ataturk Airport at 9:45 a.m. on Turkish Airlines, connecting with American Airlines in Chicago, and then continuing to San Francisco. Scheduled arrival time in San Francisco was 4:35 p.m. Samael had booked two rooms at the Hotel Sausalito—a small, out-of-the-way, boutique hotel only minutes from San Francisco on the north side of the Golden Gate Bridge in Marin County. It was the perfect location to review the details of the mission with Usman.

Samael sat and took one last sip of his coffee leaving only the sludgy grounds in the bottom of his cup. His resolve and commitment was deeper now than ever. He was ready to serve out his destiny on Earth and continue into the afterlife.

He waved a hand at a young waiter. The young man quickly approached the table dressed in the 19th century period costume.

"Yes sir." The boy recoiled slightly when light reflected against the albino's white face.

"Son, would you call me a taxi?" Samael didn't want to stand in the light of the café while waiting for the taxi. He preferred to sit under the cover of darkness until the taxi arrived.

"Yes sir."

He paid for the coffee and slipped the boy an extra five million lira note (equal to slightly more than three U.S. dollars)—enough for one person to buy lunch or dinner in a second-class restaurant. "Notify me when it arrives?"

"Yes sir. It should only be a few minutes."

"Fine."

Samael returned to his reflections, basking in the thought of returning to Istanbul in a matter of days where he would celebrate and live out the rest of his earthly life in the white body of the albino.

Sooner than expected, the young waiter returned to his

table. "Sir, your taxi has arrived."

The young man stepped back. Samael had grown accustomed to being treated like a contagious leper. The boy took another step back when Samael rose from the table; his large frame towered over the boy.

Quickly and discreetly, Samael made his way through the small café. The crowd in the café had grown in numbers with the onset of nightfall; the beverage of choice changing from Turkish coffee to raki—the Turkish national alcoholic drink. While making his escape, only a few patrons had time to notice him. The ones that did, winced after catching a glimpse of his ghostly appearance.

Safely seated in the taxi, he spoke only two words to the driver, "Hotel Daphnis." He made a point to sit in the right rear seat, hoping to avoid the anticipated stares from the driver in his rearview mirror.

Although the roads were congested, giving proof to Istanbul's thriving nightlife, he arrived back at the hotel along the banks of the Golden Horn in less than thirty minutes. He passed the driver enough money to cover the fare, plus a healthy tip, and quickly exited the taxi, into the empty lobby, and up the stairs to his room.

Samael readied for bed, said his prayers, turned out the lights, and slipped his tall frame into the small, single bed. Tomorrow he and Usman would depart for California. He planned to rise early enough to ensure plenty of time to visit three very important locations.

First, he would stop at Fatih Mosque, paying his condolences at the tomb of Sultan Mehmet the Conqueror.

Next, he would stop at the Suleymanine Mosque where the tombs of Suleyman the Magnificent and his wife Roxalena are located.

Finally, he would visit the Golden Horn River where he would fill four small jars with the water from the glorious river, the symbolic life blood of his beloved mother—

Keroessa.

The 2,600-year journey of his soul had been perfectly orchestrated and was close to an end. Before falling asleep, he thought of Usman. His technical knowledge and computer skills would ensure the success of the mission. Sadly though, Samael would have to kill the little man once his services were no longer needed. But on the positive side, death would release Usman's soul from the pitiful, little body that imprisoned him.

CHAPTER 10

Monday, May 26th

T he weak presence of dawn's first light strained to wash the black from the sky. The cry of the muezzin's call to Morning Prayer echoed from minaret to minaret—a network of antennae broadcasting high above the city's tallest buildings. Samael rose to the first of five daily calls to the faithful to pray.

After a bath, he coated every exposed inch of his body with sunscreen and dressed so as to hide his white skin. Instead of a taxi, he embraced the cool, spring morning and walked the short distance—less than a mile—to the nearby Fatih Mosque to pay his respects to Mehmet.

Located atop the fourth of the seven hills of Istanbul, Fatih Mosque was a popular place for the pious. Each Wednesday, the streets around the mosque were filled with a vast, street market. Many brought picnics and made a day of their visit.

The brisk walk invigorated him. A lone dog's bark pierced the morning silence, ricocheting through the quiet streets. Instinctively, he pulled the hood of his jacket down over his face and continued, arriving at Fatih Mosque before six, just as the sun was breaking above the horizon.

Fatih Mosque was the first of three stops. There was still plenty of time, as his flight didn't depart until 9:45 a.m., and the drive to the airport could easily be made in thirty to forty-five minutes.

Behind the mosque, in the graveyard on the eastern side, stood the tomb of Mehmet the Conqueror, a decagonal structure crowned with an imposing dome. Alongside Mehmet's tomb was the tomb of his favorite wife, Gülbahar.

Samael stopped and knelt beside the entrance to Mehmet's tomb. Thoughts of his beloved Gülbahar stimulated strong currents within his soul. The doors to the tomb were locked and wouldn't be open for visitors until 9:00 a.m. With his eyes closed, he encouraged his soul to explore the memories of his past.

After an uplifting time in meditation, he checked his watch—6:30 a.m. Suleymaniye Mosque was less than a mile away, but crossing Ataturk Boulevard—a major freeway—on foot would be impossible.

He spotted a yellow taxi parked under a tree. The driver appeared to be asleep. He slipped into the back seat and was quickly met by the startled, blood-shot eyes of the driver.

"Suleymaniye Mosque," Samael said. The driver rubbed his face, cranked the engine, and sped off.

The driver headed south to Fevzi Pasa Street, then eastbound, passing the Valens aqueduct as he crossed over Ataturk Boulevard, then left onto 16 Mart Sehitleri Street which led up to the Suleymaniye Masque behind Istanbul University, all in less than ten minutes. Samael paid the fare plus a generous tip.

"Cok tesekkür ederim (thank you very much)," the driver said.

"Bir şey değil (you're welcome)."

He exited the taxi and stood in awe of the spectacular mosque with its four minarets flanking the main building and central dome as the symbol of sultans (princes and princesses were allowed only two minarets, and others could have only one). Situated on the highest hill in the city, overlooking the domes and roofs spilling down the hillside to the Golden Horn below, it offered one of the most impressive views in all Istanbul. Considered the most beautiful of all imperial mosques in Istanbul, it stood proudly representing the greatness and strength of the Ottomans.

He made his way to the tomb garden on the southeast side of the mosque. The large cemetery had grown up around two octagonal-domed mausoleums attached to the mosque containing the remains of Suleyman the Magnificent and his most favored wife, Hurrem Sultan, later known as Roxelana.

Suleyman's tomb is surrounded by a colonnaded veranda with a porch on the east side. Roxelana's tomb is smaller and placed to one side. Samael had expected the tomb to be closed until 9:30, so he found a private place in the shade next to the building where he could reflect. With the remains of Suleyman near, Samael knelt on the concrete and began to meditate on the past—*his* past.

Time passed quickly. Sensing an urgency to move to the third stop, Samael stood and breathed a cleansing breath, then left the tomb garden.

He walked to clear his head. He navigated his way through a crisscross maze of narrow streets; a labyrinth of cobble-stoned, dirty streets filled with strange scents.

He glanced inside a smoky parlor where old men in drab, wool jackets played backgammon. One man held a glass of tea in one hand while shuffling prayer beads with the other.

Farther down the road he saw a woman leading a goat down the street. She wore a wide-brimmed hat, a white, translucent scarf wound around her head and decorated with colored trim, a red, print blouse topped with a multi-colored vest, and Turkish divided pants (salvar).

Seeing the sparkle of the Golden Horn River filled his

thoughts with a woman he'd never met but had dreamed about—his mother.

Samael found a secluded place near the river's edge, checked that no one was looking, then reached into the pocket of his hooded jacket and produced a small, vinyl, zipper pouch. He unzipped the pouch and withdrew four 3-oz, clear, glass bottles with screw-on tops. He was limited to three-ounce containers of liquids aboard the airplane.

He bent down, unscrewed each of the tops, and then set the tops on the ground. One by one, he dipped the bottles into the Golden Horn, filling them. Once filled, he secured the tops and placed three of them back in the zippered pouch, and then stood. Holding the fourth bottle up against the blue sky, he examined its contents. Unlike when he envisioned being a child and playing along the shores of the Golden Horn when its water was clear and fresh, it was now polluted from industry, shipping, and waste. Now, instead of a clear liquid, it was dark-brown, almost black. Millions of unidentifiable particles swam in the bottle. The disgusting filth of the water angered him. He viewed it as a sin against his beloved mother.

He carefully placed the last bottle into the pouch with the others, zipped it closed, and tucked it into his pocket. He then stooped down, scooped up a palm full of the murky, brown liquid, brought it to his lips, and kissed it. He rose to his feet and stared out at the river. "I must leave now, but soon," he said, "things will be as they once were, I promise. This time, I will not disappoint you."

CHAPTER 11

Sausalito, California
Tuesday, May 27ᵗʰ

Samael and Usman arrived at the San Francisco airport at 4:35 p.m. They traveled light with one carry on each, as they planned to return to Istanbul in a matter of days. Samael had booked a hotel in Sausalito, a small community in Marin County on the north side of the San Francisco Bay. While in San Francisco, they planned to purchase the needed equipment and supplies for the mission. Prearrangements had been made with black-market suppliers for certain controlled narcotics and drugs.

As the cab made its way through San Francisco and toward Sausalito, the iconic, orange towers of the Golden Gate Bridge, draped with massive steel cables, came into view. Standing tall, like a sentinel guarding the San Francisco Bay, the magnificent bridge was not only a concrete and steel path across the strait, but a monument of American pride.

Samael's face reddened with anger as the view of the bridge filled the taxi's front windshield. The twin towers pierced the blue sky like minarets. Once on the bridge, he laughed with delight, knowing that within a few, short days, the disgusting mockery of his dear mother's name would be buried in the depths of the sea.

Usman craned his neck out the window of the cab. "Amazing!" he said, the wind muffling his voice. "It's much like our Bosphorus and Fatih Sultan Mehmet Bridges."

"Older," Samael said with disgust in his voice. "As far as suspension bridges go, the main span of this bridge is only a few hundred feet wider than ours. It's basically a piece of junk ready for the scrap yard." The cab driver shot Samael a piercing glance in the rearview mirror. Samael snapped at the defensive San Franciscan, "What are you looking at?"

Within five minutes the cab turned onto El Portal Drive in Sausalito, and wheeled up in front of the Hotel Sausalito. Samael and Usman exited the cab and met the driver at the rear of the car. In his early to mid sixties, the long-haired, bearded, tattooed, love child quickly removed the two bags and said, "That'll be—"

"This should cover it," Samael said, having made note of the fare on the meter before exiting the cab. To avoid unnecessary conversation with the driver, he handed the man double the amount of the fare, then lifted his bag and headed for the hotel entrance. "Let's go," he ordered Usman, who quickly followed without a word.

Built in Mission-Revival style in 1915, the sixteen-room, waterfront hotel was rumored to have been a bordello during the era of Prohibition, an emotional escape from the drudgery of life for many railroad workers, seafarers, writers, and passing travelers. After an extensive renovation in 1996, its décor presented a flavor of the French Riviera. Strikingly accurate renditions of Matisses and Monets lined the hallways. Hand crafted furnishings, stained glass windows, and views of the park and harbor accentuated the hotel's international flavor. Samael found the quaint feel of the hotel pleasing.

The desk clerk greeted Samael with an uncomfortable

stare, "Checking in?" The clerk's voice sang with femininity. His movements were laced with twirls and twists that sickened Samael. However, unlike most that saw Samael for the first time, the clerk appeared unfazed by Samael's size and appearance. Living in the epicenter of liberalized thinking, the city had obviously conditioned him to accept the most freakish forms of humanity without casting judgment.

Samael said, "S. Jones and U. Smith. Two rooms."

The frail, young man flipped through a file box behind the counter with the most delicate touch. "Ah, yes, here we go." Inspecting the reservation card as he lifted it from the box, he raised an eyebrow and brought his index finger to the corner of his lip. "Hmm." Glancing in Samael's direction, he said, "Mr. Jones?"

"Yes."

"Both rooms appear to have been prepaid."

"That's correct. Is there a problem?"

"No, not at all. I think it's marvelous. Here are your keys."

Samael took both keys, handing one to Usman.

"Ah…Mr. Jones. I almost forgot. You have a package." The clerk placed a small, brown envelope on the desk and slid it toward Samael. The label read 'Samael Jones'. Samael took the envelope.

The clerk said, "Will there be anything else?"

"No," Samael said.

"Well then, enjoy your stay and give me a buzz if you need anything or have any questions."

Samael thought of the many guests who had stayed in the hotel since the bridge opened on May 27, 1937. Until then, the only access to Sausalito from San Francisco had been ferries or long drives around the bay. It pleased him to think that the people of Marin County and the sleepy, little town of Sausalito would soon thank him for ridding their community of nosey tourists.

In the hallway, before entering his room, Samael turned to Usman and said, "There are plenty of restaurants down the street, but I suggest you avoid the public. I'll meet you in the morning."

"What time?"

"I'll knock on your door at 5:00. Be ready."

"I'll be ready," Usman said.

Expecting the next two days to be emotionally demanding, Samael needed his rest. Tomorrow night they would stay in Sausalito, and then drive to Southern California the following morning.

After undressing, showering, and praying, he opened the envelope that the desk boy had given him. The contents included $20,000 in cash, a remote entry car key, and a one-way ticket from Los Angeles International Airport to Ataturk International Airport, Istanbul, departing at 9:55 a.m., on May 30th. Only one ticket was required, as Usman would not be making the return trip.

CHAPTER 12

Wednesday, May 28th

Instead of the cry of the muezzin's call to worship, Samael woke to the sound of fog horns in San Francisco Bay. The unfamiliar sounds caused a momentary disorientation but quickly cleared.

He smiled.

In little more than 48 hours, he would be on a flight out of LAX headed back to Istanbul, his mission complete.

Sleep was a wasteful necessity of the body that, like a thief, robbed him of valuable time. He sat up and swung his feet to the floor. He rubbed his eyes and searched for his glasses on the nightstand. The green glow of the digital clock read 4:15. He stood and walked to the window, peeling back the curtains to reveal the black of morning. No cars on the streets. No people strolling by in the park. The ferry landing was quiet. It would be at least an hour before the sleepy town came to life.

He pulled the curtains closed and walked naked across the room to the bathroom. After switching on the light, the horrid image of his reflection met him in the vanity mirror above the sink, an image he'd been forced to live with for thirty-three years. His lean, muscular physique was the only thing in which he took pride. He had the face of a monster but the body of a warrior, partly due to genetics from a father he'd never met, and partly due to a rigorous exercise program. His disgust turned to focused strength as his thoughts were refreshed with the task before him and the tattooed letters across his white chest: KEROESSA.

Once he had showered, dressed, and prayed, he removed a satchel from his suitcase, unzipped it and transferred the money into the bag. Next, he took the pouch containing the four bottles of water from the Golden Horn River, carefully removed the bottles, lined them up on the dresser, and removed the tops. He then removed the blade from his disposable razor and drew it across his thumb, squeezing five drops of his blood into each bottle. He then secured the bottle caps, returned the bottles to the pouch, and bandaged his thumb.

Now we are one—my blood and yours.

Ensuring the DO NOT DISTURB sign was on the doorknob, he left the room, crossed the hall and knocked on Usman's door. The door opened within seconds.

"Good morning," Usman said. He was clean shaven and dressed like an American tourist, as Samael had instructed. Without his beard and mustache, he looked like a child.

"Let's go, there's much to do." Samael hurried down the hall. Usman followed close behind. After exiting the hotel, Samael stood on the sidewalk, pulled the car key from his pocket, gazed into the dark, and pressed the UNLOCK button. A chirp broke the silence, along with a flash of yellow taillights. A black, Chevy Suburban was parked on the curb.

Samael smiled.

He tossed the satchel into the front seat and switched on the car. "Today," Samael said, "you will see with your own eyes the purpose for our lives. Before the sun sets on this day, all of your questions will be answered."

He pulled away from the curb, turning left onto Bridgeway Road with the San Francisco Bay to their left. As they drove clear of the small town, the sight of the orange towers of the Golden Gate Bridge, draped with its sweeping cables, pierced the morning sky. Passing under the highway leading to the bridge, they followed Conzelman Road up the twisting incline to the vista points on Hawk Hill. The location offered the most dramatic views of the bay and bridge from the north.

Usman looked back at the bridge showcased against the deep-purple, morning sky as they ascended the hill to a height equaling that of the towering 746 foot spears of the international orange towers. "Is that it?" Usman said.

"If you are referring to our target, yes, that's it." Samael pulled off at a vista point. With the Suburban facing the spectacular view of the bridge, city, and Alcatraz, he switched off the ignition. "Chrysopylae," he said.

"What?" Usman said.

"You're looking at Chrysopylae."

"Isn't that Greek?"

"Yes. In December 1845, Captain John C. Fremont and a force of thirty men arrived in the Mexican province of Alta, California, with the intentions of mapping the West Coast area. While exploring the upper coast of California, he came upon what is now known as the San Francisco Bay. Having previously traveled to Istanbul, when Fremont first saw the three-mile-long strait leading into the San Francisco Bay, it reminded him of our glorious Golden Horn.

On June 5, 1848, Fremont submitted his *Geographical Memoir* to the U.S. Senate. About this place, he wrote, was *called Chrysopylae (Golden Gate) on the map, on the same principle that the harbor of Byzantium (Constantinople afterwards) was called Chrysoceras (Golden Horn)....*"

"I had no idea the bridge was that old?"

Samael turned his head, giving Usman a disgusting stare. "Not the bridge! Fremont named the strait! The name *Golden Gate* was officially applied to the entrance to San Francisco Bay on June 5, 1848—the same day Fremont submitted his *Geographical Memoir* to the U.S. Senate. The bridge wasn't completed until 1937." Samael's jaws tightened. "Fremont said he was *inspired* by our glorious Golden Horn—Chrysoceras." The sound of his own words caused his heart to race and his skin to tingle.

Usman remained quiet, obviously sensing Samael's change in countenance.

Samael took his wallet from his rear pocket, opened it, and removed a small antique-looking black and white photo. The photo of a man had been Xeroxed from a picture he'd found in an encyclopedia at the library.

The droopy-eyed, bearded man in the photo looked to be in his early thirties. His wavy, dark hair was parted in the middle and combed down over his ears. He wore a double-breasted coat with an extremely large bowtie. The young man was John C. Fremont.

Samael crumpled the paper up into a small ball and stuffed it into his mouth. After chewing on it for a few seconds, the watery mixture of secretions from salivary, mucous glands in his mouth lubricated the paper sufficiently allowing him to swallow it into the depths of his stomach.

Samael turned and gazed down at Usman, his eyes filled with bewilderment. "This monument was built by the infidels as a mockery to our beloved Chrysoceras. The journey of my soul will finally be complete once it is removed. I failed on July 11, 2002, but with your help, I will not fail again. Let's go. We have one more stop to make.

Samael descended from Hawk Hill and parked the car at the vista point on the north side of the Golden Gate Bridge. He unzipped his satchel, retrieved the small pouch containing the four vials of water and blood mixture, removed one of the vials, tucked it into his pocket, and returned the pouch to the satchel.

"Get out, we're walking across," Samael said.

"The bridge?" Usman said.

"Yes. There's something I must do."

He slipped on his protective wrappers, pulled his hood down snug over his head, and walked briskly toward the sidewalk leading to the pedestrian footpath spanning the east side of the bridge. Usman followed, working hard to keep pace with Samael's long strides.

A stiff breeze swirled across the Bay, chilling the air, masking the growing danger of ultraviolent rays from the rising sun. Light was Samael's greatest enemy. All bright light irritated his eyes, but it was the ultraviolent light from the sun that presented the greatest danger. If exposed, any unprotected skin would fry like bacon.

Samael moved with urgency and purpose in each step. The healing would soon begin. With his beloved mother's blood, he would cleanse the infected waters passing through the Golden Gate—Chrysopylae.

Just as an antibiotic overcomes a bacterial infection within the human body, water from the Golden Horn—Chrysoceras—would cleanse the contaminated water flowing through the Golden Gate Strait.

Standing in the exact center of the bridge beneath the twin towers, facing east, Samael reached into the pocket of his jacket and retrieved the vial. After unscrewing the top to the bottle, he brought the bottle to his lips and kissed it. With the bottle in his right hand, he lifted his head toward the sky, closed his eyes, and extended his arm out beyond the orange railing of the bridge. He slowly emptied the contents of the bottle.

As the brown liquid disbursed into the air, carried off by strong winds, he said, "Oh my beloved, may you purify these waters, healing them of the poisons by which they have been afflicted." He then opened his eyes, drew back his arm, and hurled the bottle away from the bridge.

Usman stood speechless having not been informed beforehand of the significance of the ceremony. "What was in the bottle?"

Samael peered down at the little man as a teacher might a befuddled student. "The only way to purify these polluted waters is with the blood of Chrysoceras."

"You brought water from the Golden Horn River?"

"Yes. The blood of my beloved is the only way the wrongs of the past can be purified." Samael turned and faced the south tower. He gazed up at the orange steel reaching 748 feet into the air. "The last act of healing will be when this monument, a mockery to my beloved, is destroyed." He smiled, knowing his beloved mother was sure to be smiling down on him. "At exactly midnight tomorrow night, under a crescent moon, this monument will collapse into the purified waters below. No longer will there be a monument to this Chrysopylae. At that moment, my purpose in this life will be fulfilled, and I will be free to return to the afterlife."

"Tomorrow is May 29th," Usman said. "It's the day we celebrate Mehmet's victory at Constantinople." Usman peered up at Samael. "And it's your birthday. What a genius plan."

"Tomorrow will be a new beginning. Just as Mehmet found victory under a crescent moon on May 29th, we too will find victory on the same night, under the same crescent moon."

"It could not be more perfect."

"We will celebrate together." Satisfied, Samael turned and marched back toward the car, calling to Usman, "Hurry along; we have a busy day ahead of us."

PART II

"Yea, though I walk through the valley of the shadow of death, I will fear no evil; for You are with me; Your rod and Your staff, they comfort me." Psalm 23:4

CHAPTER 13

Thursday, May 29th
6:30 p.m.

Ryan rolled out of bed after a two hour nap. The view out his bedroom window was black. He moaned.

Oh boy, here we go again.

He pulled the spongy foam plugs from his ears, tossed them in the top drawer of the nightstand, slipped on a pair of jeans, then headed downstairs for dinner.

Every few days, he repeated the cycle, the same routine: nap for a couple of hours, eat dinner with his family, throw a few things into a half-packed suitcase, put on his uniform, and make the one hour, 68 mile drive to the airport.

By the time he hit the road, most of the working world had fled to their domestic nests in search of a few hours of rest before rising to the drumbeat calling them to repeat the never-ending cycle.

As a junior L.A.-based airline captain, the red-eye trans-con to the East Coast was the best trip he could hold. Pinned to the bottom of the seniority list, married to a company shrinking their way to profitability, he was forced to join the invisible brotherhood of workers who performed their trade and earned their living under the cover of darkness; the likes of burglars, grave-diggers, and prostitutes.

After fifteen years, he'd imagined a different life. Instead of all-nighters, he'd dreamed of flying day trips out of LAX to Hawaii. Early arrivals to the Islands in time for relaxing dinners at sunset, eight hours of sleep, and late-morning departures back to the Mainland the next day. But the fallout from 9/11 had forced the airline industry into a nosedive, taking with it any hope of a better quality of life for all airline employees.

The bright, kitchen lights, smell of fresh bread, and the clatter of dishes helped bring him out of his half-dazed state. A glimpse at the black of night beyond the sliding glass window leading onto the patio was a sobering reminder of what lay ahead.

"Hi, Honey." Keri said, greeting him with a kiss. "Were you able to sleep?"

"Remind me to kill the neighbor's dog," he growled. "I'm sure I'd be doing them a favor."

Keri's face scrunched with empathy. "I'm sorry."

"While I'm over there, I'll be sure to put a knife in their kid's basketball."

Keri placed a plate in front of him with baked chicken, rice, and broccoli. "What would you like to drink?"

"Water's fine."

As ice cubes clunked into the glass from the dispenser, she said, "So, is it New York, Boston, or Miami tonight?"

"New York," he grunted.

Regardless of the destination, it was all the same. Drive to the airport, complete a routine preflight, takeoff into the darkness, climb to cruise altitude, stare into the black of night for five to six hours while fighting the urge to sleep. Then approximately thirty minutes from landing, tank up on enough bad coffee to last through the descent and landing, make the bag drag from the arrival gate through the terminal to the crew van to the hotel, find the room, pull the curtains, crawl into bed and hope for a few hours of rest. His two greatest enemies were the noise of departing guests in adjacent rooms and the dreaded, mistaken knock on the door: "Housekeeping!" It was a constant battle with circadian rhythm, chronic fatigue, and living in an upside-down world.

Keri set his water glass on the table and took a seat. "Thanks," he said.

After the debacle with her father's inheritance, Keri returned to work. However, not willing to sacrifice her time with her young son, she waited until David had entered the first grade. In the shadow of 9/11, the idea of continuing as a flight attendant was unsettling, plus being on the road and away from David was not acceptable. She decided to return to school for a nursing degree.

Between the time David started first grade and the birth of their daughter, Martha, Keri completed a bachelor's of science degree in nursing and had worked two years as a nurse at a local emergency clinic located only a few minutes from their house. With qualified nurses being in short supply, she had been fortunate to find the perfect job with the perfect hours. Her added financial contribution helped to pare Ryan's 30 percent pay cut at the airline.

Financial catastrophe bred a new form of corporate greed. Airline managers began to look on the tragic events of 9/11 as a trump card in a bigger scheme aimed at breaking the backs of labor unions—a form of unorganized conspiracy.

With the help of inflation, a flying public conditioned by lowered air fares and less frills, a younger workforce willing to accept lower wages in exchange for the promise of job security, skyrocketing fuel costs, and the use of bankruptcies to shed expensive pension obligations, corporate executives worked frantically to spin the negative events so as to forever blur the actual value attached to the professional responsibilities of being an airline pilot.

Ryan and Keri were blessed by what most would call a *good* marriage in a day when most marriages are little more than a mini vacation down the highway of lust, littered with offspring created from the *8-12% possibility of failure* as read on the warning label of most condom packages.

"Hi, Dad," David said and signed, walking into the kitchen and slipping into his chair at the table. His guttural voice sounded strained.

"Hey, Buddy," Ryan said and signed. "Where's your sister?"

"Coming."

A moment later, small arms squeezed his waist. "How's my sweetheart?"

"Fine." Martha took a seat beside him. "Daddy," she said, signing while she talked, "do you *have* to go on another trip tonight?"

"Yes. But when I get home, we get to take that vacation we've been planning."

"Can't you just miss this one trip? Pleeease!"

"Darling, I wish I could."

David added, "Yeah, Dad, miss it. We go tomorrow. Vacation."

"You guys know there's nothing I'd like more." He glanced over at Keri, meeting her wishful gaze. "This is the last one and then I'm off for two whole weeks." He put a bite of chicken in his mouth.

The horrid images from his dream still lingered—they always did. Ryan and Keri had made a point not to share the events of his recurring nightmare with their children.

Once David and Martha finished their dinner, Keri said, "You guys can be dismissed."

After they left, Keri turned to Ryan and said, "Are you going to be okay?"

"Is it that obvious?" He pushed the remaining food

around on his plate.

"I worry about you."

Still looking down at his plate, he said, "It's the nightmares." Resting his fork on his plate, he turned and met Keri's concerned eyes. "I just can't let it go. Rex should've never died."

"Honey," she said, placing her hand on his arm, "it's not your fault. Just like you told *me*, you've got to let it go."

"I know."

"You can't do this to yourself. You have to know there's nothing you could have done to stop what happened."

"And Emily...."

"I know...." Her eyes filled with a watery glaze.

He glanced at his watch, "I need to get ready."

He felt trapped by circumstances beyond his control: his company always wanting more for less, pushing him to his physical, mental, and emotional limits; his insides being eaten away by guilt and remorse for the circumstances surrounding Rex's death; the needs of a handicapped child.

If only there was something he could do to make it all go away. He couldn't bring Rex back, and he had few options to deal with his work schedule other than calling in fatigued or sick—neither a fix for the emotional hemorrhaging that plagued him.

He took one last drink of water before heading upstairs to dress and finish packing.

7:35 p.m.

Dressed and packed, he loaded the car and gave Keri a kiss. "I'll see you tomorrow night, late. Don't wait up."

Her eyes searched his soul, seeing things only a wife could see. "I love you," she said. "Ryan, everything's going to be okay."

"I know." He slipped into the driver's seat, pulling the seatbelt across his chest, snapping the buckle. He looked up at her, forcing a smile. "I love you."

Leaning down, she gave him one last kiss, and then walked to the door leading back into the house. He backed out of the garage and onto the street. The night was damp. The black asphalt shown under the mist-cloaked, street lamps while fog, carried by a cool breeze, drifted beneath the tops of the trees like ghosts.

One last glance at Keri standing at the door tugged on his heart like a cord refusing to let go. He eased away against the slight grade in the street. Within five minutes, he merged into a sea of traffic on Interstate Five. He checked the time—7:45. He should roll into the employee parking lot at 8:50 in time to catch the 9 p.m. bus to the terminal. He normally allowed more cushion in case there was any unexpected traffic or an accident on the freeway, but, this time, he found it extra hard to leave Keri and the kids. As long as there were no delays, he had plenty of time to make his 9:30 sign in.

He clung to Keri's departing words and the sweet lingering taste of her lips. One last trip stood between him and two weeks of needed rest with his family.

He pushed through the dark among a herd of speeding automobiles driven by blank faces masking complex and mostly troubled lives.

CHAPTER 14

7:40 p.m.

The sight of Ryan driving away tore at Keri's heart. She had watched him drive away thousands of times before, but this time it was different. He was hurting. Life was out of balance. Something had to change.

She returned into the house. In for the night, she checked the doors, engaged the bolt locks, and flipped off the foyer light, and front porchlight. Hearing the children upstairs, she took a breath, accepting the challenge of getting them bathed and in bed. Tomorrow she'd promised they'd do something special together, just the three of them.

"Okay, time for baths," she said, signing her words as she spoke.

"Not now," David spoke in a guttural tone.

"Yes, now. Tomorrow is a fun day and we all need to get to bed early." She noticed David brighten.

"Yay!" Martha said. "What are we going to do, Mommy?"

Keri took Martha's hand and led her towards the bathroom. "You can think about it tonight, and we can decide in the morning."

The doorbell chimed, followed by a light knock. Keri checked the time—7:45.

Who could that be?

Martha looked up at Keri, "Mommy, someone's at the door. Let's go see who it is."

Keri checked her watch. "No, Honey, I'll get it. You get ready for your bath. I'll be back in a minute." Keri turned to David and signed, "Doorbell. You and Martha bathe."

"Mommy, please let me go with you," Martha pleaded.

"No. You start getting ready for your bath."

Keri descended the stairs, flipped on the foyer light, then the porchlight. She glanced quickly through the small peephole, remembering that the porchlight was out—something Ryan had told her he would fix. The glare from the foyer light made it hard to see into the darkness.

She unlatched the bolt lock and opened the door slightly. A man's shoe slid into the small opening between the door jam and the door, blocking it from being closed. The door jerked violently, pushing her back against the stairway banister. Two men rushed into the house and closed the door.

"Who are you?! What do you want?!"

One man towered over her, his shoulders wide, his arms like tree trunks. His head was buried in the shadow of a hooded jacket, his eyes hidden behind narrow glasses. In his right hand he gripped a black handgun. His large paws were sheathed in latex gloves. The other man was small and frail, at least a foot shorter, maybe more.

He's going to kill me! Then the children!

"Mommy!" Martha screamed from the top of the stairs. "Mommy!"

Keri glanced up at the children, both clinging to the banister at the top of the stairs. "Go to your room! Lock the door!"

David, unable to hear, sensed the danger. He pulled on Martha but could not break her grip on the banister. She screamed louder with each pull. "Stop! I want my Mommy!"

The tall man, unaffected by the child's screams, calmly said, "No, no, no…everything will be just fine." He looked up at the children. "Children, why don't you come down and join us. I think your mommy would like that…wouldn't you, Keri?"

Martha's cries grew louder, unable to process her fear, "I WANT MY MOMMY!"

"Keri," the tall man said, remaining calm and contained, "please tell your children to come down here, now."

Keri turned to the hooded man. "How do you know who I am? What do you want?"

"Mrs. Mitchell, forgive my manners…" he said in a relaxed and soft voice, "…may I call you, Keri?"

"Who are you?"

"There will be plenty of time for that later."

Keri yelled, "Martha, you and David go to your room! Lock the door!"

The tall man stepped in closer to Keri, clamping his monstrous, free hand around her throat, squeezing ever so slightly, pinning her against the banister. The hot, rubbery palm pressed against her windpipe causing her to hack and gasp for air. Something jammed into her ribs, inches below her left breast.

The gun!

She flinched. Desperately searching for relief, her eyes darted to the man's face, now illuminated by the light from a lamp in the den. His ghostly-white face caused her to gasp. She coughed. His tight grip cut off her attempt to draw needed air into her lungs.

"Now, Keri, dear, everything will be okay if you simply do as I say. Do we understand each other?" Through clinched teeth, the man repeated, "Do we understand each other?"

His warm rancid breath hit her face. She caught a foul whiff of onions and coffee. She wanted to vomit. His grip tightened around her throat. Desperate for air and unable to speak, she nodded to indicate she understood.

"Good," he said, loosening his grip and removing his hand.

Keri gulped in air. Coughed. Her hands reached for her throat, massaging it where the man had left his latex imprint.

Martha screamed, "Mommie!" She broke free of David's grasp and raced for her mother. David followed. Martha latched onto Keri with both arms. Keri pulled her close and put her other arm around David.

"Now, Keri, you and the children follow my little friend into the den and have a seat on the couch."

The children remained glued to her side as she struggled to the couch. Martha's cries turned to whimpers.

Keri looked at the small man. He appeared less threatening, almost normal. He was wearing dark slacks, a black-collared shirt, and latex gloves. He was clean shaven with neatly-trimmed, black hair. The lenses of his glasses were unusually thick. His dark skin, heavy brow, and general features made him appear to be Middle Eastern. So far, he hadn't spoken a word.

The tall man appeared unaffected by her near-death experience as he sauntered over to her. "Keri, I want you to call Ryan."

How does he know Ryan's name?

"I have something I would like to discuss with him. Of course, the moment he hears a man's voice coming from his wife's cell phone, he will suspect something is wrong. He'll, no doubt, insist that I let him talk with you. I will let him speak with you, and you will tell him to please do what the bad man tells him to do. Keri, do you understand?"

"What do you want? Why are you here?"

"Keri, you need to calm down." He leaned down, his face only inches from hers. "Just do as I say. Do you understand?"

She nodded, afraid he might grab her throat again.

"Good." He stood up, stretched, and smiled down at Keri. "Now, where is your cell phone?"

"In my purse." Her eyes glanced toward the table in the foyer. "Over there."

The short man said, "I'll get it." His high-pitched voice was as Keri had imagined. He quickly retrieved the phone and handed it to the tall man.

The tall man flipped open the phone and started pressing buttons on the keypad. "Here it is: RYAN. How convenient."

"I can't do it," she said.

"Of course you can, dear."

"What do you want him to do? Is it money? Do you want money? I'll give you money."

"Like I said, dear, all you need to do, now, is tell your husband you're okay. If he wants you to *remain* okay, he'll need to do what the man wants."

"What happens if he won't do what you want?"

"We don't need to talk about that now. What you need to do *now* is agree to do exactly as I tell you."

Martha's head was buried under her mother's protective wing. "Mommy, I'm scared. I want daddy."

Keri pulled her in tight. "Honey, everything's going to be fine."

"Let me explain something, Keri." The tall man leaned down, his eyes peering over the rims of his narrow spectacles. He whispered, "If you can't do this for me, I'll not only kill you and your children and leave you for the police to find, I'll make it look like your husband did it before he left for work."

Suddenly, she thought of Emily. A chill raced up the back of her neck like some creature crawling under her skin looking for a safe place to hide. She couldn't help but wonder if this was the same lunatic that murdered Emily. A wave of dizziness swept through her head. Keri said, "Who are you?"

"Keri, I'm sorry. Forgive me for not properly introducing myself. I guess we can take a minute. You can call me Sam." He turned toward Martha. "You know…like the cat with the hat: *Sam I Am*." He smiled at Martha. She gripped her mother with all of her might and buried her face in her side.

"This is all wrong," she said. "What do you want with us? My husband can't help you." Her body trembled uncontrollably. All she could think about was Emily and Rex.

Samael took a deep breath then stood. "Keri, I'm starting to lose my patience with you. I don't have all night."

"What do you want with Ryan? Just tell me."

"I think you'd better start thinking about your two beautiful children and all the other children who will die if you don't cooperate. Because after I kill you and your children, I'll kill another family, and another, and another. I'll keep doing it, Keri, until I find a pilot and his wife who will make the right choice."

She said nothing.

He must be the one who murdered Emily.

"Keri, do you want me to continue killing?"

She said nothing.

"You see, Keri, you are not the first and, if you don't cooperate, you won't be the last. Think of it this way, if you help me, you will not only save yourself and your children's lives, but you will save the lives of others. I know you don't want to be the cause of the deaths of others, now do you? I'm certain once your husband weighs the alternatives, he will be more than happy to sacrifice his life for the lives of his dear wife and children."

"Are you serious? I can't put him in that position."

"What position?"

"Choosing who's going to die. You must be mad! You want him to do something with his airplane, don't you? You want him to kill innocent people. I can't do it. I won't do it."

"Keri, they're just people. People you don't even know."

I knew it! It's him!

"Keri, it's an easy decision. I'm sure your husband will be willing to save the lives of his family in exchange for a few hundred people he doesn't even know; people who could care less about him or his family. Besides, he'll be dead. It's not like he'll have to live with the guilt of killing those people."

"I know Ryan. He won't do it. You might as well kill us now."

"Do you really believe he'll choose strangers over you?"

"If he chooses us," she said, "who says you won't kill us anyway?"

"Well, I guess it comes down to trust, doesn't it Keri? But for now, that's something you don't have to worry about. Your husband is the one who will have to make a choice. Life is all about making choices and taking risks. I suspect if given the choice, most people would sacrifice their life for the lives of their loved ones. As for me, I personally don't see the dilemma. I'd much rather choose death."

She met his eyes.

This freak is seriously deranged.

"Keri, what's your problem? I'm quite certain your husband will make the right decision."

David could read the man's body and facial expressions, but could not hear his words. Martha heard everything. The thought of her five-year-old daughter hearing this man talk about death and killing was more than Keri could stand. If only to stop the morbid talk, she surrendered. She met the pendulous eyes of the albino man and said, "Go ahead, call him. I'll do what you want." She could only hope Ryan would think of something.

The tall, white freak smiled. He pressed a button on the cell phone's keypad then moved the phone to his left ear.

CHAPTER 15

8:05 p.m.

Ryan glanced down at the speedometer. The digital readout glowed—73—eight over the posted 65 mph limit. It normally took ten or more over the posted limit to wake any patrolmen that might be hiding in the shadows.

Ahead of schedule and assured of arriving at the airport with plenty of time to spare, he piloted the car through the darkness like a wingless jet. The flow of traffic was steady, but thin.

The one positive about flying all-nighters was the relatively quiet drive to the airport. During the day, the hyper-dynamic circulation of vast freeway arteries throughout Southern California was notorious for producing toxic levels of needless stress and rage.

Ryan stored a mental map of the journey from his house to LAX. He measured his progress with methodical perfection. The car's on-board computer provided a wide range of information which fed his insatiable thirst for details: average fuel consumption, average speed, range till empty, driver-defined speed limit warnings; all accessed with the touch of a finger from a control stalk on the steering column and viewed in the car's central instrument display.

The 68 mile trek unraveled in orderly parcels delivering a satisfying sense of accomplishment. After countless trips to LAX, he habitually, almost subliminally, compared the passing of key landmarks with the tripometer. At any given point, he knew the exact number of miles and minutes that remained.

Droning through the dark, he preferred silence to music or mindless talk radio. An occasional chirp emitted from the radar detector mounted high on the windscreen. The CHP (California Highway Patrol) normally used tactics that make a radar detector worthless, but more than once, the detector had saved him from the jaws of a speed trap. The radar guns used by the CHP send out signals that are loud, clear, and constant. There is no mistaking them for a lost electron from a local, retail establishment searching for a patron to strike.

His thoughts drifted to his family. Keri had said she planned to take the kids out tomorrow, possibly to the beach or a movie. He had a vacation to look forward to, once he put this trip behind him. He had booked reservations at the Hilton Waikoloa Village on the Big Island of Hawaii. The kids had been looking forward to it all year, especially the Dolphin Quest and hotel sponsored day camps for keiki, or "little people". He had promised they'd make the trip once Martha turned five.

He snapped from his trance when his cell phone rang. The familiar ringtone told him it was Keri. Had he left something: his identification badge, wallet, keys? In a matter of seconds, his free hand touched the critical items: his back pocket, his right, front pocket, the lapel on his coat lying in the passenger's seat beside him. Everything was there. He also distinctly remembered loading his suitcase, kitbag, and gun in the trunk.

A second ring sounded. He lifted his cell from its holder, clipped on his belt. Flipping it open, he pressed TALK. "Hi baby, what's up?"

"Hello, Captain Mitchell," an unfamiliar man's voice said, "I must say…you are a lucky man."

"Who is this?"

"There's no need for alarm, Captain Mitchell, or do you mind if I call you, Ryan?" The strange voice was unnervingly calm. "Your family is safe…and will remain so, as long as you do exactly as I say."

Ryan's chest tightened. His heart raced. "Let me talk to my wife."

"Certainly. Let me put her on."

Keri's voice quivered. "Ryan, we're alright," she said. "The children are here with me. They're fine. He says if you follow his instructions, he won't hurt us."

Martha cried out, "Daddy! I'm scared!"

"Martha! I'm right here!"

Click!

Did I lose her?

Louder and clearer than before, the eerie calm of the lunatic's voice returned, "Captain Mitchell, you heard your wife."

He transferred the cell to speaker.

"If you do exactly as I instruct, your family will remain safe. Otherwise, they will all die, starting with your youngest child. Do you understand?"

"I don't know who you are, but if you lay one hand on my family—"

"CAPTAIN MITCHELL! LISTEN TO ME! This is not a negotiation! I don't have time for your games! You either do as I say, or your family dies. It's that simple. This is the last time I'm going to ask you. Do you understand?"

"YES! YES! I understand. What do you want?"

Silence.

Ambushed by the deepest darkness known to man, the very essence of Evil incarnate, Ryan fought to hold tight to the only thing on Earth that mattered: his family. Trapped in a vacuum of denial, everything real vaporized. His eyes locked on the beams of light carving a path through the black of night while images and circumstances surrounding Keri, Martha, and David flooded into his mind.

How did the lunatic enter the house? Is he alone? Where in the house is he holding them? The children must be horrified. Why is he doing this?

"Good," Samael said in a calm voice. "Mitchell, don't test me again."

Ryan hammered the accelerator to the floorboard. He'd passed PACIFIC PARK exit a few miles back. EL TORO exit was next. Only minutes away. He would exit there, reverse course, and be at the house in less than twenty minutes. He would call 911 once he hung up with the lunatic. SWAT (Special Weapons And Tactics) would surround the house. They were trained. They knew what to do. If he beat them to the house, he had his gun.

Anxiously waiting for the exit, Ryan said, "What do you want me to do?"

CHAPTER 16

8:10 p.m.

U sman scurried like a weasel from outside to inside, busily converting the Mitchell house into a mini command post. A folding table was erected in the den on which he positioned two laptop computers. With a 20-foot Ethernet cable and a Y-connector, he married the computers to the existing high speed Internet service.

"Captain Mitchell," Samael said, speaking into the cell, "I want you to do exactly what I tell you." He looked down at Keri, then over at the children, pausing briefly. "If I haven't already told you, you have a beautiful family, but I'm sure you already know that."

"Who are you?" Ryan's strong voice forced Samael to move the cell away from his ear. "If you touch my family, I swear I'll hunt you down and kill you with my bare hands!"

Keri whimpered at the sound of Ryan's voice.

In the background, the computers beeped as their screens filled with color. Usman moved between the two keyboards, clicking furiously at the keys, connecting them each to specific sites.

"Captain Mitchell," Samael calmly said, "I don't think

you understand. It's not about who lives or dies—you kill me; I kill you; I kill your family; whatever…it's about you doing *exactly* as I tell you. We're all going to die, sooner or later. The only choice you must make is who dies now, and who dies later, or if we all die together. Are we on the same page?"

"Why are you doing this? Is it money?"

"We mustn't digress. We're on a schedule, something I'm sure you're very familiar with. You have a flight to catch. Remember?"

"What do you want?"

"For now, you just drive. Don't even think about turning around and trying to be a hero, because if you feel brave and choose to deviate, it will cost you one of your family members, starting with the youngest and working up. One life for one mistake. I think that's fair, don't you, Captain Mitchell? So, I guess you could say you have three chances to get it right."

Keri pulled the children close, attempting to shield Martha's ears from the vicious threats.

"How do you know I'm not heading back home right now? Have you thought about that?"

"Captain Mitchell, don't be foolish. Think of me as God. I know everything." Samael glanced over at Usman. The little man nodded. One computer screen displayed a map of the west coast of California from Los Angeles to San Francisco. The other monitor displayed a map of the California freeway system from San Diego to Los Angeles.

Samael walked over to the computers. His poor vision required him to lean in close to examine the screen. A small, blinking, red light moved slowly along a blue line representing Highway 73. "A very sophisticated satellite, tracking device is bolted to your car. Being a military man, you will appreciate the fact that this device was originally designed for military use and is capable of following you

around the globe. In ten seconds you will be passing the EL
TORO exit on State Road 73."

The EL TORO exit was next after PACIFIC PARK, which
Ryan remembered passing only moments after receiving the
call…and there it was: EL TORO. He checked the time.
Exactly ten seconds from the mark.

The man's voice returned. "Not only am I watching your
progress on the freeway, but I know the exact speed of your
car and the average speed and congestion on the freeway. I can
tell you your ETA (estimated time of arrival) at the employee
parking lot with an accuracy of plus or minus ten seconds.
Your speed was 76 miles per hour until you pushed it up to 91
a few minutes ago."

Ryan looked down. The digital readout glowed 91.

"I think you should slow down. I would hate for you to
be pulled over. We don't have time for any unnecessary
delays caused by your stupidity. Just so you understand, here
are the rules—if you exit the freeway, stop, or attempt to be a
hero, one member of your family will die. Understood?"

"Yes." Ryan quickly removed pressure from the
accelerator. The digits started to fall: 90…85…78…74…70.

"Good. It's all about trust, Captain Mitchell. We need to
trust each other. The next thing you need to know is that if
anyone shows up at your house, I will start killing your
family in the order I previously described."

"How can I control that? What if a neighbor or friend
comes by?"

"Don't be alarmed, Captain Mitchell. The house is dark
and I would expect any visitor to leave after no one comes to
the door. My concern is that you might attempt to get word to
someone to send help to your house. Although we are
monitoring your cell phone, I don't want you to think that

you can pass a note or ask someone to place a call for you. If you do, someone will die. Am I clear?"

"Yes. I understand."

"Good. Remember, it's all about trust. In order to trust each other, we must first believe in each other. Captain Mitchell, do you believe I will do what I am telling you?"

"Yes."

"Good. When you arrive at the airport, I want you to conduct business as normal. Park your car. Ride the first available employee bus to the terminal. Go to flight operations. When you check your mailbox, you will find an envelope. That envelope will contain the specific instructions of what I want you to do. Don't waste your time trying to understand why you are being asked to accomplish this task, just do it. Remember, your lack of cooperation will result in the death of your family. Do you understand?"

"Yes. I understand. I have a question."

"Captain Mitchell, that's all the time I have for questions. Remember what I've told you. Complete your part and your family lives. Fail…and they will die. I will contact you once more before you board the plane. Remember, it's all about trust. Don't let me down, Captain Mitchell. I trust you."

A buzz replaced the lunatic's voice. Ryan slapped the cell closed and dropped it in the passenger's seat. He pounded the steering wheel with both palms. "WHY, LORD, WHY! YOU CAN'T DO THIS TO ME!"

Calm down. Don't panic. Think, Ryan, think.

He took a deep breath and exhaled. Every minute took him one mile further from his family. Each mile sliced away another layer of hope that he would ever see them again. "Think, Ryan! There's got to be a way."

Winding through the San Joaquin Hills, the five-lane toll road ran parallel to the Pacific Coast Highway to the west, and the San Diego Freeway to the east.

Like an animal clawing under Ryan's skin to escape, the urge to exit the freeway, turn around, and race back to his family was unbearable. Smacked by the first link in the chain of grief—shock and denial—he grasped for denial.

With each mile, the gravity of his situation weighed heavier on his mind and emotions. His every move being watched like some lab rat working its way through a vast labyrinth with but one true exit, and many wrong turns; a maze of deception, bewilderment, confusion, choice, and uncertainty.

Paralyzed in the grip of the lunatic's do-or-die demands, Ryan held the lives of his family in balance. Regardless of what the freak had said: "Your family is safe as long as you do exactly as I say." He feared for their lives.

Crazed maniacs never leave survivors and often find martyrdom an added act of heroism.

The sudden, unexpected remembrance of his friend, Rex Dean, ambushed his thoughts. Cold chills ratcheted up his spine. Could this be a replay of the night Rex died? Could this be the same lunatic that was responsible for Rex's death and the murder of Emily?

If so, Rex would've gotten a similar call on the way to the airport while Emily was used as bait to force him to do something with the airplane. But what?

The reporter on TV the morning of the crash had said the plane had been shot down because officials suspected it was headed toward a target in San Francisco. The lunatic must've known the jet went down and subsequently murdered Emily. Rex did not murder Emily. It had to be the same lunatic! The same maniac that murdered Emily was in his house. It was too weird to be a coincidence.

It didn't take a genius to surmise that the plan had included the use of the jet that Rex was scheduled to fly to New York. Filled with 60,000 pounds of fuel—enough to fly from LAX to JFK—made the jet a flying bomb capable of massive devastation.

Unless he could find a way to foil the plan of the crazed killer, his family would be murdered. However, if he complied with the lunatic's demands, he and hundreds of passengers, along with possibly thousands of innocent bystanders, would die.

This couldn't be happening. Anger filled his emotions. He slammed his hands against the steering wheel. "No!"

There has to be a way.

"Think!"

But with every attempt to think of variables, options, strategies, and solutions, thoughts of Keri, David, and little Martha took priority, pushing back possible solutions to the crisis. Tears spilled from his eyes as he imagined his family in the same room with a deranged lunatic who had nothing on his mind but death.

If he made an attempt to save his family and *not* do as the killer demanded, thousands of people would be saved, but how could he stop the killer from doing as he said he would. He quickly rationalized that if he broke the lunatic's rules, his family would be killed. The morbid thought levitated in his mind as he continued searching for every possible variable that might spoil the killer's plan.

He checked the tripometer. Twenty-eight miles separated him from his family. Within two miles, the toll road would merge with the 405, leaving 38 miles until he would arrive at the employee parking lot.

Thirty-eight miles...approximately 42 minutes, plus or minus...depending on the traffic lights on the airport perimeter road.

Since the call from the lunatic, his emotions had been pulled and jerked in a torturous roller coaster ride filled with gut-wrenching falls and unexpected hairpin turns: fear, anger, hate, and compassion. As the paralytic fear subsided, his watery eyes burned. His chest tightened. He was resolved to find a way out of the maze.

Keri, I will NOT let anything happen to you!

The rules given to him by the lunatic were: do not exit, stop, or attempt to be a hero. He had been warned about being stopped for speeding, but said nothing about the speed he must drive. Based on the obvious sophistication of the lunatic's tracking system, any decrease in speed based on traffic should be acceptable, but otherwise, it might cause alarm. If he sped up, he would have more time to digest the contents of the instructions and formulate a plan after arriving at the airport.

Red taillights in the distance indicated a flat stretch of road ahead and few places for speed traps. He pressed down on the accelerator...75...80...85. Getting pulled over by the CHP would be the perfect opportunity to alert someone of his situation; someone with a radio that the lunatic probably wasn't monitoring. A simple radio call from the patrolman would dispatch an army of help to his family's aid.

But what if he was wrong? What if the maniac did as he said he would do and started the killing, his daughter first? The thought of it shot ice through his veins. It was too great of a risk. Driving with the traffic flow would keep from drawing any attention.

But no sooner than he relaxed the pressure of his right foot did the rapid and distinct chirp of his dash-mounted radar detector start to sing out. He'd been nabbed by a steady stream of invisible electrons being fired from a patrolman's radar. Though the digital speedometer was falling through 80, it was too late. Ryan's heart pounded in his chest.

The silhouette of a car parked in the median of the highway beneath the shadowy darkness of an overpass burst into a disco of red and blue lights.

CHAPTER 17

8:15 p.m.

The two men huddled in the corner of the room, speaking in low voices. Keri held tight to David and Martha, trying to calm their fears. With her children safely tucked under each arm, Martha said, "Mommy, I'm not afraid."

Keri turned and forced a smile. "That's right," she said, "everything's going to be okay."

Anything to comfort the children.

Parents are quick to lie to their children to avoid subjects that are incomprehensible for their innocent minds.

"Mommy, do you know why I'm not afraid?"

"Why, Honey?"

"It's like the movie."

"What movie, Darling?"

"The movie about the monsters."

There was only one movie her five-year-old daughter could possibly be thinking of. "Do you mean MONSTER'S, INC.?" It was Martha's favorite movie. A computer animated feature film aimed at helping children overcome their fear of nighttime monsters in the closet. Two, not-so-scary monsters,

Sulley (James P. Sullivan)—a lovable, furry, blue behemoth-like giant, and his best friend and sidekick, Mike (Wazowski)—a short, one-eyed, green alien meet their match in the form of a fearless, little girl called Boo (Mary).

"Remember," Martha said, "monsters are not really bad people...like in the movie." She pointed her tiny finger toward Samael. "The big man is white, not blue, and the little man has two eyes, not just one—just like in the movie."

Martha truly believed what she was saying; possibly a subliminal coping mechanism attempting to dissociate her from an inescapable traumatic situation. Keri had read studies concluding that amnesia, multiple personalities, and even mental illness were chronic forms of dissociation. What Martha was experiencing was a normal defense mechanism, more common to daydreaming. Children often dissociate when they become frightened or overwhelmed.

Keri decided to play along. "So, you must be Boo."

Martha giggled. "Mommy, you're funny."

Samael glanced toward the couch. He smiled. "So, I see we're having a good time? That's nice." He turned and spoke a word to the little man, who then quickly left the room. Keri heard the front door open and the sound of steps fading. "We don't have much time," Samael said. "We should probably think about getting the kids to bed."

Keri said, "I'll take them up to their rooms."

"That won't be necessary, dear."

Keri heard the front door open, followed by a noisy clatter; the rattle and banging of something. Something on wheels. Around the corner appeared the little man, rolling an ambulance gurney. He positioned it carefully, next to the computer table, pressed the locks on the four castors, and quickly returned outside.

A chill shot through Keri when she noticed the black nylon straps dangling from the sides of the aluminum frame.

Two more trips outside produced two more identical

gurneys. He positioned them side by side, their back supports angled up 45 degrees. The little man made one last trip outside, returning with three identical suitcase-size aluminum cases and, what appeared to be, collapsible IV poles. He placed one case and IV pole at the foot of each gurney. He then flipped the latches open on the three cases, lifted the tops, and removed a handful of colored computer cables and electrical connectors from each case. He then closed the cases and secured the latches, but before he did, Keri caught a glimpse of what appeared to be an infusion pump and three pre-filled bags of fluid in each case. She was too far away to determine what was in the bags.

Working with speed and in a precise manner, the little man unrolled nine colored cables. He then clipped one end of each cable into a hub that was connected to one of the computers. The loose ends were then separated into three groups, each containing a red, blue, and yellow cable. He twisted each group together making a rope and ran one rope of cables alongside each gurney.

Keri watched with growing concern. Without a doubt, she and her two children would soon be strapped to the gurneys. Her biggest fear was the contents of the plastic bags.

She glanced at David. The confused look on his face made her heart race. She signed to him: "Not worry. Be calm." She wanted to scream at the lunatics, cursing them for any thought they might have of harming her children.

The horrid thought of what this monster had done to Emily Dean terrified her. She needed Ryan. He always had answers. She might never see him again. She fought to hold back the tears.

I need to be strong for the children.

The lunatic must want Ryan to crash his airplane, like he did Rex. She knew the freak would kill her and the children, just like he did Emily. He would never let them live. How hard would it be for her, even the children, to identify a giant albino with a birthmark on his face?

She had to do something, and fast. Once the freak strapped them to the gurneys, she'd be helpless.

The little man had moved to the kitchen and was probing through the pantry, obviously looking for something to eat. The albino was hunched over the computer screens with his back to her. His handgun was on the table beside the computers.

The albino's face was inches from the computer screen. The little man was rummaging through the pantry like a rat. If she moved fast enough, she might be able to leap for the gun before the albino could react. Then, after putting distance between her and the albino, she might be able to get off a shot.

Her knowledge of guns was limited to one trip to the firing range with Ryan. She remembered Ryan's gun did not have an external safety switch. Instead, it had a double-action trigger. If the albino's gun had a mechanical safety, she would have to locate it before the gun would fire. If she fumbled while trying to flip it off, she might lose her only chance for freedom. What did she have to lose?

"Usman! Quick! He's slowing! It looks like he might stop!" The albino announced. "This is not good."

Keri knew something was wrong. She knew Ryan wouldn't risk doing anything that would endanger his family.

The little man came running, munching on something crunchy he'd found in the pantry. With the two men distracted, this might be her chance. Her eyes locked on the gun. The muscles in her body tightened. Her heart raced. Seconds before she uncoiled, the big man rose from the chair, turned and faced her. He flipped open her cell phone and pressed a button, then listened. After four unanswered rings, the phone transferred to voicemail. Samael turned the speaker towards Keri letting her hear her own voice: "Hi, this is Keri. Please leave me a message."

He flipped the cell closed. "Keri, your husband has stopped and doesn't seem to want to answer. You know what that means." His eyes glanced at Martha then back to Keri.

"Try again!" she pleaded. "Sometimes the reception in that area is bad. It's the hills."

The albino tried again. After four more rings: "Hi, this is Keri. Please leave me a message."

"I'm sorry, dear, but he's not answering." He flipped the cell closed and started toward Martha. "You see, Mrs. Mitchell, it's all about trust. We can't trust if we don't first believe, now can we? Apparently, your husband is not a believer yet."

CHAPTER 18

8:18 p.m.

The interior of Ryan's car splashed with alternating red and blue lights as the patrol car closed in from behind. Should he speed up? Make a run for it? If he did, the freak would surely call and ask about his speed, not to mention what the cop would do when he finally caught him.

With the cop now on his bumper, flashing the headlights of his Ford Crown Vic, Ryan had no choice but to ease to the side of the freeway.

He put the car in PARK and switched off the engine. The knots in his stomach twisted tighter. His cell phone rang. It was his wife's familiar ringtone.

Not now!

He glanced in the rearview mirror. The patrolman was out of his car, his flashlight beaming a path toward the driver's side of Ryan's car.

Ryan reached to his belt, the phone was missing. On the second ring, he remembered he had tossed it in the passenger's seat.

A third ring.

He fumbled in the dark, finally locating the phone. On

the fourth ring, he flipped open the cell and pressed TALK. "I can't talk," Ryan said. "A cop just pulled me over for speeding. I swear I won't tell him anything. I'll call you back." Without waiting to hear the lunatic's response, Ryan closed the cell just as the cop's light saber swirled through the interior of his car, half blinding him.

"Well, Skipper," the patrolman said, obviously noticing Ryan's four-strip epaulets on his uniform shirt, "looks like all you need is a pair of wings and you'd be airborne."

The tall figure towered above Ryan's window, in the unmistakable khaki-colored uniform, seven-pronged gold badge, and shiny black belt. "Officer, I must've been distracted. I normally don't—"

"Driver's license and registration," the patrolman snapped. "Do you have any weapons, firearms, or drugs in the car?"

As Ryan passed his driver's license and registration to the cop, the familiar melody of his wife's cell phone filled the car. Ryan reached and silenced it. "Ahh... No drugs, but I do have a handgun. It's in the trunk. It's my authorized duty weapon."

"Got a permit or some ID authorizing you to carry the weapon?" the cop said.

Ryan pulled his credentials from his back pocket and offered them to the cop.

"What kind of handgun?"

"Forty-caliber Glock." Ryan nervously waited while the patrolman's light zeroed in on the credentials. Hopefully the cop wouldn't ask too many questions. However, he might call his dispatcher; time Ryan couldn't afford. Ryan glanced at the in-dash clock. Every minute gave the lunatic an excuse to fulfill his promise—youngest to oldest.

"Captain Mitchell, you might want to ease up on your wingless jet." The cop handed Ryan his license, registration, and credentials. "It's not that I don't think you can handle the speed, I'm more concerned with you surprising grandma from behind.

Understand?"

"Yes sir, I understand."

"I'm not going to write you a ticket. The way I see it, we're on the same side." The cop leaned down meeting eyes with Ryan. "I appreciate what you're doing to make it safer for us all when we fly."

"Thank you. And I'll be sure to watch my speed."

The cop acted like he wanted to chat. "You know, it pisses me off about what those ragheads did. My wife and I only fly once, maybe twice a year, but every time we do, I can't help but think about 9/11."

"I know what you mean."

Come on! I've got to go.

Every muscle in Ryan's body was screaming, drawing tighter as the seconds ticked away. He had to call the lunatic.

"You just can't afford to let your guard down. Lots of crazies out there. We see it every day in this job. Just the other day—"

"Listen, I'd love to chat, but I've got a flight to catch."

The patrolman stepped back from the car, quickly losing his air of friendliness.

Ryan reached for the ignition. He hesitated.

Should I tell him? It's my last chance.

Any thought of asking for help vaporized when the familiar melody from Keri's phone filled the car. His throat tightened.

"I'll let you take that. Drive carefully and have a nice flight." The officer turned and walked away.

Ryan pressed TALK on his cell as he raised it to his ear.

"Captain Mitchell,"—the lunatic's voice sounded pleasant, almost cordial—"don't you think we should be moving along?"

"Listen, I didn't tell the cop anything!"

"Did you forget, Captain Mitchell? It's all about trust. I'm afraid you are not a believer yet. I cannot depend on you to trust if you don't believe."

"Okay, I understand…I know, but I swear, I didn't tell the cop anything!"

"That would've been a very stupid thing to do." The lunatic's voice was too calm. "Trust is very important. We need to trust each other, don't we, Captain Mitchell?"

"Yes, of course. You can trust me. Just don't hurt my family."

"I want you to trust me, the same way I want to be able to trust you. It makes for a healthy relationship." The lunatic's voice firm, focused. "Captain Mitchell, what did I tell you I would do if you deviated from the plan? Remember the rules? Don't deviate. Don't try to be a hero. And don't…what was the last one? "

"I had to stop! I didn't have a choice! The cop—"

The lunatic's voice grew stronger. "What did I tell you, Captain Mitchell?"

"I had to stop! I promise, I didn't tell the guy anything! I swear!

"Captain Mitchell, it's all about trust, isn't it?"

"Yes, and I'm doing exactly like you asked. You can trust me!"

"Well, I certainly hope so, because you know what I will do if I find some cop snooping around outside your house in a few minutes, don't you?"

"Yes, but you won't. Trust me, you won't."

"Good, then I won't have to kill your son."

"My son?"

"Yes. Your son. You're not too sharp for a jet pilot. Have you forgotten, Captain Mitchell? Youngest to oldest."

"No! No!" Ryan's heart pounded from the inside of his chest like a sledgehammer. His head tightened. His eyes filled with water.

"Oh, didn't I tell you?" the lunatic said calmly. "Your daughter is dead. When you didn't answer my call, I killed her. Youngest to oldest. Remember, Captain Mitchell, it's all about trust."

CHAPTER 19

8:28 p.m.

The albino closed the cell, picked up the handgun, and eased over in front of Martha. He squatted, bringing them eye to eye. "You're not afraid of me, are you?"

"No."

"I didn't think so." He rose and gazed at Keri.

The lunatic could have killed her, but he didn't… not yet. His calm, slow movements eased Keri a bit, making her believe he was only messing with Ryan's mind.

Poor Ryan.

The thought of Martha being dead must be torturing him. "Why did you do it? Why did you tell my husband…?"

"Interesting, don't you think, Keri? Only through the eyes of a child are we able to see fear for what it is…completely subjective. Fear is nothing more than a fabrication in the mind. It's not real. The greatest weapon against someone is their own mind. You see, Keri, there's nothing to be afraid of…not even death. You live, you die, you live again; what is there to fear? Because of a few simple words spoken in a calm tone, your husband's mind is tormenting him. With just words, Keri, that's all."

"You're sick," Keri said, "You need help."

"Do you like to read, Keri? Do you ever read fiction? Do you ever wonder how a good novel can raise the tension in your emotions to such levels that you *feel* afraid or hopeless, just like the characters on the page? Words. That's all they are—words referring to other words."

"Please, I beg you, call my husband and tell him his daughter is still alive. Please! If you do, I'm sure he'll be more likely to do what you want. I know him, and right now he can't even think. How is he going to be able to help you if he can't think?"

"Keri, I've decided to do things differently this time. No more bloody mess like with your friends, the Deans."

Keri gasped. "I knew it! It was you!"

"Captain Dean and your husband are a lot alike, except for one thing: Captain Dean didn't seem to be as attached to his wife as your husband is to his family. Dean didn't respond to words like I wished he had."

Keri's eyes filled with tears. She tried to hold back any sound, knowing it might give Martha a reason to see the white monster as the evil man he really was. David couldn't hear the man's words, but she was certain he sensed the fear in her quivering body and facial expressions.

Samael called to Usman, "Is he moving yet?"

"No," the little man said, his mouth full of chocolate chip cookies.

Samael flipped open Keri's cell and pressed the speed dial for RYAN. With the phone against his ear, he sighed, shaking his head in disapproval while staring at Keri. "I thought your husband understood what I meant by trust. If he doesn't believe, he won't trust. Somehow, I need to make him a believer."

Keri's stomach wrenched in torment with each waiting second.

Ryan pick up...please...pick up.

8:31 p.m.

The lunatic's words—"Your daughter is dead"—paralyzed Ryan. If he didn't get moving, the lunatic promised to kill again. His son would be next. Then Keri. He glanced in the rearview mirror. There was still time to spill his guts to the cop.

I can't. I need to keep going.

He checked the tripometer—36 miles to go; then the clock—8:31. With no traffic problems, he would arrive at the employee parking lot by 9:15. His scheduled departure was 10:30 p.m., but he was required to sign in one hour prior at 9:30. The shuttle bus departed the employee lot every twenty minutes for the ten-minute drive to the terminal. If he didn't catch the 9:20 bus, he would be late for sign in. Not signing in on time would generate a call from crew scheduling. If they couldn't reach him by 9:45, they might reassign his trip to another pilot.

Mentally exhausted and emotionally distraught, he had difficulty processing. Every fiber of his emotions grasped to convert words into reality, while every cell in his brain refused to accept it as truth.

The trooper switched off the red and blue lights atop his Ford, his headlights pierced Ryan's eyes in the rear view mirror. Should he stop the cop and tell him what was going on? There was still time. One last chance.

But before Ryan could sort through the consequences, the cruiser pulled out onto the freeway and raced off. Ryan was alone in the dark.

His cell rang.

Ryan reached to his belt. The cell wasn't there. A second ring sounded from the passenger's seat. He found the phone. Fumbling in the dark to open the flip, he dropped it on the floor.

It rang a third time.

He probed in the dark beneath his feet, stabbing his hand around until he found the small block of plastic. As he brought the phone to his ear, he flipped it open with his thumb. "Hello…I'm here!"

"Captain Mitchell, why aren't you moving? I hope you're not talking to that cop? Do I need to kill your son, too?"

The lunatic's voice was too calm for someone who had just murdered a five-year-old girl. A sliver of hope crept into Ryan's thoughts.

"Please," he pleaded, "I'm going." Ryan turned the ignition. "Just tell me you didn't do it? Tell me my daughter is alive. Please…."

"Yes," Samael said, "your daughter is alive."

"Oh, dear God…." Ryan whispered. "Thank you, God."

"Captain Mitchell, your God doesn't hear you. If he did, you wouldn't be in this situation, would you? I'm your god now, and next time I won't be so merciful. Now, drive! I want to see you moving."

"Okay! I'm moving!" Ryan stomped the accelerator, spinning the tires, gravel clinking against the wheel wells as the car fishtailed onto the highway. "I'm driving! See! Look at your screen! I'm moving!"

The cell went dead. The lunatic was gone.

CHAPTER 20

8:34 p.m.

The tiny, red light inched slowly across the computer screen. "He's moving," Usman said.

The albino smiled. He turned to Keri and the children. "Keri, I think it's time the children went to bed."

Looking at the gurneys was enough to "fabricate" fear in her heart. She quickly offered, "I'll take them to their rooms."

"No, Keri. I went to a lot of trouble to bring some very special beds just for you and the children." He looked at the children. "You can all sleep together tonight. It will be like camping out. Won't that be fun?"

Keri protested, "What are you doing? Let me take them to their rooms."

"Keri," Samael said, moving closer, "you can make this easy, or you can make this difficult." He looked at David. "See how quiet your son has been." Turning to Martha, he said, "And your beautiful little girl has been especially brave." In a low, calm voice, he said, "Now, Keri, if you work with me, your children will have no reason to be afraid. Remember, fear is nothing more than a fabrication in the mind."

There was no use resisting. It would only make things

worse for the children. If she cooperated, it might open up an opportunity to snatch the gun, kill the little cookie-munching midget, and blow the albino into his next life. She signed to David as she spoke, while Martha watched. "The man wants us to lie down on the cots and rest. Understand?"

David signed back, using guttural-sounding words, "All three?" He pointed to the gurneys. "There?"

Keri's hand, balled into a fist and nodded, meaning yes. David stood, holding his mother's hand. Within his quiet world, having not heard a single word spoken all night, Keri realized that David had less reason to fear. He trusted his mother because he believed in her—principles that even the twisted and evil mind of the albino understood. Thankfully, Martha continued to dissociate, comparing the giant, white freak and his weaselly, little friend to Sulley and Mike from Monstrapolis.

As they all three stood and moved to the gurneys, Keri focused on the gun in the albino's latex-covered hand. She glanced at the little man. He appeared content, staring into the computer screen at the blinking, red dot as it progressed along the freeway to the airport.

Samael encouraged David to lie down on the gurney. He released his mother's hand and sat on the edge of the bed. The albino lifted David's legs onto the bed, and gently eased his upper body against the 45 degree incline. He patted the thin mattress of the middle gurney. "This one is for the brave little girl. You will be between your brother and mommy."

Before reaching to help Martha up, the albino placed the gun on the table next to the computers. Though six feet away and well out of Keri's reach, she couldn't believe he put the gun down. This was her chance.

She glanced back at the little man. He seemed happily hypnotized by the blinking dot on the computer screen. It was a million-to-one chance—probably impossible—but what did she have to lose? Soon, she would be helplessly strapped to the gurney.

As the albino lifted Martha onto the gurney, she would move quickly: grab the gun, shoot the midget, then the freak. She'd have to be fast. Her heart broke into a stampede; her peripheral vision narrowed. It was her last chance.

Her eyes turned to Martha's feet as the albino bent over to cradle her legs and lift her onto the gurney.

Do it now!

Keri lurched for the gun, grabbed it, swung around, and raised the muzzle at the little man's head. Hearing the disruption, he turned. His eyes, as large as dinner plates, staring at the muzzle of the gun only three feet from his face. She pulled the trigger, but instead of the expected boom, the hammer made a dry, stick-breaking *click* as it fell on an empty chamber.

Panicked by the silence, she swung the pistol toward the albino, hoping for a second chance. The albino whipped around, but she was faster. Seeing Martha in his arms, she hesitated, then quickly raised the muzzle to the freak's head.

Staring at her through fearless eyes, he said, "Go ahead, see if you're lucky."

Her finger pulled the trigger.

Click.

"I guess not," he said.

Click.

Smiling, he came straight at her as she squeezed the trigger a third time.

Click.

With Martha still cradled in the albino's left arm, he grabbed the pistol with his right hand and tore it out of her grip with such force that she thought her finger broke before it slipped through the trigger guard. She squealed in pain.

"Bad girl," he said, still smiling. He tapped the butt of the gun against her skull. "Did you really think I'd put a loaded gun within your reach? He tucked the pistol in his pocket and turned, gently placing Martha on the gurney. He then turned back to Keri. "Guns are loud and messy. There are other ways to kill." He nodded to the little man. "Help me strap them down."

Usman rose and assisted strapping the children to their gurneys.

David met Keri's stare, his eyes growing watery with tears. Martha appeared calm, less frightened than David, possibly still imagining the two men as innocent scarers sent on a mission from the scare factory in Monstrapolis—a city powered by little children's screams; screams she was not going to provide.

Painfully, Keri watched her children being strapped to the beds like animals. Martha's silence was a sign she was in shock.

"No! *Please!*" she pleaded. "They're just children! They can't hurt you. For God's sake, my son is deaf, he won't talk."

The men continued until the children were securely strapped to their gurneys. The little man produced a roll of duct tape and began tearing off slices from the roll, taping the children's mouths closed.

Keri's instincts took over. Blood pumped through her small frame, her muscles tightened. All fear was forgotten— erased from her mind. Unconcerned for her own life, she struck like a viper at the little man, knocking him to the floor. Her fisted hands pummeling his face, knocking his glasses across the room; then his chest, stomach, and anything she could make contact with.

"Help! Samael! Get her off me!"

Keri continued her assault like a jackhammer, relentlessly beating the man's body. "Don't touch my children!"

The albino spun around, his arm like a coiled spring, his hand like a claw, he grabbed the back of Keri's blouse, pulling her back, lifting her to her feet like a puppet. "Keri!

What did I tell you?" He slammed her on top of the gurney. She kicked wildly, struggling against the inevitable nylon straps, but there was no use. The albino had ten times her strength.

"They're just children!" she cried, tears welling in her eyes. "Please!"

In less than a minute, she was immobilized; her arms and legs secured to the gurney by black nylon straps.

The little man, assured of bruises from his beating, happily tore a strip of the wide gray duct tape off the roll. He stretched it across Keri's mouth and pressed it hard, running his fingers over the tape, pushing it as if he wanted to work it into her pores. His fingers moving back and forth across her lips made her want to scream—pushing and rubbing. Keri almost fainted.

"That's enough," the albino said to Usman. "Get back to the computer."

Keri inhaled deep through her nose, her heart pounding in her chest. She blinked furiously, clearing her tear-blurred vision.

"Keri, until you calm down, the tape stays on."

Samael retrieved a satchel she'd not yet seen, and carefully removed a zippered pouch. From the pouch he withdrew three, small, clear bottles filled with a dirty-looking liquid, and placed them reverently on the mantle above the fireplace. With his back to her, she watched him standing quietly with his head bowed.

He turned and moved back to Keri's side and leaned down, bringing his face level with hers. She caught a glimpse of his eyes over the narrow rectangular lenses. She flinched. His blue eyes flickered uncontrollably. Her head pushed back against the thin mattress as he moved closer, fearing what he might do. He didn't move for the longest time as he stared, first into her left eye, then into her right. He leaned closer, now only an inch from her face. He sniffed, smelling her.

He straightened and stepped back. "Keri, I want to show you something."

He pulled off his hooded cloak and his undershirt. He stood naked from the waist up. His cadaverously, white body towered over her. His muscles bulged beneath tightly-drawn, white skin. Cold and inhuman, he resembled a marbleized, museum double of Michelangelo's sculpted perfection of *David*.

Tattooed across his chest in flowing script was the word *KEROESSA*.

Her stare lingered. She found it difficult to look away. Never before had she seen anything like it. He pressed his fingers against his chest beneath the black letters of the tattoo, from the *K* to the *A*.

"My beloved Keroessa," he said. The corner of his mouth curled into a smile. "This is why I'm here. I wanted you to see it before you sleep."

Keri felt confused. The words meant nothing to her. Perhaps it was the name of his lover.

How could any woman love this creature.

Samael pulled on his shirt and cloak, leaving the hood down, then leaned close. Her heart raced.

He placed his hand on her shoulder.

Keri jerked against her binds, twisting her head, arching her back, feeling the bite of the straps digging into her wrists and ankles as she tried to scream through the tape.

Samael squeezed her shoulder once, firmly, as if he were testing the bone beneath her flesh, and then he drew away.

Returning to the satchel, he pulled out a flexible, rubber tube and white, plastic case. The case held hypodermic syringes and several ampoules containing an amber solution.

Her eyes widened. Unable to speak, she moaned against the burning tape stretched across her mouth.

"Keri, don't be concerned, it's only a little sodium thiopental to help the children sleep. Nothing more."

She knew a small amount was harmless and would only induce sleep, but repeated injections would be required. Too much could put the children in a coma. An excessive amount would be lethal.

While being careful to keep the hypodermics out of the children's view, he stripped the sheath off the needle, pierced the cap of one of the ampoule, drew a measured dose of the solution into the barrel of the syringe, and squirted some of it down at the floor to be sure no air remained in the needle.

Easing up next to Martha, he turned her right arm palm up. He used the flexible tubing as a tourniquet to make a vein clarify in the girl's small arm. She whimpered and strained against the straps, closing her eyes tight, tears pouring down her cheeks. When he stuck the vein—she flinched. He slowly pressed the plunger and slipped loose the tourniquet. As the amber solution receded from the clear barrel of the hypodermic, the girl's body relaxed, her whimpering ceased.

He refilled the hypodermic and then repeated the procedure with David.

With both children now sleeping, he rose and turned to Keri. "Would you like to join your children, or stay with us for a while?"

She shook her head repeatedly back and forth.

CHAPTER 21

8:50 p.m.

Ryan drove into the night, every mile separating him further and further from Keri, David, and Martha. His encounter with the cop had cost him valuable minutes. Driving over the posted speed limit was no longer an option. Assuming the freeway was clear, there was just enough time to make it to the employee lot, hop the bus to the terminal, and sign in for his trip before crew schedule started looking for him. He remembered the lunatic's words—"Next time I won't be so merciful."

With his mind clouded in a fog of fatigue and stress, the remaining thirty-five miles clicked away unnoticed as he subconsciously navigated the 73, the 405, and then onto the 105 leading to the airport perimeter road.

Anxiously waiting at a traffic light on the perimeter road, heading west, he gazed off into the black sky. Seeing a crescent moon launched his tired mind into the past, recalling nursery rhymes and bedtime stories. *Wee Willie Winkie, Hey Diddle Diddle, Twinkle Twinkle Little Star*, and Martha's favorite: *Goodnight Moon*.

> *Goodnight room. Goodnight moon.*
> *Goodnight cow jumping over the moon...*

She loved identifying the objects in the great, green room—the red balloon, the comb, the kittens, the mittens, and especially the mouse—as he, or Keri, would read. Glued to each page, she would watch as Bunny's room got continuously darker, the moon rose higher in the sky, and the time on the clock ticked later…

Goodnight stars. Goodnight air.

until the last page was turned…

Goodnight noises everywhere.

Pleasant memories, happy moments, and sweet thoughts spun his mind far away from reality. His body relaxed as the charge of adrenalin subsided, replaced by a sensation of near euphoria. Thoughts of death abated, if only for a short few moments—like the eye of the hurricane offers a moment of calm and peace to its tormented victims before striking another blow. For Ryan, the fears in his mind had receded and he was no longer a part of them.

Focused on the wispy thin clouds floating past the crescent moon, he basked in the sweet memories of quiet moments with his children before bedtime; a time free from evil and stress.

His heart ached, thinking of his deaf son. While reading bedtime stories, Ryan would sign to him. David's little hands and fingers would join in with Ryan and Keri, signing words as they spoke.

In the beginning, David would study each picture, signing the words, while anxiously waiting for the page to turn.

Good—the open right hand moving away from the lips.

Night—the left arm horizontal pointing to the right (representing the horizon); the right wrist resting on the back of the left hand; right fingertips pointing down (the direction of the setting sun).

Room—flat hands, palms facing each other, fold in, one behind the other (marking the four walls of a room).

Good—night...

Moon—index finger and thumb of right hand forms a modified C (representing the crescent moon), below the right eye.

With practice, David's hands moved faster and faster, anticipating the words on each page and quick to point out when a page was skipped or a word forgotten—

Good night room, good night moon.

A car horn from the anxious driver behind him blasted, jolting Ryan back into reality. He had not noticed the traffic light had turned green. He jammed his foot on the accelerator, and sped off. He checked the clock on the dash— 9:11. He should make it to the employee lot in time to catch the 9:20 bus to the terminal, arriving at flight operations before his 9:30 sign in.

He parked in the lot at 9:16, unloaded his bags, and locked the car. The thunderous sound of a departing jet climbing into the inky-black night caused him to look up. An encroaching, marine layer of fog masked all but the jet's navigation, strobe, and landing lights moving across the sky from east to west.

He boarded the employee bus and waited an excruciating three minutes before it departed. Other than his brief encounter with the cop, the short bus ride to the terminal would be his first contact with people.

He contemplated telling someone of his predicament; possibly passing a note with his home address, asking them to call for help. He surveyed the faces of employees; mostly crewmembers and maintenance workers preparing for the graveyard shift. There was not enough time. What if the lunatic had someone on the inside working with him—riding the bus? All it would take is a phone call and his family would be dead. Every urge he had to cry out for help was snuffed out by his unwillingness to risk the lives of his family. There had to be a way.

The employee bus jerked and jolted as it crossed the ramp and joined a service road that paralleled a taxiway. Tugs pulling multiple baggage carts, like little trains, whizzed past, racing to take passenger bags to their connecting flights.

The bus slowed as it approached a B-767, the jet's taxilight carving a path into the night, its engines spooling up to push the monstrous machine forward. Ryan gazed up at the silhouettes of the two pilots in the cockpit, appearing relatively small in comparison to the machine they piloted. Soon he would be in their place, taxiing his plane for takeoff on a mission of death. The lunatic had made it clear—"You have a choice to make. You either do as I say, or your family dies. It's that simple."

As far as he knew, his every step was being watched. The tracking device on his car would show that he'd arrived at the employee lot. No outgoing calls had been placed from his cell. The freak must be happy. The only question haunting Ryan was if the lunatic had kept his end of the bargain. Was his family *all* still alive?

Then, out of nowhere, the idea hit him. Perhaps it was a gift from *Wee Willie Winkie*, or *Diddle Diddle Dumpling*, or perhaps, even, the *Man in the Moon*, himself. He now had a plan, a long shot, but a plan. If it worked, he could save his family *without* endangering the lives of hundreds of innocent people.

The bus stopped. He jumped up, almost knocking a flight attendant down. "I'm sorry. Please forgive me." Eager to see what awaited him in his mailbox, Ryan rushed off to flight operations.

CHAPTER 22

9:16 p.m.

The family room at the Mitchell house looked more like an intensive care unit than a place of refuge and peace from the struggling world outside. Fear, not peace, filled the air—fear of an unknown future.

"He made it," the little man called out. "The car is in the lot."

Samael left Keri's side and moved to the computers. He leaned down, his face inches from the screen. "Finally."

He raised up and patted the top of the second computer—the one monitoring the progress of the jet. "Make sure the car stays put, and start focusing your attention on this one. I want to know the second the jet backs off the gate, or if that car moves." Samael brought his watch on his left wrist up close to his eyes and checked the time—9:18. "I'll call Mitchell, once he's had time to read my instructions."

From Keri's position, with the back of her gurney raised at a forty-five degree angle, she could clearly see both computer screens. The albino had more than likely positioned her that way on purpose so she could "fabricate" some more fear. She rolled her head to the left, David appeared to be asleep, his breathing steady. Martha was also asleep and breathing, a slight smile on her face. The thought of the albino's next move caused her heart rate to take off. She breathed deep to accommodate her racing heart's demand for oxygen. The sticky tape glued across her mouth forced her to draw air solely through her nose. Salty tears burned her eyes.

"The albino moved to Keri's side. "Are you comfortable, dear?"

She narrowed her eyes in anger, wanting to curse the man. A muffled noise groaned in the back of her throat like an angry Pit Bull.

"I would be more than happy to remove the tape, but it appears you need a bit more time to calm down. You're a feisty one to be so small, much more so than your friend, Emily Dean." He stared off at the ceiling in thought. "If I recall, she was much more passive, almost submissive. Killing her was much like killing a sacrificial animal. She squirmed a bit at first, but who wouldn't. I guess it was fear playing tricks on her mind."

Keri struggled against her straps, grunting and groaning, wishing for just one of her arms to break free. Her fight was useless. She released her body, her chest heaving, her nose burning from rapid, sharp breaths, her eyes blurred and burning from the flood of fresh tears. The freak was torturing her on purpose, breaking her spirit.

"Keri, if I haven't said so, yet, you have a lovely home. I think I'll show myself around, if you don't mind."

Amid all the excitement, Samael had made the mistake upon his arrival of not thoroughly checking the house. The only possible visitors he might have missed at this hour would have been children invited for a sleepover, now hiding.

If one of Keri's girlfriends had been upstairs when he

arrived, possibly using the toilet, she might have attempted to call for help. If she'd attempted to use the house phone, she would have discovered it was dead. The thought made him question the stupidity of the phone company to install the phone box on the exterior of the house. Since no one had come to the door, he ruled out the possibility of a dawdling visitor having a cell phone, or if there had been a visitor at all.

The beige-colored carpet on the stairs showed signs of wear, indicating the house to be at least six-to-ten years old, maybe older. All three bedrooms were upstairs. He walked through each, checking the closets and underneath the beds.

Nothing.

The bathrooms and shower stalls were empty. A small study adjoined the master bedroom. A large oak desk with a high-back leather chair took up most of the space. The desk was cluttered with the usual assortment of pens, papers, unpaid bills, and notes scribbled on yellow sticky pads. At first, he assumed it to be Ryan's office, though, a more careful examination showed signs the space was shared by Keri.

Bookshelves drew his attention—colored albums of matching size, all with neatly labeled spines:

OUR WEDDING
RYAN'S AVIATION CAREER
MARTHA
DAVID
FAMILY VACATIONS
HOLIDAYS

Samael pulled down the album labeled, OUR WEDDING, opened it, and examined the photos closely. He flipped through a few pages recognizing a younger Keri. The man standing beside her in the black tux, her arm interlaced in his, had to be Ryan. "Hmmm. Very handsome." He then placed the album back on the shelf, ensuring to align its spine with the others.

He selected another one—RYAN'S AVIATION CAREER. Hoping for more interesting viewing, he moved to the leather chair and sat down, pushed aside an obstruction on the desk, and opened the album. Starting at the beginning, he slowly turned the 12x12 laminated pages, taking time to study the pictures, reading the neatly penned journaling—no doubt a woman's writing; Keri's, he suspected.

The pages told a story of a young man's love for flying. Samael estimated that the boy in the first picture, with the big grin, standing beside the small single-engine plane, could not be more than twenty years old. The entry beside the picture read *Ryan's First Solo*. A few pages forward revealed an older, more mature Ryan, in a military flight suit, under one arm a helmet, the other leaning against a U.S. Navy, F-14 fighter jet. "Ryan, you must be so proud of yourself."

After replacing the albums, all spines perfectly aligned, he went downstairs. Finding Usman in his place staring at the computer screens, the children resting quietly, and Keri, no longer struggling against her straps, he flipped open Keri's cell. "Keri, I'm calling your husband. He will want to know that you and the children are alive and well. I will remove the tape to let you speak with him. You will need to tell him everything is fine and for him to do as he is instructed. Do you understand?"

She nodded.

Samael warned, "If you do anything crazy, your daughter will die. Is that perfectly clear?"

Again, she nodded.

Samael pressed the number on the keypad designated to speed dial Ryan.

Ryan picked up after one ring. "Yes."

"Captain Mitchell, I assume you've had time to review my instructions."

"You're insane!"

"From your perspective it might appear so, but I have my reasons."

"I want to talk to my wife!"

"First, let me confirm that you understand. I am watching your every move. Remember? I am your god, I see all. I know when your plane leaves the gate, when it takes off, and will be watching it every mile of the way until it reaches the target. I remind you, *if* the plane does not reach the target, or for some reason it does not take out the target, your family will *all* die. Do you understand?"

"Yes. I understand. Now let me talk to my wife."

Samael peeled the tape away from Keri's mouth, and then held the cell phone to her lips.

"Ryan, it's me," Keri said, her voice low and subdued.

"Are you and the children okay?" he said.

"Yes, but the children—"

Samael pulled the cell away. "Everything is fine. Keri wanted you to know that the children are asleep."

Ryan pleaded, "I'm going to do what you want, just don't hurt my family. You can trust me. I promise."

"Wonderful. We finally trust each other. Now, go fly your final mission and your family will live—a picture-perfect ending. Perhaps your Keri might want to add and album to her collection after this is over. As the story says— "And they all lived happily ever after." Well, not everyone, but the important ones. Isn't that right, Captain Mitchell?" Samael closed the flip on the cell. He peered down at Keri, "My dear, it's time. Once we get you and the children all hooked up, I'll let you go to sleep—hopefully it won't be forever."

Keri's rage returned. "You're going to pay for this! You may kill us all, but you'll pay!"

Samael reached down and stretched the silver tape back across Keri's mouth, pulling it tight, pressing it against her face. She struggled wildly. "Keri, I was in hopes we could visit; share some of my views on this life and the next, maybe have a cup of tea, but I guess not."

David moaned. Keri turned and saw his head move. She fought hopelessly against her bindings and grunted.

The sound drew the albino's attention. He reached into his satchel and pulled out the hypodermic and ampoule of sodium thiopental. He walked to David's bed and administered another injection. He then leaned down and checked Martha. "She should be okay for a few minutes," he said, "but it looks like we need to go ahead and get everyone hooked up."

Keri pulled and strained.

CHAPTER 23

R yan exited the employee bus, hurried into the terminal building through a secure checkpoint, and up the stairs to the main concourse. His heart raced faster and faster with each step.

After navigating around and through a stream of passengers, he slipped into an obscure corridor that led to a single-door elevator reserved only for flight crews. He inserted a key into the key access switch located beside the steel door. As he turned the key, he pondered how the lunatic might have obtained access to the secure area. Secured areas throughout the terminal building were limited to those employees that worked in that specific area—with one exception: cleaners. The cleaners had full access for cleaning, emptying trash cans, and vacuuming carpets, duties conducted mostly at night. Perhaps the lunatic had paid a cleaner a few hundred bucks—maybe less—to drop the package in Ryan's mail slot.

After an agonizingly slow ride to the second floor, the door opened to a cold room as quiet as a morgue. Ten computer terminals, evenly positioned on waist-high counters, lined the far wall. A ceiling to floor map of the world spread across the adjacent wall.

Ryan headed for the mailroom, a labyrinth of slotted shelves alphabetized with the names of pilots and coded by their crew position and aircraft type. He quickly located MITCHELL, R. and pulled the contents from the narrow slot. He moved to a table in the adjacent room where he could review the contents of the package in private. He hesitated, as another pilot moved listlessly through the dimly lit room, but he paid Ryan no attention.

Ryan flipped through his mail—chart updates; company memos warning of discipline for extended sick absences; fuel saving suggestions. There it was, as promised. He pushed everything else aside, tore open the envelope, and pulled out a folded piece of paper with typed instruction:

✓   THE PROFILE MUST BE FLOWN EXACTLY
      AS SHOWN.
✓   YOUR PROGRESS WILL BE TRACKED.
✓   DEVIATIONS WILL RESULT IN UNWANTED
      CONSEQUENCES: YOUNGEST TO OLDEST.

Load the following latitude and longitude points into your flight computer. Speeds and altitudes will be flown as indicated.

POINT A: $N34^0$ $W120^0$ – Speed: 250 knots; altitude: 10,000 feet.
POINT B: $N37^0$ 42' $W123^0$ – Cross at 500 feet. Then increase speed to 325 knots to the target.
TARGET: $N37^0 48.5$' $W122^0 28.4$' – Arrive at the target at an altitude of exactly 500 feet above the water, and a speed of 325 knots.

FLY THE PROFILE EXACTLY! ARRIVE AT THE TARGET AT EXACTLY **12:00 (MIDNIGHT).**

At first glance, Ryan had no idea of the exact location of the latitude and longitude coordinates, however, the increasing latitude for each point—N34^0 to N37^0—told him the locations were somewhere north of LAX.

Using the jet's global positioning and inertial reference systems, the on-board flight management computer could easily be programmed to navigate to the exact points, including the altitude, airspeed, and time constraints the lunatic had listed. Ryan's concern was how to convince air traffic controllers to allow it. Arbitrary deviations from the flight plan, unless small and quickly corrected, would create panic for the controllers, and in extreme cases—such as with the lunatic's proposed flight profile—could result in the launch of nearby escort fighters sitting on alert.

Taking the lunatic's instructions, he rushed over to the flight-planning table. Underneath a clear, Plexiglas top was a navigational chart stretching from Dallas to as far west as the Hawaiian Islands, and from the border of Mexico to a point 100 miles north of San Francisco. The chart included a grid of latitude and longitude lines evenly divided into increments of two-degree blocks.

Ryan quickly located LAX airport (N33 56.0 W118 25.9). A thin green longitude line crossed from right to left just above the airport. Following the green line, his eyes darted to the edge of the chart at the left, reading N34^0. He then zeroed in on the markings for the lines of latitude along the bottom of the chart, moving from east to west, right to left: "N118^0...N120^0."

He followed the thin green line back up until it intersected with the N34^0 line of longitude. Holding the spot with his right finger, he checked the paper in his left hand: POINT A: N34^0 W120^0.

The point beneath his finger was located above a small group of islands approximately 130 miles west of LAX—The Channel Islands.

Holding his spot, he checked the paper. POINT B: $N37^0$ 42' $W123^0$.

His eyes jumped to the edge of the chart, moving up...$N36^0$...$N38^0$...and then to the right...$W124^0$...$W122^0$.... toward the coast.

The lines were marked in even numbers. He split the small block in half, estimating the midpoint: $W123^0$. The navigational fix named FARRA, conveniently marked with Lat/Long: N37 41.8 W123 00.9, was practically the exact location of the lunatic's POINT B.

FARRA.

Ryan knew FARRA to be short for the Farallon Islands; a nearby collection of ten islands—211 acres of inhospitable, craggy rocks towering to 350 feet—located west of San Francisco. Though only thirty miles from Macy's in Union Square, the islands remain unknown by many of the seven million Bay-area residents. The mysterious landscape, filled with myth and nightmare, juts from the Pacific like the fangs of a sea monster, aptly dubbed by sailors in the 1850s as the *Devil's Teeth.*

Ryan first learned of the Farallon Islands while watching the Discovery Channel series, *Shark Week.* The cold Pacific waters, along with the island's blubbery carpet of seals, attract the largest great white sharks in the world. The Farallones lie within a particular 100 mile stretch of coastline—from San Francisco to Monterey—named the Red Triangle. It has been estimated that of all documented great white shark attacks on humans, more than half have occurred within the infamous Red Triangle. The Farallon Islands form the corner of this triangle. He wondered if the lunatic had chosen the forbidding place as some sort of eerie message of death.

It wasn't the sharks that concerned Ryan. Something worse—birds, lots of birds. As a wildlife and wilderness refuge, he knew that the airspace above the islands, up to

1,000 feet, was a protected no fly zone. The lunatic's instructions called for the jet to descend to 500 feet over POINT B: the exact coordinates of FARRA.

Home to hundreds of thousands of seabirds, the inky-black sky above the Farallones was guaranteed to be filled with nocturnal seabirds—a jet engine's worst nightmare. At 300 miles per hour, a surprise attack by a flock of gull-size birds could equate to a shotgun blast with bowling ball-sized pellets. The jet's engines, unable to digest multiple hits from the feathery, foreign objects, would burst into flames, rocketing turbine blades in every direction, easily slicing through the thin walls of the fuselage. Depending on the size of the bird, cockpit windshields could shatter possibly decapitating the pilots.

With his finger now resting on FARRA, a point approximately twenty nautical miles west of San Francisco, he checked the paper for the final point. TARGET: $N37^048.5$' $W122^028.4$'.

Seeing $W122^0$, his heart leaped in his chest. The longitude for the final point decreased from $W123^0$ to $W122^0$, meaning the target was to the east, toward the coast.

Ryan slid his finger slowly across the top of the glass to the east toward San Francisco. He double-checked the paper, and then looked closely at the chart beneath his finger. He noticed the navigational aid for Sausalito, the small harbor town across the bay to the north of San Francisco. The lat/long coordinates for the navigation aid were printed on the chart: N37 51.3 W122 31.4. He checked the paper again. TARGET: $N37^048.5$' $W122^028.4$'.

The *degrees* for the two sites matched exactly: $N37^0$ and $W122^0$, but the *minutes* were slightly different.

Knowing that nautical miles are based on the size of the Earth, by dividing the circle of the Earth at the equator into 360 degrees, traveling one degree around the Earth was equal to traveling 60 nautical miles. Then, by dividing each degree into 60 minutes, one minute of the Earth's arc is equal to one nautical mile.

Ryan quickly did the math, calculating the distance from the Sausalito coordinates to the target: 51.3 minus 48.5, and 31.4 minus 28.4. That put the location of the target at a point 2.8 miles south and 3 miles east of the Sausalito navigational aid.

He examined the chart closer. He remembered a romantic weekend he and Keri had spent in Sausalito while touring the wine country to the north. He knew the navigational facility would not be located in the valley near the town, but to the west, toward the coast, possibly on a hilltop. The higher elevation allowed for enhanced reception of the radio beams, as they rely on line of sight.

He suddenly realized the target.

"Oh my God, the bridge!"

Ryan quickly turned and scanned the room to see if his outburst had been noticed.

He remembered the shock he felt that morning, hearing the reporter attempt to justify why Rex Dean's flight had been shot down by U.S. fighters: "Officials believed the plane was headed for a target in northern California".

The lunatic did it! The lunatic killed Rex! He's already tried this once, and failed. Then he murdered Emily. He's not joking. If I don't do this, he will kill my family.

Now certain that the lunatic's target was the Golden Gate Bridge, certain that the lunatic had murdered Emily, and certain that Keri and the kids were in grave danger, he began to sweat. His throat tightened, holding back a wave of nausea. His legs felt like they might give way. He gripped the counter to steady himself.

The wall clock read 9:42. He steadied himself, then moved to a computer and pulled up the crew list. His copilot, Charles Smith, had already signed in. He should be somewhere in operations, or possibly on his way to the plane.

Ryan needed time to explain the plan to Smith. Without Smith's help, Ryan was certain that Keri, David, and Martha would die.

CHAPTER 24

9:30 p.m.

Chuck Smith's watch alarm began chirping repeatedly at 9:30 interrupting dreams of palm trees, crashing surf, and Hawaiian dancing girls waiting on his every need. He wiped the drool from the corner of his lip and retracted the extended foot of the recliner where he'd spent the last two hours.

After rubbing his face, his eyes still unable to make out shapes in the dark room, he stabbed around on the floor until locating his Rockports, slipped them on, and eased out of the recliner, being careful not to wake the other pilot stretched out on the sofa in the corner of the room. The guy was snoring loud enough to buffer any noise Chuck might make opening the door and exiting the small, closet-like room.

He squinted hard at the burst of fluorescent light that met him on the other side of the door.

At least six times each month, Chuck commuted to LAX from Fresno to fly the red-eye to JFK. After fifteen years as a first officer, all-nighters were the best he could hold. If he ever did upgrade to captain, he was destined to spend the rest of his career nailed to the bottom of the seniority list—on reserve—flying the same crappy trips. At least now, he had a schedule, something reserve didn't offer.

His weekly routine consisted of non-reving down from Fresno, crashing in the sleep room—a converted closet in the corner of flight operations—for a couple of hours, waking in time to sign in for his trip, locating the captain he was assigned to fly with, then racing to Starbucks before they closed at 10:00 p.m. for a venti bold drip with a double shot, then out to preflight the jet.

The LAX to JFK red-eye was a two-day trip with a scheduled landing in New York at 6:36 a.m. followed by a glorious layover at the airport Best Western next to the freeway. The return leg to LAX late that afternoon, if on schedule, would arrive back at LAX in time for Chuck to catch the last flight to Fresno. If he missed it, he would have to bunk down in the nasty sleep room—provided other pilots had not already taken claim to the three recliners—and catch the first flight to Fresno at 6:05 the next morning. Every two days, he repeated the cycle.

Chuck blamed the airline for his wife divorcing him ten months ago. She said she didn't get married to live alone. She might have never left him if Chuck hadn't come home unexpectedly to find a big brown delivery truck parked in front of his house, and the UPS guy upstairs making a special delivery of his own.

A chatty neighbor's wife later told him she found it strange that, when he was out of town, the same delivery guy dropped off a load once, sometimes twice a day. It didn't help that the UPS guy made twice the money Chuck did and was home every night.

After leaving the sleep closet, Chuck stopped off in the men's room to relieve himself and freshen up. He brushed his teeth, splashed water on his face, and ran a comb through his thinning blond hair. He paused, peering at his image in the mirror, questioning how life had taken such a toll on his appearance.

At forty-one, he could easily pass for fifty. The dark shadows under his eyes normally cleared up after a few days off, but the rest of it was permanent. He might not be the catch he was ten or fifteen years ago, but he still knew how to please the ladies.

He checked his watch—9:40. The line at Starbucks was guaranteed to be out the door as passengers and crewmembers queued up for one last caffeine rush before scattering to the far ends of the Earth.

He still had to meet the captain. He would make one swing through the flight planning room. If the captain wasn't there—screw it—he'd meet him at the jet. The thought of watered down airplane coffee made him shake.

He strolled into flight planning and saw one lone pilot, a captain, staring into a computer screen. Chuck didn't recognize him, but by the strained look on the guy's face, it promised to be an interesting night.

Ryan glanced over his shoulder. A pilot with three-striped epaulets on his shoulders was headed his way.

Must be him. Should I tell him now, or wait? If I tell him now, he might try to call someone. I'd better wait until we are locked up in the cockpit, checklist complete, and ready for takeoff.

"New York?" the pilot said.

With only a handful of outbound red-eyes, it was often easier finding a pilot headed to a certain destination than it was finding a name.

"Yeah." Ryan turned, extending his hand, forcing a smile. "Ryan Mitchell."

"Chuck Smith."

They shook hands, Ryan feeling his sweaty palms

against Chuck's spongy grip.

Chuck was a good head taller than Ryan, skinny as a rail with a dark tan. His thinning, blond hair looked more like a skull cap than hair, combed back with well-defined rows, held down with water, spray, or some type of gel or mousse, curling at the neck. Ryan turned back to the keyboard and clicked a few final keys, sending a request for his flight plan. Chuck eased his lanky frame up next to the counter and propped on an elbow. "Hey, Cap'n, I don't believe we've flown together."

Continuing to stare into the monitor, hoping to hide the distressed look on his face, Ryan said, "I don't think we have."

"You live local, or commute?"

"I'm down in Orange County. What about you?"

"Commute. Fresno."

Ryan nodded, acknowledging Chuck's response with a cursory glance.

"I didn't get a chance to check out the rest of the crew," Chuck said. "Maybe we'll get lucky tonight and have a couple of hot stews,"

Ryan shot Chuck a questioning glare.

Hot stews?

In all of his years at the airline, he'd never heard flight attendants referred to as "hot stews".

"Oh, don't worry, Cap'n," Chuck patted Ryan's shoulder, "I'd never use that term in front of the ladies. The last thing I want to do is piss off the help or end up being counseled for sexual harassment."

Ryan's concern escalated. He needed a copilot with more of a military-type attitude—someone that understood war—not some has-been, laid-back, skirt-chasing surfer dude.

Chuck eased off the counter and checked his watch. "Hey, I'm gonna hit Starbucks before they close. Can I get you anything?"

Nice gesture, but how would you carry two cups of coffee plus drag your roller bag?

"No, I'm good. I'll meet you at the plane."

"Great. See ya there." Chuck hurried off.

God help me.

CHAPTER 25

10:05 p.m.

When Ryan stepped aboard the plane, Chuck was standing in the first-class galley engaged in meaningless conversation with two flight attendants. He wondered if Chuck had even started his preflight duties. Normally, when Ryan arrived at the plane, most copilots were in the cockpit busily flipping switches and loading the flight computer.

Chuck turned, proudly gripping his venti-size Starbucks cup. "There's the man."

Looking past Chuck, Ryan greeted the two flight attendants. "Hi, I'm Ryan."

The young, attractive brunette Chuck had cornered responded, "Tina." He guessed her to be in her early 30's.

The stout, blond woman in her late 40's, standing beside Tina said, "Hi, I'm Bev. You got anything for us, Captain?"

As the lead flight attendant, she wanted to know if there were any special briefing items: security issues, expected delays, ride reports.

"No, nothing unusual. No delays and it should be mostly smooth. Possibly some chop crossing the Rockies. Let me know if you need anything during boarding."

Hearing passengers coming down the jet bridge, he dragged his kitbag and suitcase through the narrow hallway leading into the cockpit. He stowed his roller bag, securing it with floor straps, and then slung his kitbag into the small space to the left of the captain's seat.

He checked the time—10:05. In exactly twenty-five minutes the agent would seal the cabin door, and they would push back from the gate. The lunatic said he would be watching his every move. Any delay might cause alarm.

After checking the logbook, Ryan climbed into the left seat. A quick glance around the cockpit told him that, surprisingly, Chuck had already completed the preflight; he'd even loaded the flight plan into the computer—a flight plan that would not be flown.

After checking over his shoulder to ensure he was alone, Ryan took the lunatic's instructions and quickly loaded the profile into the computer's secondary route. The secondary route was normally left blank, but if used, could be activated with only a couple of key strokes.

Chuck eased into the cockpit at the same time Ryan completed loading the computer. Chuck moved in a certain sloth-like manner, calm and laid back, almost as if time had no meaning. Ryan glanced over to see Chuck staring out his side window into the dark. Not until he raised a hand, running it slowly along the top of his blond helmet, did Ryan realize Chuck was using the window as a mirror.

With ten minutes remaining before scheduled departure, Ryan said, "Let's get started."

Chuck came to life and rattled off the checklists with the ease of a seasoned veteran. It was Ryan's first inkling of hope that beneath Chuck's apathetic shell was a skilled and competent professional.

With the checklist complete and the passengers boarded, the gate agent closed the jet's entry door at exactly 10:29.

Chuck radioed ramp control for pushback clearance. Once the clearance was received, Ryan released the parking brake and advised the ground crew on intercom that they were cleared to push. At precisely 10:30 p.m., the jet pushed off the gate.

Ryan knew his only hope of saving Keri and the kids depended on Chuck. The plan he had dreamed up required Chuck to fly the jet solo, while Ryan raced home. The lunatic would never suspect it. Once the cockpit door was bolted closed, post 9/11 security procedures prohibited the flight attendants from entering the cockpit without permission from the pilots.

Ryan would have until midnight to get home—exactly one hour and thirty minutes from now. If Chuck flew the lunatic's profile perfectly, Ryan would be able to climb out through the cockpit window, hop a ride on the back of a baggage cart to the employee parking lot, and race home— hopefully before Chuck reached the Golden Gate Bridge.

After the ground crew disconnected the tug, Chuck called the tower for taxi clearance. The tower cleared them to taxi to Runway 25R. Ryan began carefully maneuvering the big jet through the dimly-lit taxiways toward the runway. He glanced at the clock—10:35.

The 68 mile drive back to his house would normally take 55 to 60 minutes. At this time of night, he didn't suspect that traffic would be a problem. He knew his only real problem would be convincing Chuck to fly the profile solo— especially after what happened to Rex's flight, ten months earlier. Never before had a commercial airliner been shot down by military chase planes. There was a high probability they would do it again—especially if the plane was descending and heading toward the Golden Gate Bridge. Hopefully he could convince Chuck otherwise.

Ryan eased along the dark taxiway, responding to the checklist items as Chuck called them out.

"BEFORE TAKEOFF CHECKLIST is complete," Chuck said.

A United B-747 thundered by in the opposite direction down Runway 25R. "Cap'n, you want me to tell the tower we're ready?"

"Tell 'em we need five minutes."

Ryan felt his chest tighten with every minute. Once the tower approved the short delay, he would unload his plan on Chuck.

"Tower, Angel 54 needs five minutes."

"Roger. Hold where you are and let me know when you are ready."

"So...what's up?" Chuck said.

Ryan checked the time—10:38. He turned to Chuck.

"Chuck, I desperately need your help, and we don't have a lot of time. I need you to listen carefully to what I'm about to tell you."

CHAPTER 26

The albino stooped down at the foot of Keri's gurney. She craned her neck to watch. He rose with a two foot long IV pole. With a jerk, the pole telescoped to twice its length. He clamped it to the aluminum tubing of her stretcher, just to the right of her head.

He leaned down again and picked up the silver case and placed it between Keri's spread legs. He flipped open the latches and raised the lid. He lifted three pre-filled plastic bags of fluid from the case, all complete with drip chambers and a long tube with a regulating clamp. He hung the three bags of fluid on hooks at the top of Keri's IV pole.

Keri's eyes widened as she read the labels taped to the bags:

SODIUM THIOPENTAL
PANCURONIUM BROMIDE
POTASSIUM CHLORIDE

The same three chemicals used to perform lethal injections.

Talking in a calm voice as Samael fiddled with the tubes dangling from the bags of chemicals hanging above Keri's head, he said, "Keri, I'm going to hook you up first, then the children."

He removed an infusion pump from the aluminum case and clamped it to the IV pole.

"Being a nurse, I'm sure you're familiar with all this," he said, "and you've probably read the labels on the bags by now. But you have no reason to worry. The chemicals will only be used if your husband fails to do as I have instructed him."

Samael worked with the tubes as he connected them to separate channels of the infusion pump.

"These multichannel infusion pumps are set to automatically sequence the chemicals," he said. "The pumps have been interfaced with our computer and will only be activated under certain conditions. The circuitry is tied to a simple program, similar to a light switch. If the conditions are met, the circuit is switched on, activating the infusion pumps. The chemicals will flow through the tubing and into you and your children's bloodstreams, one bag at the time." He paused and met Keri's stressed stare. "Don't worry, dear, you and the children won't feel a thing. The sodium thiopental is first, and it will put you into a deep sleep."

He moved to the foot of the children's gurneys, each having their own silver case and IV pole, and repeated the setup. When he'd finished, he called to Usman. "You can connect the pumps now."

The little man connected the loose ends of the three colored roped cables to its respective infusion pumps. He then checked the connections at the hub and to the computer's processor.

"Keri, there are two conditions that will turn these pumps on. The first is if your husband does not complete his mission at exactly midnight. Secondly, once we activate the program, if the infusion pumps are disconnected from the computer or power is lost, the pumps will switch ON."

She and the children's lives hung in the balance of a set of conditions that might or might not turn *their* lights out—forever. From the way it looked, the albino and his little friend were setting things up to, at some point, leave them alone.

"You see, Keri, I didn't want to leave a bloody mess this time."

"I'm finished," Usman said. "Do you want me to activate the program?"

"Not yet."

Usman returned to his chair and continued monitoring the computer screen.

Samael retrieved the three bottles of brown water from the mantle, and returned to Keri's side. She watched as he disconnected the tube extending from the bottom of the bag marked, POTASSIUM CHLORIDE, removed the top from one of the bottles, poured the contents of the fluid into the tube, and then reconnected the tube to the bag. He repeated this procedure with the bags hanging from the children's IV poles. He then returned the empty bottles to his satchel.

"Keri, if the worst happens, and of course we hope it doesn't, you can now be assured that your bodies will be cleansed from the evils of this life."

Keri looked up at the tube filled with the dirty liquid. When released, the brown sludge would flow into her veins, followed by the last deadly chemical, potassium chloride. At that point, it really wouldn't matter what the freak had poured into the tubes, because if they made it that far, they'd all three be dead, unless the infusion pumps malfunctioned, or—worse—less than the lethal dose of the chemicals made it into their bodies.

Just as with execution by lethal injection or physician-assisted suicides, the sodium thiopental—a powerful sedative—would cause unconsciousness, the pancuronium bromide—a paralytic agent—would stop their breathing and all muscle movement, except the heart, and the potassium chloride would ensure the end by inducing a cardiac arrest, stopping the heart.

"Keri, for death row inmates this process would only take

a few minutes, but for you and the children, since I am using drip bags, it will take a bit longer."

The amount of thiopental the freak had in the drip bag far exceeded what was needed for medically-induced coma protocols. If none of the other drugs made it through the infusion pumps, the thiopental alone would kill them. Due to its high lipophilicity, it would only take one circulation through the brain before they were in an unrecoverable state of unconsciousness.

The albino placed the cloth satchel on Keri's stomach. She squirmed. "Easy, Keri." He withdrew the flexible rubber tube from the bag. "It's time for you to sleep."

She moaned and shook her head violently.

The albino studied her eyes. "Would you like to stay awake?"

She nodded.

"Can you behave?"

She nodded.

"Okay, but I still need to hook you up to the IV."

He used the rubber hose as a tourniquet to make a vein clarify in her arm. She watched as he slid the hollow IV needle out of the plastic cover. His fingers traced along the crease of her arm, looking for a vein. Next came the expected sting of the needle stabbing through her skin. Her jaw muscles clamped down hard. She sucked in a breath. He pushed the needle in deeper, then pulled back.

"Sorry, Keri, I missed. My vision is not the best." He leaned in closer, putting his face inches from her skin.

She watched, his fingers pressing in the crook of her arm, searching for a new place. He stuck her again, harder this time. She flinched with the sting of the needle, sucking in more air, her left hand gripping the thin mattress.

"There we go, dear, I think I got it that time."

He snapped off the rubber tourniquet, attached the tube dangling from the infusion pump, and then anchored everything to her flesh with strips of adhesive tape.

He then moved to the sleeping children and repeated the process. Once he had the children's IV's in, he pressed a few buttons on their infusion pumps. "That should keep them under," Samael said. He glanced at Keri. "Just a slight drip of thiopental, that's all, don't worry."

Keri did worry. She worried that the freak had no idea what he was doing with the drugs. A "slight drip" too much could put the children into a coma.

He stepped back to admire his work. "Usman, you can activate the program now."

With an unobstructed view of the computer screens, Keri watched as the little man clicked away at the keyboard. The right monitor, which was previously used to track Ryan's car, was replaced with a large, digital clock showing the current time in hours, minutes, and seconds—10:18:52.

The infusion pump strapped to the IV pole on her gurney beeped once, followed by beeps from the pumps connected to each of the children's poles.

"Done," Usman said.

"That looks nice," Samael said, admiring the large, digital clock on the monitor. "Even I can read those numbers. How about you, Keri?" He walked over and stood beside her. "Yes, you have a perfect view. Now you'll know if your husband does what he's supposed to do. Since I won't be here, you'll be the first to know." He looked down at her. "When the clock reaches midnight, if you hear that pump click ON, you will know your husband has failed us. Of course, you know what that means. I'll have to do this all over again with another family. But on the other hand, if you don't hear a click, you and your lovely children will live…that is, if nothing goes wrong with the automation before someone finds you."

Keri glanced over at the children, thankful that they were asleep and unaware, and then back at the clock—10:19:32. Her thoughts drifted to Ryan and what he must be thinking;

what he must be going through—alone.

God, why?

The computer monitor to her left displayed a map of the west coast of California from Los Angeles to San Francisco. On top of LAX airport was a small, airplane symbol— assumedly the plane Ryan would be flying. A line was drawn from the airport out over the Pacific Ocean and then up the coast to a point abeam San Francisco. The line then turned to the east, stopping at the coast.

The albino and the little man stared at the computer screens, waiting. The scheduled departure time for Ryan's flight was 10:30 p.m. The clock on the right monitor ticked away the seconds:

10:29:56
10:29:57
10:29:58
10:29:59
10:30:00
10:30:01

"He's off the gate," Usman said.

The small airplane symbol moved, indicating the flight had pushed off the gate.

"That's good," Samael said. He turned to Keri. "Looks like you might be around to see another sunrise—not that I think that is such a good thing, but I'm sure you do."

Keri swallowed hard, her heart pounded in her chest. Fresh tears filled her eyes.

God, I beg you! Please stop this evil man.

CHAPTER 27

10:38 p.m.

Ryan looked across the dark cockpit at Chuck. It was a long shot. If he couldn't convince Chuck to help him, all hope would be lost.

"I'm all ears, Cap'n. What's up?"

Here goes...

"Chuck, my wife and kids are being held hostage by some lunatic who says, if I don't fly this jet into the Golden Gate Bridge at exactly midnight tonight, he'll kill them."

"Seriously?"

"Yes! I'm serious! I'm pretty sure this maniac is the same guy that murdered Rex Dean's wife?"

"What are you talking about? I thought Dean murdered her."

"Listen, we don't have time to get into it. I need you to fly the profile the maniac gave me."

"By myself? Solo? Where are you going?"

"To try and save my family."

"Let me get this straight. You want me to fly the jet, solo, into the Golden Gate Bridge while you go home to your family? Have you lost your freakin' mind?"

"I'm not asking you to fly the plane into the bridge. When you reach the bridge, fly over it and land at San Francisco or Oakland." Ryan hit two keys on the flight computer's keypad. The secondary route displayed on the screen. "I've loaded the route exactly like he wants us to fly it—nav points, altitude, and speeds. All you have to do is couple the auto pilot after takeoff, and when you reach the bridge, just pull up. If you don't help me, my wife and two kids will die."

"This is crazy!" Chuck said. "You've got to come up with another plan. Have you tried calling someone? You need to call 911, the police, the FBI! Call somebody! There are people trained to handle this kind of stuff."

This is why I didn't tell him inside.

"You don't understand, if anyone shows up at my house, the lunatic said he'll start killing, starting with my daughter, then my son, then my wife. I can't call anyone. Please! If you'll do this, I'll have time to make it home before you reach the bridge."

"Maybe he's lying."

"NO! He knows everything. He's tracking the plane right now. He tracked my car, he's tracking my cell phone, and I'm not even sure he isn't tracking *me*...or even you!"

Chuck stared at the navigational display—similar to a small TV—in front of him. The secondary route was mapped out, giving him a bird's-eye view of where the route would take the jet. "How am I going to get ATC to let me fly up the coast, when we are supposed to be going to New York? They'll have fighters on my butt in a nanosecond. What do you propose I do then? Have you forgotten what they did to Dean? They blew his ass right out of the sky, along with over 200 innocent passengers."

"After you take off, declare an emergency. Tell them you're having flight control problems, and it's taking full left control to fly level. They'll never know. Tell them you can only bank right. Make them believe you need to stay out over the ocean to troubleshoot the problem. They'll never suspect terrorists if you hit 'em with the flight control problems."

Chuck listened.

"The navigation points will keep you out over the ocean and away from land. Then somewhere up the coast, tell them you're going to fly abeam San Fran, let down, and make a wide circle to the right and come back for a landing at Oakland. I know it'll work! As long as you stick to the flight control problem, you'll never see any fighters."

After a moment of silence, Chuck said, "I'll do it."

"Thank you!"

Ryan ripped off his seat belt, reached above his head, popped open a plastic panel in the ceiling and pulled a nylon bag from the cavity. The bag contained a twenty foot rope used for emergency evacuation from the cockpit, one end attached to an anchor point in the ceiling. He then unlocked his side window and cranked it open. As the window opened, the rush of jet-engine noise filled the cockpit. He tossed the bag out the window, taking the knotted rope to the ground.

"Get your coat," Chuck said. "It'll hide that white shirt."

"Good idea."

Although it was pitch black, the lights of a vehicle or airplane would reflect off the white shirt like a billboard. He slipped on the dark jacket. He put his right hand on his hip. The .40 caliber Glock 23 was secure in its holster. He tossed his cell phone to Chuck. "One more favor…"

Chuck stared at him. "What?"

"Do you have a car?"

"Yeah, but it's a beater."

"I need your keys and your cell phone. My car and cell have tracking devices on them. I'll use your phone to call for help once I get close to my house."

Chuck dug his keys from his pocket and located his cell phone and handed them to Ryan. "Like I said, it's a beater, but it should get you there."

"I'm sure it will get me there." Ryan tossed his car keys to Chuck. "After this is over, you might need a ride." Ryan stepped up in his seat, grabbed the rope with both hands, and sat on the ledge of the cockpit window.

"Remember, fly the profile. You must arrive at the bridge at exactly midnight."

Ryan pushed his body out of the window. The noise of the jet's left engine was deafening. Hand over hand, he lowered himself to the ground. Once on the ground, he looked up to see Chuck give him a thumbs up as he reeled the rope back into the cockpit, and cranked the window closed.

Ryan scurried, half-crouched, into the uncut grass at the edge of the taxiway, running like a convict escaping prison. The bright lights in the cabin prevented passengers from seeing a man running. The control tower was too far away to spot him in the dark.

Luck was on his side. A tug pulling six baggage carts was approaching from the right, one headlight burnt out, the other casting a weak beam. Ryan lowered himself to the ground, hoping the driver would not think to scan the dark, grassy median.

The train of carts passed, then began to slow. Thinking he might have been spotted, Ryan fell spread-eagle in the grass. He heard the tug rattle to a stop. He lifted his head slightly to see that the driver had not spotted him, but had stopped at a stop sign on the service road. Ryan sprang up and sprinted for the last cart on the train. He dove into the cart, half full of luggage, just as the driver hammered the accelerator, sending a roller bag crashing down on top of Ryan. The driver, oblivious that Ryan had hopped a ride, sped off to deliver his load of bags.

Ryan closed the side curtains on the cart, shielding him from being spotted. The tiny wheels of the baggage cart telegraphed every crack and bump in the pavement through its metal floor to Ryan's butt. The caboose fishtailed like an out of control garden hose. Under cover of darkness, the tug driver pushed the tug's engine to its limit, racing to deposit the load of bags.

After one last abrupt stop and start, the train veered off the service road and toward the ramp area, coming to a jolting stop beside a parked Boeing 737, its baggage doors open wide like the mouths of baby chicks waiting for food.

Ryan hopped out of the cart, unnoticed by the driver and meandering ramp workers, straightened his coat, and blended into the scene as a pilot performing a routine preflight. He scanned the area near the terminal spotting an employee bus stop, a bus just approaching. He broke into a run, waving at the driver. Luckily, the driver looked up.

Once at the employee lot, Ryan stepped off the bus and scanned the sea of cars. He froze. He'd forgotten to ask Chuck what kind of beater he drove or where he'd parked it. "Great!"

This can't be happening to me.

Ryan pulled the key from his pocket. Thankfully, the car had a remote door locking system. He raised the key fob above his head, swinging it left and right, repeatedly pressing the unlock button.

Nothing.

He ran up and down the rows of cars, continuing to press UNLOCK, searching for taillights, listening for a chirp or beep.

Finally, yellow taillights flashed. "Yes! Thank you Lord!"

He ran to the car. Chuck was right, it was a beater. A dark green Dodge Omni built in the early 80's. The key fit. He wrestled with the door, wondering why Chuck bothered to lock it.

He removed his holstered gun and tossed it into the passenger's seat, sat behind the wheel, and slammed the door closed. He probed in the dark with the key, searching for the ignition, found it, inserted the key, and turned it.

Nothing.

"Crap!" Dead. He pounded the steering wheel. "Not now!"

The thunder of a jet pulled his eyes in the direction of the black sky above the runway. It was Chuck.

"Com'on!" He turned the key again. The starter caught, and after a cough and a pop, the engine fired. He pumped the accelerator, forcing fuel into the faltering pistons. Fumes of exhaust filled the car. Finding reverse, he backed out of the spot, shifted into drive, and punched the accelerator. The beater stalled and died.

"NO!"

He slammed the shifter into park and turned the key. The battery struggled against the load, seconds seemed like minutes. The engine fired.

"Yes!"

He found drive, hammered the accelerator, sending the car lurching like a rabbit. He exited the parking lot and began the 68 mile drive. Without traffic, he was looking at 55 to 60 minutes.

Too dark to see his wristwatch, he searched the dash for a clock. No clock. He flipped the switch for the overhead light. Burnt out. After another scan of the dimly-lit instrument panel, confirming the beater was clockless, he spotted the fuel gauge.

No!

"Chuck! Why? I don't have time for this!"

The needle was bouncing off the top of the 'E'. In desperation, he calculated. The engine was small, probably under 100 horsepower. Even with its sick condition, it should squeeze out thirty miles per gallon. Two gallons was all he needed.

Assuming the gas tank held somewhere between 12 to 14 gallons, the distance from the top of the 'E' to bone dry should be at least two gallons—60 miles. He needed 68.

CHAPTER 28

10:43 p.m.

Chuck unbuckled his seat belt and shoulder harness, climbed into the captain's seat, and reeled the escape rope back into the cockpit, leaving it piled on the floor. He saw Ryan glance up, gave him a thumbs up, then cranked the window closed.

"Good luck," he said, knowing he was talking to himself.

He strapped into the copilot's seat, took a deep breath, and called the tower.

"Tower, Angel 54 is ready."

"Angel five four heavy, two five right, position and hold."

"Roger, Angel five four heavy, two five right, position and hold."

Chuck released the parking brake, and eased the throttles forward. The plane shook as it rolled. With only one nosewheel steering tiller, located across the cockpit on the captain's side, Chuck had to maneuver the jet onto the runway by using differential thrust and tractor breaking.

After lining up, best he could, on the centerline of the runway, he glanced over at the empty captain's seat.

What am I doing? I must have lost my mind.

"Angel five four heavy maintain three thousand, runway two five right cleared for takeoff."

"Maintain three, cleared for takeoff on two five right, Angel five four heavy."

He pushed the throttles to takeoff power. The engines rumbled to life, pressing Chuck against his seat as the jet thundered down the runway and up into the dark night. He retracted the landing gear and engaged the autopilot.

"Angel five four heavy, contact departure."

"Angel 54 going to departure."

Chuck flipped the radio to the departure frequency.

"Departure, Angel five four heavy passing three, for five."

"Angel five four heavy, climb and maintain one zero thousand."

"Roger, Angel five four heavy, 10,000."

Chuck planned to wait until just prior to reaching 10,000 feet before declaring an emergency—approximately two minutes. He engaged the secondary route in the flight computer. The navigational display instantly changed, showing the new route. The small TV-like computer screen displayed a colored line from LAX to the first turn point, approximately 150 miles west, out over the Pacific, just past the Channel Islands. Clicking the display to a range of 320 miles, Chuck could see that the course turned north after passing the Channel Islands.

"Angel five four heavy, turn left heading two two zero."

He couldn't turn left. If he did, he'd fly through the course displayed on the nav display. He had to declare the emergency, now.

"Departure, Angel five four heavy is unable. We have a flight control problem…can't turn left."

"Angel five four heavy, I understand you have a flight control problem?"

"Affirmative! We can't turn left!" Chuck tried to sound stressed, which wasn't hard.

"Angel five four heavy, state your intentions."

"We need to continue straight out, heading two seven zero! We're declaring an emergency! I'm leveling at 10,000 feet."

"Roger, Angel five four heavy, state fuel and souls on board."

"It's all we can do to keep it level! Standby on the fuel and souls!"

"Roger, Angel five four heavy, let us know your fuel and souls on board when you're able."

"Angel 54, we need some space to troubleshoot the problem."

"Roger Angel five four heavy, we will clear the airspace. Keep us advised of your intentions."

"Roger."

Chuck connected the autopilot to the nav computer ensuring that the jet would precisely fly the alternate route's course, speed, and altitude. He pressed a button on the flight computer's keypad showing the calculated arrival time at the final destination of 12:00 a.m. Chuck glanced at the clock on the forward instrument panel—10:50.

So far, ATC was buying the emergency as the real deal. Next, he needed to contact the company and inform them he had a problem. They would get tech support and company maintenance involved. The more realistic he could make the mechanical problem appear to the world, the less chance of fighter jets being launched.

The interphone chimed twice.

"Crap!" He'd forgotten about the flight attendants. He lifted the handset.

"This is Chuck."

"Chuck, this is Bev. Is it okay if we get up?"

Normally, the captain signaled the flight attendants with a chime to indicate it was safe to begin their cabin duties. Chuck forgot.

"Ahh…listen, Bev, we're working a small flight control problem. Maybe it would be best if you stay seated for a while."

Bev peppered him with questions, "Are we returning to L.A.? Do I need to make a safety briefing? Should I make a PA and let the passengers know?"

"No! Just stay seated, and DO NOT make a PA! We'll get back with you in a minute."

In a stern voice, Bev said, "Let me talk to the captain."

Chuck glanced at the empty captain's chair. "He's sorta busy right now. He can't talk."

Chuck slammed the handset into its cradle.

The jet leveled at 10,000 feet with the flight computer married to the autopilot. From this point on, the computer would send signals to the autopilot and autothrottle systems to ensure the jet flew the path Ryan had programmed into the alternate route.

Chuck dialed the company dispatch frequency into the number two radio. He paused momentarily, reviewing how he would present the make-believe problem to the company. He had to make it sound believable. Some type of flight control problem that would only allow him to bank the jet to the right. That way, once he hit the first checkpoint, he could fly north up the coast to the second checkpoint without alarming ATC. If they suspected he was under duress, they might launch the fighters if only as a precautionary measure. He wondered if Rex Dean had tried a similar stunt. If he had, ATC would definitely be putting the fighters in the air, *again*.

"Dispatch, Angel 54."

"This is dispatch. Go ahead 54."

"We've got a flight control problem. We need you to connect us to tech support."

"Roger, 54. Standby."

Chuck looked out his side window at the lights of Santa Barbara sparkling on the coast. A quick check of the flight computer showed he would cross the first checkpoint, on schedule, in twelve minutes.

"Angel five four, we've got tech support on the line. Go ahead."

"Tech, this is the first officer on flight 54." Chuck tried to act cool with a touch of panic.

"Go ahead Chuck, this is Tom in tech support. What've you got?"

"After takeoff, once the flaps were retracted, we had to add full left aileron to keep the jet level. If we release any pressure, it banks right. It's taking all we've got to keep it flying straight and level."

"What about the rudders? Can you bank it with rudders?"

"No. The pedals are stiff. I can move them, but when I do, all it does is put us into a slip."

"Sounds like it could be a split flap. Do you have any other indications; any advisory or caution lights?"

Chuck failed to think about the numerous warning systems that should accompany his make-believe flight control problem. Telling tech that there were not any warnings to accompany the problem would make it harder to sell. He was in too deep.

"Nothing."

"Are you sure?"

"There are no warnings, and both the flap and slat indicators are normal."

"What about pitch control?"

"There's nothing unusual with the pitch. We're level now and there was nothing unusual with the pitch during the climb until the flaps were retracted."

"Strange you didn't get a warning. Are you sure the flap and slat indicators are normal?"

"No warnings and the indicators are normal."

When Tom keyed his mike, Chuck could hear voices in the background. He suspected Tom was not working alone.

"Chuck, have you got enough ailerons to keep it level?"

"Yeah. But the captain wants to try and bank it right to a more northerly heading to stay close to the coast."

"Sounds like a good idea. Let us know how it acts in the turn."

"Roger. I'm going back to ATC to coordinate."

"Okay, we'll keep working on it from our side."

Chuck turned the volume down on the number-two radio, and up on the number-one.

"Departure, Angel five four heavy."

"Angel five four heavy, this is departure. Go ahead."

Just as Chuck spoke, the jet crossed the first checkpoint and started a smooth bank to the right, following the course line to the second checkpoint.

"We're turning north and plan to fly along the coast while we troubleshoot the problem. We plan to maintain 250 knots and 10,000 feet. We are talking with our tech support."

"Angel five four, we'll clear the airspace. You are cleared as requested. What's your fuel and souls on board?"

"Two-hundred and twelve souls, ten crew, and seven hours of fuel."

"Angel five four heavy, we copy, two twelve plus ten, with seven hours of fuel."

Chuck returned to the company frequency. "Tech, this is Angel 54."

"Go ahead, Chuck. This is Tom."

"The jet banked smoothly to fifteen degrees."

"How much did you relieve the controls?"

"About half."

That sounds about right.

"Are you level now?"

"Yeah. We're level at 10,000 and holding our heading fine. The captain wants to talk with me, standby."

Chuck was stressed and tired of all the back and forth, but so far it seemed to be working. Everything was cool. He would fly over the bridge, circle around and land at Oakland. Until then, he only needed to feed ATC and the company enough information that they would buy the lie. That's all he could do. He checked the computer. Only 45 minutes remaining.

Downhill from here. Sit back and chill.

The interphone chimed three times—two was normal— three was urgent. Chuck forgot about the flight attendants, *again.*

Instead of using the handset, he selected the interphone button on his audio panel. This would allow him to speak to Barb using his boom-mounted microphone while still monitoring ATC and the company.

"This is Chuck."

"What's going on up there?" Barb said. "I've got passengers back here going crazy! They see the lights on the coast and want to know why we're flying so low! Let me talk to Captain Mitchell!"

"Listen, Barb! The captain is doing all he can to keep the airplane right-side-up! He doesn't have time to talk to you!"

"Well, someone needs to talk to these passengers, now! If you don't, I am!"

"Okay. We'll say something."

He needed to tell the passengers something to calm them down. The last thing he needed was a mutiny. He selected the PA button on his audio panel, continuing to monitor ATC, the company, and Barb on the interphone.

He spoke in a calm, controlled voice. "Ladies and gentlemen, this is the captain. Some of you have noticed we've been flying rather low. The captain and I are troubleshooting a minor flight control problem—nothing serious. Once we get things worked out, we'll be returning to Los Angeles. Please follow the flight attendant's directions. We'll keep you updated."

Before he could punch off the PA button, the interphone

chimed.

Ding, ding, ding.

"This is Chuck."

Barb's voice started immediately. "What did you mean 'this is the captain'! And then you said 'the captain and I'? That was a real confidence builder for the passengers. I want to talk to the captain! Now!"

Barb's whining started to irritate him. He needed to get her off his back. He had enough to worry about without having to nurse her. He keyed his mike.

"Barb, the captain is not here! I'm flying the freakin' jet by myself. And there's no flight control problem, I'm faking it. The captain's family is being held hostage by some freak who says he will kill them if we don't crash this plane into the Golden Gate Bridge. The captain is somewhere down there on the 405 racing home, hoping to stop the lunatic from killing his family. So you can tell the passengers anything you want; just keep them calm for 45 more minutes and, hopefully, this nightmare will be over for all of us."

In a shocked voice, Barb said, "Check your PA button."

Chuck glanced down at his audio panel. The tiny button marked PA was lit. "Oh crap!" Now the passengers knew everything. He had just announced everything to the passengers. The blood drained from his face, sweat bursting from pores he didn't even know he had. He could hear muffled screams of passengers coming from the cabin.

Barb screamed, "So you're telling me...*us*, there's no captain up there?! You're all alone?! And we're all gonna die in forty-five minutes? What am I supposed to do now?"

The phone went dead. He could hear more screams, closer this time, just outside the door, then banging—fist beating against the cockpit door.

CHAPTER 29

11:28 p.m.

The Mitchell house was deathly quiet. Keri's eyes were frozen on the computer screen watching Ryan's plane move slowly north along the coast.

The albino startled her when he crept up alongside her gurney. He placed one hand on her arm, attempting to calm her, and then lifted a finger to his lips. "Shhhh."

Like I can say anything with my mouth taped close.

He cut his eyes toward the little man, before reaching into his satchel. He then took something with him and disappeared behind her, out of view, headed toward the kitchen. She heard the refrigerator door open and a cabinet door close. He then appeared with a glass of orange juice, which he handed to the little man.

"Here, you should drink this," he said.

The little man turned from the computer with a smile. "Thank you." Perhaps it was the salty chips or junk he'd eaten earlier, but he must have been parched, turning up the glass of juice and guzzling it down in a matter of seconds. The albino took the empty glass and returned to the kitchen.

"So, everything is looking good." Samael called out to

Usman from the kitchen.

"Yes. Not much longer and the plane will be making its final turn toward the target."

Samael returned to the computer and leaned down close. "Beautiful. Whatever Captain Mitchell has done, he has kept the fighters on the ground." He turned to Keri. "Your husband is doing a wonderful job. You should be proud."

The thought of her husband minutes from sacrificing his life for his family, her two children drugged to within an inch of their lives, and Evil incarnate standing in her presence saying 'everything is looking good' made her nearly faint. Any faith she had left was sucked from her spirit.

How can a loving God allow this?

"Perfect," Samael said. "Well, it looks like your job is done, little man. Thank you for your help."

"My pleasure."

Within a matter of minutes, the little man began to fidget and squirm. She heard a noise she couldn't identify, possibly gas erupting from the frail man's body. He turned, searching for the albino.

"Samael," he called, "I need to go to the bathroom. Can you come watch the computer?"

Samael said, "Are you okay?"

"Yes, I think so. It's my stomach."

"Your IBS acting up again?"

"I guess. Could have been something I ate earlier."

"That's too bad," Samael said. "I believe there's a bathroom just off the foyer."

The little man scurried off.

The albino met Keri's stare. "He has a bowel problem, among other things. I decided that once his services were no longer needed, I'd do his soul a favor and free it from that miserable little body."

The albino's eyes revealed a hollowness that was not of this world.

Samael explained, "The little cocktail I prepared him will ensure his body is purified once his soul slips away. The body, you know, is only good for a season."

The freak had put something in the man's juice, possibly a dose of the same dirty liquid he poured into the IV tubes. It must have triggered the little guy's IBS. Of course, the smorgasbord of junk food he inhaled earlier didn't help.

With the midget in the bathroom busy tending to his spastic colon, the albino pulled a syringe and a glass ampoule from his satchel. He twisted off the needle guard, and pierced the cap of the ampoule. Keri strained against her straps. Terror filled her eyes. She didn't want to sleep.

Focusing on the hypodermic as it filled with fluid, he said, "Oh, dear, this is not for you, it's for Usman." He drew the plunger deep, filling the barrel of the syringe. "Lidocaine is my favorite."

Although adverse drug effects from lidocaine were rare, if administered correctly, the dose the freak had sucked into the barrel of the syringe would stop a person's heart in a matter of minutes. It was definitely not a pretty way to go.

The albino squirted some of the solution into the air then headed in the direction of the foyer, disappearing from Keri's view.

She listened intensely.

Voices first, then a couple of thuds against a wall, very little struggle. Keri imagined the large albino had little trouble subduing the man before lancing him with the lethal dose of barbiturate, especially if the man had been seated on the toilet with his pant legs down, acting as shackles around his ankles.

The sound of the bathroom door closing against its frame, like a coffin, was followed by footsteps. The albino strode calmly into the room as if he'd simply been to the bathroom to relieve himself, nothing more.

A dead man was in her bathroom. She felt sick, nauseated. She forced her mind to think on something else, knowing the tape across her mouth might cause her to drown on her own vomit.

The computer screen. The little airplane. Ryan.

"It looks like it won't be much longer now." He moved next to Keri's bed. "I'll ask you one last time before I go." He leaned in close, taking a deep breath through his nostrils, smelling her like a flower. His voice lowered to a whisper. "Do you want to sleep?"

Keri shook her head.

"As you wish." He raised up. "Keri, death of the body is not something you should fear. Your body is nothing more than a shell. Your soul will live on." He stroked her head. "We all have a purpose, which I have learned can take more than one lifetime to discover."

After picking up his satchel, he made one last look around the room and then flipped off the lights. The glow from the two computer screens provided enough light for Keri to keep watch over David and Martha. They were sound asleep—hopefully not in a coma. The freak disappeared behind her, headed toward the foyer.

She heard the front door open followed by the freak's voice "Good luck dear." The door slammed closed.

She checked the glowing digital clock on the computer screen:

11:32:05
11:32:06
11:32:07
11:32:08

Less than 28 minutes remained.

With his work finished, Samael checked the door after pulling it closed.

Good. Locked tight.

From the street it would appear to a passerby that the Mitchell household had turned in for the night. He embraced the cool, fresh, night air, taking a full breath, filling his lungs, and then exhaling. It was a wonderful night. He smiled as he strolled to the Suburban, whistling quietly as he walked.

He gazed into the sky, rewarded by the sight of a crescent moon—the same crescent moon that, as Mehmet, he had seen in 1453. It was the beginning of a new month, the end of his long struggle. No more hiding. No more shame. He would finally be whole, just as his beloved grandmother, Io, had been changed back from the hideous white heifer and freed from the maddening stings of the gadfly—the curse of Hera—he too would soon be rid of the torment of the white carcass that imprisoned his soul.

Before climbing into the Chevy, he looked back at the Mitchell house. Thanks to him, three more souls would soon be freed from their earthly bondage. At midnight, the computer program would activate the three infusion pumps.

He had lied to Keri about the two conditions that would trigger the infusion pumps. Regardless of what happened to the jet, she and the children would die. It was the only way.

He closed the door to the Chevy and cranked the engine. He thought of Usman, knowing the little man's soul must be rejoicing. The thoughts of death made him jealous. He shifted into DRIVE, pulled away from the curb, and eased through the quiet streets lined with darkened houses, bodies sleeping, souls resting, all waiting for their glorious day of death and release.

The clock in the dash read 11:40. He flipped on the radio and scanned the channels, searching for a local news broadcast with a clear signal. Shortly after midnight, every station across the country would be broadcasting the crash. He didn't want to miss the frantic drama.

His drive north to L.A. promised to be exhilarating. Assured there were plenty of hotels near the airport with vacancies, he looked forward to a restful night before his flight back to Istanbul in the morning.

CHAPTER 30

11:25 p.m.

Ryan pushed the Omni hard, the accelerator spending most of its time against the floorboard. But even with that, the sick engine could do no better than 70. If he slowed, he might be able to conserve fuel, but the minutes lost could make the difference between life and death for his family.

The fuel gauge needle had eased ever so slowly below the top of the 'E'. Every muscle in his body was wound tight as a spring. With 28 miles to go, he prayed the dregs of the tank would offer up at least one more gallon.

Three thoughts constantly revolved in his head, all interconnected: time, fuel, family. He raised his wristwatch and, using the headlights from the car behind, checked the time—11:26. If the vapors in the tank would last, he should arrive at the house approximately ten minutes before midnight.

The thought of killing felt wrong, but he had no reservations. He took Chuck's cell phone, flipped it open, and punched in 9-1-1 on the keypad. He lifted it to his right ear and heard the first ring, then a beep. He looked at the face of the phone. It was black. The battery was dead.

"Great!" He threw the phone out the window. "I guess

I'm on my own."

He felt his pocket to learn of another problem. His house key was on the ring with his car key. Chuck had both. "What else?"

He raised his left arm into the beam of light from behind— 11:28. Each agonizing minute knotted his stomach tighter. He reviewed possible scenarios. He would park the car a couple of houses away, then ease around to the back of his house. The sliding glass door, leading in from the patio, should be unlocked. If not, his only other choice was the outside door that led into the garage. From the garage, he could enter through the mudroom. Other than that, his entry would be noisy robbing him of any advantage over the lunatic.

A flicker of light on the car's instrument panel drew his attention inside. Everything looked normal. He stared for a minute, hoping to see the flicker. The thought of the engine overheating and seizing crossed his mind. He dismissed the thought. Suddenly, a yellow light next to the fuel gauge burst from the darkness. It was the fuel low-level light.

"Come on! You can make it!"

The needle had plummeted well below the bottom of the 'E'. He turned the steering wheel slightly from side-to-side, causing the car to gently swerve in the lane. If any fuel was trapped in a crease in the bottom of the tank, he might be able to slosh it into the fuel line. With most cars, the warning light meant there was enough fuel for twenty to thirty miles; with the beater, there was no guarantee. He needed twenty.

There is no time to stop.

He pounded the steering wheel. "You'd better not die on me! Not now!"

CHAPTER 31

11:35 p.m.

Chuck ignored the screaming and banging coming from the cabin. The reinforced door should keep them out of the cockpit. He also stopped answering Barb's calls. She'd have to deal with it the best she could.

The thought of passengers scrambling for the phones to call for help sent a shock of panic. If a passenger called the local news media or 911, they would discover the captain's name, where he lives, and alert the police, FBI—the world. Ryan's family would certainly die.

He reached for the overhead panel, pulling a circuit breaker, disabling the air-to-ground telephone system. Chuck knew it was still possible for a passenger to connect with the outside world using a cell phone.

He checked the flight computer. POINT B was 84 miles ahead—twenty minutes to go. Glancing to the navigation display, he noticed the name FARRA. He knew the location to be near the Farallon Islands. The ETA to POINT B was 11:55. He checked the clock—11:35. Once the jet made the turn over POINT B, the computer would increase the speed to 325 knots. At that speed, the last leg would take five minutes, arriving at the bridge as planned—12:00 a.m., midnight.

"Angel five four heavy, this is SoCal Center."

Chuck had forgotten about the bogus flight control problem. ATC probably wanted an update. He really didn't have time for games. He needed to get the jet on the ground.

"SoCal, this is Angel five four. Go ahead."

"Angel five four, we received information that you might have a situation on board. Is this correct?"

"NO! All we have is a flight control problem. No 'situation'. I repeat, no 'situation'! Everything is under control. We plan to turn toward the coast, circle east, and land at Oakland."

Silence followed.

Chuck feared what was coming next.

"Angel five four heavy, as a precautionary, we've alerted Fresno Air National Guard."

No!

"SoCal, there is no need. We have control of the jet and will be landing at Oakland. I repeat: There is NO situation!"

A passenger must have made a call mentioning the chaos erupting on the plane. That's all it would take to scramble the fighters. Since 9/11, knowledge of a disruptive passenger would be enough to warrant a fighter escort.

Chuck knew the 144th had F-16s sitting on alert, able to be airborne in five to ten minutes. Using their afterburners, they could be over the Pacific within fifteen minutes after liftoff. If the fighters had already launched, they could be on site in less than ten.

Chuck had friends at the airline that also pulled guard duty at the 144th Fighter Wing at Fresno. The 144th was the same unit that shot down Rex Dean's flight on July 11th, 2002. The guy that pulled the trigger lived in Chuck's neighborhood. The poor guy eventually cracked and went out on a medical. The guy hadn't flown since.

"Center, call them back! We don't need an escort! We'll

be on the ground in twenty minutes."

"Angel five four heavy, the escort is airborne. ETA approximately seven minutes."

Ding. Ding. Ding. Ding.

Four chimes. Bev was panicked. Chuck ignored her.

Hammer-like bangs sounded against the cockpit door. Unrecognizable muffled screams followed. "DON'T DO THIS! MY WIFE AND BABY ARE BACK HERE! PLEASE!"

Chuck pressed the PA button on his audio panel and keyed the mike. "Listen! Nobody is going to die! Everybody sit down, buckle up, and shut up!"

He checked the nav display and the clock. In nine minutes—11:43—the jet would start it's programmed descent from 10,000 feet, so as to cross POINT B at 500 feet. The fighters would be on him by the time he made the turn toward the bridge.

"Angel five four heavy, we've got the escort on radar. They should be joining up with you in less than five minutes. Request you continue flying your current heading. Do not, I repeat, do not turn toward the coast. Monitor GUARD frequency. The fighters will contact you."

Chuck didn't reply. If he maintained his present heading, Ryan's family would die. If he made the turn toward the bridge, especially at 500 feet, he was a goner; the fighters would blast him out of the sky. He and his crew, plus 212 innocent passengers, would join Rex Dean in the abyss below.

At exactly 11:43, the throttles retarded to idle as the jet slowly nosed over; the altimeter started to unwind. Chuck had minutes to decide what to do—disconnect the autopilot and maintain his present heading to the north, hoping to avoid the same fate of Rex Dean, or make the turn toward the bridge and pray for mercy.

The muffled screams and cries from passengers in the

cabin continued. Chuck ignored them.

The jet's computer was handling the descent into the blackness perfectly. With the airspeed needle frozen on 250 knots, and a descent rate of 3,000 feet per minute, the jet would fly the remaining four miles to POINT B—FARRA— in exactly one minute, leveling at 500 feet as scheduled. Based on the speed of the jet and the upcoming sharp ninety degree change of course to the east, Chuck expected the jet's computer to anticipate the turn at FARRA by initiating a bank approximately half a mile before reaching FARRA.

Just as the jet banked right toward the coast, a voice crackled in Chuck's headset, a new voice he'd not heard before.

"Angel five four heavy, this is Shark Zero One on GUARD. How copy?"

The fighters.

He looked down to the audio panel on the consol. With his trembling, index finger, he selected the button connecting him to the GUARD frequency. "Shark Zero One, this is Angel five four heavy. Everything is cool here. We're okay."

The jet leveled at 500 feet, Chuck was pressed back into his seat as the throttles automatically moved forward to max power. The airspeed needle eased off 250, headed for the targeted 325 knots. The black ocean below offered no sense of how low he was, however, through the front windshield, less than twenty miles away, the bright lights of San Francisco glowed on the horizon.

"Angel five four heavy, turn left immediately to a northerly heading. I repeat, turn to a northerly heading, now!"

Chuck reached for the control yoke, one side of him fighting the urge to follow the warnings from the fighter pilot, the other side screaming to click the autopilot off and turn north. Surely if he turned north now, the last few minutes would not make a difference. He'd given Ryan plenty of time.

Before he could act, the jet jolted from a riveting blast against the cockpit equivalent to ten to twenty bowling balls. His heart rocketed into his throat, blocking his sudden gasp for breath.

They fired! We've been hit! We're gonna die!

A short silence followed before a second hammering of twenty or thirty blows on the windshield. The captain's windshield shattered. The blast of glass, propelled by the 300 mile per hour wind, shredded the fabric back of the captain's chair.

Chuck saw blood everywhere, but, thank God, it wasn't his.

I'm still alive!

The plane was still flying.

Birds! We've been hit by birds!

Bird feathers swirled through the cockpit. Dead birds everywhere—big birds.

The deafening shrill of wind muted the constant commands in his ear. Chuck reached blindly to the audio panel and swiped his hand across the volume controls, pushing them all to their maximum levels.

"Angel five four heavy, turn north now, or we'll be forced to shoot!"

Caught in a conundrum of indecision, the California coast less than ten miles away, he reached for the controls. If he continued, the fighters were certain to fire their guns, or worse, launch a missile, sealing Chuck and his screaming passengers in a watery grave.

Chuck gripped the control yoke with both hands just as another volley of birds—five to ten—hammered the cockpit and windshield. The windshield held, but simultaneous to the pops against the glass, the nose of the jet yawed abruptly to the right, the right wing dipped, fire bells and flashing, red, warning lights followed, sending Chuck into a frenzy.

Instinctively, he called out, "ENGINE FIRE!"—his

voice muted by the deafening hurricane of wind rushing through the captain's windshield.

Wrestling with the controls, he had not noticed his death grip on the control wheel which encompassed the transmit button. His words: "Engine Fire" had been transmitted to the world.

"Angel five four, Shark Zero One! We copy and confirm! Your right engine is on fire! I repeat, your right engine is on fire!"

Chuck clicked off the autopilot, shoved hard against the rudder pedal with his left foot, bringing the jet's nose back to center. While holding pressure against the pedal, he rolled the wings level, slapped the fire warning light on the glareshield—silencing the annoying fire bells—identified the right engine fuel control lever by the glowing red light in the handle, pulled and twisted the lever—sending fire extinguishing agent into the right engine nacelle.

He looked ahead. Through the blood-smeared windshield, he could make out the lights of the Golden Gate Bridge less than a mile away. He gently pulled back on the control wheel. The jet climbed...1,000...2,000 feet. He leveled at 2,000 feet.

"Shark Zero One, I'm landing at Oakland on Runway eleven."

"Roger, Angel five four."

Based in San Francisco for his first five years with Freedom Airlines, Chuck knew the Bay area airports. He could land at San Francisco, but it was a few miles further south than Oakland. He had Runway 11 at Oakland in sight. Even with a slight tailwind, the 10,000-foot runway would give him plenty of room to stop the jet.

"Angel five four heavy, this is Oakland Tower on GUARD. We have you in sight and you are cleared to land on Runway 11. The rescue teams have been alerted."

"Roger Oakland. We should be on the ground in two to

three minutes."

"Angel five four, this is Shark Zero One...Good luck, Chuck."

Even with one engine out, wind whistling through the captain's windshield, and his window smeared with blood and guts, Chuck made a perfect touchdown and brought the jet to a smooth stop. A thunderous round of cheers and applause broke out in the cabin.

The first thought that popped into Chuck's head was...

I hope Ryan made it.

CHAPTER 32

11:48 p.m.

When Ryan exited the freeway, the fuel needle was resting at the bottom of the fuel gauge. It was a miracle the car hadn't run out of gas. Only three stoplights and five miles separated him from the house and his family. Each mile was a gift.

Passing under a street light, he checked his watch—11:48. If Chuck had done his part, there still might be a chance. The neighborhood streets were quiet, the first two traffic lights were green, but it didn't matter. There was no way he was stopping for a traffic light, and he would welcome any cop that was unlucky enough to be stuck on duty at this time of night.

He didn't know if the lunatic was alone. There could be others. He couldn't think about it now. The last traffic light came into view, 100 yards ahead. When he reached it, he would turn left. From there it was only a mile to his house.

A car approached the intersection from his left, paused, turned right and drove past. It looked like a high school kid, probably dropping off a date. In response to the kid's car rolling over the sensors in the pavement, the traffic light turned red. Ryan didn't slow. He took the turn hard and fast, tires screeching.

The slight incline in the road caused the Omni to slow. He jammed the accelerator against the floorboard. Then it happened, without warning, one cough, and it died. "NO!"

The dead engine, combined with the slight incline, quickly slowed the Omni to a crawl. He slammed on the brakes and shifted into PARK.

Maybe he could restart it.

He turned the key, pumping the accelerator. "Please, God, please!"

Nothing.

He was approximately one mile from his house. He checked his watch—11:54.

A six-minute mile. Can I do it?

With the right shoes and clothes, yes, but with street shoes and long pants it was iffy.

He jumped out of the car, breaking into a sprint, stretching his legs with each stride, muscular arms pumping close to his side. One minute...two minutes, sweat poured from his face, soaking his shirt, his heart knocking so fiercely that his vision blurred with each surge of blood. The thoughts of his family—Keri, David, and little Martha—drove him beyond his human abilities.

He turned the corner leading into his subdivision, sprinting frantically up a slight incline, one foot after the other, forcing his muscles to perform against building lactic acids, acting like concrete, hardening the fibers in his thighs. Like a bad dream, he feared he would be too late, finding his family slaughtered, or discovering that the lunatic was not alone, all with guns—lots of guns.

"My gun!"

He'd left it in the passenger's seat of the car. He staggered and slowed, but only for a few steps, realizing there was no time. He charged on. He'd kill the freak with his bare hands or possibly one of Keri's garden tools—a spade, a claw, anything.

As he approached the house, he slowed to a jog, panting heavily. The house was dark, as were all the houses on his block. He remembered Keri asking him yesterday to replace the porchlight, but he hadn't. Normally, at this time of night, he expected his neighborhood to be sealed in darkness, but "normal" was far from what he expected to find within his own house.

He stopped, bending at the waist, sucking in several, large breaths of air, his legs rubbery, threatening to collapse beneath him. He checked his watch—12:00. Hopefully it was fast.

He worked to control his breathing and regain composure. No time to look for a tool in the garage, he'd have to find something in the house to bludgeon the lunatic's head.

Sheathed in cold sweat, his breathing now under control, he eased around the side of the house to the back patio. The curtains on the sliding glass door were partially drawn, but he found a small break. He cupped his hands on the glass and peered in. Two computer screens illuminated the den, revealing the horrid scene. Keri and the children were strapped to gurneys, lying still, possibly dead. Anger and fear collided within, opening the stopcock on his adrenal glands, charging his veins with a fresh supply of fluid. The shadowy figure of a man leaned over Keri, his back to the glass door.

That's him.

The man appeared to be alone. Ryan quickly scanned the patio for a garden tool. There was none. He grabbed the handle of the sliding door. If it was locked, attempting to jerk it open would do nothing more than alert the man. He tested the lock with a gentle pull. It moved enough to tell him it was not locked. His heart pounded against his sternum. He breathed deep, yanked the door hard, burst into the house, and headed for the lunatic.

CHAPTER 33

11:49 p.m.

With the windows down, the night air swirled through the car, washing away the strain of the night and replacing it with a peaceful sense of satisfaction. Although Samael ultimately longed for the day that death would free his soul to be joined with the spirit of his beloved mother, Keroessa, he found his present state a blissful compromise. He whistled a relaxing tune.

Minutes from the freeway, his attention was drawn to the increasing sound of a strained engine approaching in the opposite direction. A small, green car zoomed past traveling well above the speed limit. At such a late hour, he assumed it to be a teen driver hopped-up on drugs or buzzed from too much alcohol; a worthless soul destined for an early departure from his empty life. In some ways Samael was jealous.

After merging onto the freeway, he checked the digital clock in the dash—11:51. By morning, every media outlet around the globe would be hard at work spreading fear into the hearts of every living soul. He added volume to the radio, eager not to miss the news of the disastrous plane crash in San

Francisco.

"Ladies and gentlemen, we've just received news that a Freedom Airlines Boeing 767 has been hijacked out of Los Angeles International Airport!"

What?

Samael added volume to the radio.

"Less than ten minutes ago, one of our reporters, who happened to be a passenger on board the hijacked plane, called, telling us the pilot had announced he was going to crash the plane into the Golden Gate Bridge at midnight!"

Samael switched to another station.

The reporter was in midsentence. "...the word is that the Freedom Airlines jet is being flown by only one pilot."

One pilot!

The reporter continued, "The pilot flying the plane apparently made an announcement to the passengers telling them the captain was no longer in the cockpit, but, instead, somewhere on the 405 freeway trying to get home...something to do with the captain's family being held hostage. We're not yet sure if the two incidents are connected. Stay with us for more."

Samael punched the accelerator, looking for the next exit off the freeway. Plastered with a strong dose of déjà vu, a dark cloud entered his soul. He remembered the horrified face of Rex Dean's wife when, instead of hearing that a commercial airliner had crashed into the Golden Gate Bridge, the TV news reporter announced that a commercial airliner had been intercepted and shot down by military fighter jets. The news had left Samael with no choice but to end the life of his hostage. He'd made it look as if Captain Dean had murdered her before leaving for work, complete with a suicide note and a nice little poem.

After exiting the freeway, Samael checked the time— 11:55. He calculated he should arrive at the house at approximately the same time the infusion pumps were scheduled to switch ON. If he had not heard that Mitchell was headed home, he would have continued to L.A., letting the lethal drugs take care of the family. It would be after midnight before the authorities would arrive at the Mitchell's house. By then, the wife and children would be well on their way to a better place.

He checked the time—11:56. Once he ensured Mitchell had not yet arrived at the house, and it was past midnight, there would be no reason to enter the house. If, however, Mitchell happened to be at the house when he arrived, which he doubted, he would kill them all. In and out. He'd be quick.

Keri trembled as she watched the seconds on the digital clock tick away. She rolled her head to the left to see both children sound asleep—or in a comma.

11:59:55
11:59:56
11:59:57
11:59:58

The freak had promised that if Ryan's jet hit the bridge at midnight, the infusion pumps would not turn ON. She listened, waiting for the sound of the pumps to click ON.

11:59:59
12:00:00
Click
Click
Click

The pumps were running.
12:00:05

Keri started to sob, partly because she was happy that her husband might still be alive, but mostly because she and her two children would never see him again.
12:00:15

Her eyes grew heavy with sleep. She fought it. She strained against the drugs pulling her into darkness. She tried to remember all she could about Ryan: the sound of his strong voice, his laugh; the tender way he held her; the way his skin felt; all their happy moments together.

12:00:33

It was useless. The thoughts slipped away. The hand of darkness tugged harder.

12:01:01

It was too much for her. She let go and closed her eyes.

God, please take care of Ryan, wherever he is. Let the children not be in pain as they leave this world.

The fear that had earlier consumed her was now gone. Peace had replaced the worry. A sensation of warmth covered her.

The opening of the front door was the last sound she heard before her world went black. Unsure if it was the freak returning, or rescuers coming to save her...she could care less.

CHAPTER 34

12:03 a.m.

Ryan breathed deep, yanked the door hard, and burst into the house, rushing the lunatic.

Two seconds, maybe three, the lunatic straightened from a crouch. Catching him off guard, Ryan jumped on his back, clamped his left arm around the man's neck, squeezing like a nutcracker on a pecan, pressing hard against the sides of his neck, clamping off the life-giving blood flowing through his jugulars into his brain.

The man stammered, clawing at Ryan's arm, thrusting his elbows wildly like battering rams. The blows to Ryan's sides made him cough and wince from the pain. He had to hold the pressure on the man's neck and not let the animal shake him off. He squeezed tighter. The man should drop in less than a minute.

Continuing to absorb blows to his side, Ryan refused to loosen his death hold on the maniac's neck. It was his only hope. The crazed man spun round and round.

Ryan caught a glimpse of his family—Keri, David, and Martha—strapped to stretchers with IV's in their arms. Each bed was identical, a small motor buzzing, fluids flowing through clear lines, but he couldn't let go.

"Drop! Drop! Drop!"

Seeing his family stretched out on deathbeds sent a fresh burst of adrenalin through Ryan's muscles. The lunatic kept spinning, grasping, and pumping his elbows, growing weaker by the second.

The man thrust backwards against a wall, pounding Ryan into the sheetrock with such force, the wall cracked, leaving an indentation of Ryan's back in the powdery structure. Off the wall, the lunatic's legs grew wobbly, he stumbled.

Latched to the lunatic's neck like a hungry viper unwilling to release a juicy dinner rat, Ryan squeezed harder. The man spun around, now facing a mirror hanging above the fireplace.

Ryan pulled with all his might, one last time, amazed the lunatic was still standing.

A momentary glance over the man's shoulder and into the mirror riveted chills up Ryan's back. There were two men in the mirrored reflection; one was his; the other—a red-faced bearded man, gasping for air, seconds from unconsciousness.

Impossible!

He must be delusional.

"Rex! Is that you?"

Unable to talk, the man's chin moved up and down.

Ryan released his scissor grip on Rex's neck. Both men collapsed to the floor.

"It is you! You're alive! How is it possible?"

Rex Dean gasped and coughed, sucking in quick, sharp breaths, nodding rapidly.

Ryan wrapped his arms around Rex. "I thought you were dead!"

Ryan quickly remembered his family, jumped up, and raced to the gurneys.

"They're good!" Rex said, coughing and fighting to get the words out. "I stopped it."

Ryan, already by Keri's side, said, "They're not moving!"

"They're breathing." Rex coughed. "Good pulse. They're fine." Finding traction with his words. "I got here just in time." Rex struggled to his feet, still rubbing his neck. "If I hadn't, they'd be gone by now."

Ryan gently stroked Keri's cheek, her body lying motionless on the gurney, as were the children's. The clear lines attached to the infusion pumps dangled free, buzzing, and pumping the drugs through the clear tubes and onto the floor.

"We need to get them to a hospital," Ryan said. "I'm calling 911."

"I've already called. They should be here in a couple of minutes."

Ryan looked at Rex. "I don't understand. You're supposed to be dead. We went to your funeral."

"I'll explain later." Before Rex could say another word, SWAT agents burst into the den from the open patio door. Helmeted, dressed in black, with raised assault rifles, yelling, "GET DOWN! ON THE FLOOR! FACE DOWN!"

Ryan and Rex dropped to the floor. With his ear against the hardwood floor, Ryan felt the reverberate sound of more booted feet drumming into the room from the direction of the foyer. Someone grabbed his hands, pulled them behind his back, his shoulders pulling at their sockets, followed by the cutting sting of plastic flex cuffs being cinched around his wrist. He winced.

"You've got the wrong guys!" Ryan said. "This is my family! This is Rex Dean! We're both pilots with Freedom Airlines! Some maniac was holding my family hostage, threatening to murder them! I'm the captain on the plane that was hijacked tonight!"

While two agents helped Ryan and Rex to their feet, EMTs rushed into the den. Ryan watched as medical personnel wheeled away the gurneys with Keri and David. Martha was unstrapped from her bed and carried out.

"That's my family!" Ryan pleaded. "The lunatic that did this is still out there somewhere! I must go with them!"

The agent said, "Calm down. They're in good hands. Before I can let you go, I need to see some identification."

"My wallet is in my back pocket. Hurry! I want to go with my family!"

The agent dug Ryan's wallet out of his pocket and flipped it open. He studied it briefly. "Okay, Mr. Mitchell. Let me cut those cuffs off."

Once the cuffs were off, Ryan turned to Rex with a look that required no words. Rex said, "Go! I'll be fine. Go be with your family!"

Ryan ran out of the den.

The shrill sound of sirens faded in the distance. The agent asked Rex, "Did you say your name was Dean?"

"Yes, Rex Dean."

After a moment of thought, the agent locked eyes with Rex. "Rex Dean is dead. I was the lead agent on that case. I'll never forget it."

During the weeks that followed the unprecedented shooting down of a commercial airliner, Rex's picture and the horrid story hit television news stations and all forms of print media from coast to coast and around the world. With his scraggly beard and hair over his ears, Rex was almost unrecognizable from the earlier pictures.

The agent searched Rex for a wallet. He pulled one from his back pocket and flipped it open. He studied the California driver's license photo carefully—clean shaven, hair cut close.

He glanced up at Rex's face, studied it for a moment, then back at the wallet. Adjacent to the DMV mug shot was a photo of Rex and Emily together.

The agent closed the wallet. "And now you're alive. How convenient. I don't care how you did it, your twisted plan didn't work."

"No, you idiot!" Rex said, "You've got it all wrong!"

The agent snapped back, "Don't get smart with me—"

"We've got a body in the downstairs bathroom!"A voice called out from the foyer.

PART III

"You prepare a table before me in the presence of my enemies; You anoint my head with oil, my cup runs over. Surely goodness and mercy shall follow me all the days of my life; and I will dwell in the house of the Lord forever."
Psalm 23:5, 6

CHAPTER 35

12:15 a.m.

Samael arrived back at the Mitchell's house only minutes after midnight. He positioned the Suburban on the opposite side of the street, a few houses down. Seeing no sign that Mitchell had returned, Samael was relieved and decided to observe the house a moment longer. By now, Keri and her two children would be pumped full of drugs and well on their way to the afterlife.

It would be nice to see Mitchell wheeling up to the house, about now, frantically rushing in to save his family. What better way to leave him with a visual message of the meaning of trust—something he was obviously having trouble with.

The silence of the night was suddenly stirred by darkened silhouettes of images rushing across the front lawns of the neighborhood houses—like roaches in a darkened kitchen scurrying about searching for a tasty morsel of food. The stealth-like invaders moved swiftly.

He counted: two, four, eight, perhaps ten men. As one man passed beneath a pool of light from a street lamp, the white letters on the man's back screamed out: SWAT.

Samael chuckled at the gung-ho macho men, with their

hope for the best, plan for the worst mentality. Beneath each Nomex flame-retardant combat suit, the knights in shining ballistic armor were merely children, trembling boys, hiding behind their guns, driven against their fears by the rush of adrenalin.

An ambulance screeched around the corner, pulling to the curb in front of the Mitchell home. He checked the time— 12:17 a.m. By now, the infusion pumps had filled the three bodies full of lethal drugs. It was too late.

A soldier positioned at the front door of the Mitchell's house waved to the ambulance crew, signaling for them to come. Five men took off in a sprint toward the house. Moments later, four men emerged from the house with two gurneys. The flimsy beds rattled down the short driveway as the fifth man trailed with the little girl cradled in his arms. The ambulance workers retracted the legs of the gurneys and slid them into the ambulance. The man carrying the little girl joined them.

There is no way they are alive.

Within minutes, a man wearing a white shirt burst from the front door of the Mitchell house. He sprinted across the front lawn, yelling and waving his arms, calling to the ambulance workers, "Wait! Wait for me!"

His behavior was frantic. He was definitely not a member of the SWAT team, and he was definitely not an EMT. The man piled into the rear of the ambulance. The rear doors swung closed, and the big box on wheels sped off, siren shrieking, red lights spinning.

Samael contemplated what he'd witnessed. The urgency of the ambulance crews and the fact that the heads of the bodies atop the gurneys were not covered with sheets was not a good sign. They might be alive.

Impossible!

The panicked man running and waving his arms had to be Ryan Mitchell. He must have made it to the house in time.

Samael took a deep breath, exhaled, and rolled his eyes in frustration. He started the Suburban, shifted into DRIVE, and followed the flashing red lights.

Only minutes ago, the night had seemed gracious, filled with promise. Now it loomed with heaviness—a burden from under which he'd hoped by now to be free. The thought of having to do it all over again depressed him, but he had no choice. After killing the family, he'd be on his way back to LAX, and then off to Istanbul in the morning as scheduled.

The ambulance raced north on I-5 toward Mission Hospital—a regional trauma center—after learning from dispatch that the local community hospital's emergency department was requesting bypass of all patients. After the lead paramedic relayed the situation and pertinent patient information to the base hospital physician, the bypass request was honored. None of the patients exhibited any uncontrollable problems, and the estimated time to reach Mission Hospital was twenty minutes.

Sirens screamed while red lights stirred the black of night like infrared mixers as the thundering diesel wheeled up to the emergency entrance at Mission Hospital. The driver jumped out and moved to the rear of the ambulance and opened the double doors. Ryan jumped out, followed by an EMT cradling Martha in his arms. EMTs unloaded the two gurneys and quickly rolled them into the emergency room.

Walking alongside the gurneys, the lead paramedic called out the situations to the ER charge nurse. "We've got a mother and two children unconscious and unresponsive after being removed from their house approximately twenty-five minutes ago. They appear to have been sedated with an unknown substance. The mother, a forty-seven-year-old female—temperature 36.9 degrees C; heart rate 77, strong and regular; BP 130 over 78; pupils equally dilated and reactive to light. No signs of trauma or bleeding."

The nurse said, "Put the woman in room five." The EMT pushing Keri's stretcher was assisted by a waiting nurse.

The lead paramedic continued his verbal report. "A fifteen-year-old boy—temperature 36.6 degrees C; heart rate 68, strong and regular; BP 118 over 79; pupils equally dilated and reactive to light. No signs of trauma or bleeding."

"Put the boy in room eight," the nurse said. The EMT wheeled David's gurney toward room eight with the help of a nurse.

The paramedic and charge nurse turned to the third EMT, standing, waiting, cradling Martha's limp body in his arms. The paramedic said, "A five-year-old girl—temperature 36.7 degrees C; heart rate 74, strong; BP 116 over 77; pupils equally dilated and reactive to light. No signs of trauma or bleeding."

"Let's take the girl to room nine." The nurse led the EMT and the paramedic to the empty room and placed Martha on the bed. Each glass enclosed room had a large window making it easy to view the patients from a central observation center.

Dr. Daniel Aulden, the attending emergency room physician, moved from room to room examining each patient and assimilating all the details available from the paramedic. After a careful review of the patient's vitals, skin color, and breathing, he ordered a battery of blood tests and continued the normal saline intravenous infusion started by the ambulance crews.

Following close behind the screaming ambulance, Samael raced toward the hospital with only one thought on his mind: how he would finish it.

He parked the Suburban and watched from a distance as hospital workers rushed to meet the ambulance. The driver jumped out and raced to the rear of the vehicle and swung open the double doors. The first one out of the ambulance was the man in the white shirt—Mitchell—followed by the EMT cradling the little girl. The other EMT's unloaded the gurneys and rolled them into the hospital.

Entering the hospital emergency room would certainly draw the attention of medical personnel. His freakish appearance and enormous size would make it impossible for him to blend in. He needed a uniform—a form of camouflage or disguise—that would allow him to enter the hospital without being questioned.

A white, lab coat with one of those colored, surgeon caps would be nice; maybe a stethoscope dangling from his neck, and a mask to hide his face. Masquerading as a nurse or doctor would ensure him easy access into the hospital. Unnoticed, like a viper coiled in the brush, he would strike. Perhaps he could wait and catch a doctor leaving the hospital after finishing his nightly rounds, or perhaps a late-night surgery. He'd follow the unsuspecting scientific healer to his car, then "borrow" his stethoscope and iconic, white coat.

As he imagined the plan, he realized it was no good. First, it would be a rarity to find a physician wearing his work clothes. Second, it would probably be impossible to find a man his size.

Scanning the parking lot, Samael noticed a security car parked at the curb beneath a street lamp. Stuffed behind the wheel of the subcompact, security cruiser, a robust man sat motionless. The guard appeared to be on break, perhaps sipping a coffee or stuffing down a cream-filled donut before continuing his graveyard shift at the hospital. Based on the silhouette of the man's broad shoulders and large head, which appeared to be scrunched up against the ceiling of the small car, Samael believed the man might have what he needed.

Samael unzipped his satchel and removed a pouch containing several hypodermics he had preloaded with lidocaine. He took one of the hypodermics, returned the satchel and the pouch to the passenger's seat, and exited the Suburban, gently closing the driver's side door. He moved quickly and quietly along the sidewalk towards the parked cruiser. Approaching the car from the rear, it appeared that the guard was napping. As he walked, he removed the protective, plastic cover from the needle. An injection of lidocaine would ensure that Humpty continued his blissful sleep into the next life.

The driver's side window was down, the guard's head was propped against the raised headrest with his mouth hanging open. Samael positioned the syringe between his index and middle finger, his thumb on the end of the plunger.

Careful with his steps, he eased up to the window and jabbed the needle into the exposed neck of the exhausted guard, quickly pushing the plunger flush with the barrel of the syringe sending the overdose of toxic liquid into the unsuspecting defender of the night. Within seconds the guard slumped forward. His head pounded against the top of the steering wheel.

He dragged the guard's limp body into the street. Sizing up the man, Samael smiled. "Perfect." He stripped the uniform from the corpse and wrestled the body onto the backseat of the car. After changing into the guard's uniform, Samael adjusted the car's side mirror and admired his appearance.

Nice.

The shirt was a bit snug—stretching tight against his wide chest, shoulders, and bulging biceps—but that was good. Samael smiled at the official-looking patches and ID badge. The security company had done a great job in designing a police-style uniform—minus a gun.

He wished for something to cover his bald head and white face. He scanned the inside of the car for a hat. The passenger's seat and darkened, floor area was littered with a Krispy Kreme bag, a Big Gulp cup, and assorted food wrappers and newspapers. He opened the rear door. After checking the area behind the front seats, he reached in and rolled the guard's naked body to the floor. On the back seat was the guard's uniform hat—slightly crushed from the weight of the guard.

He retrieved the hat, reformed it, and checked the size. Luckily, the guard had a fat head. He adjusted the brim of the hat to hide his forehead, as much as possible, and checked it in the mirror. He smiled—especially impressed by the official-looking badge on the hat's crest. The dark-colored, police-style uniform was certain to convey power, strength, and authority, demanding cooperation while inducing feelings of safety.

Camouflaged as a defender of the night, Samael would waltz through the unsecured entrance to the emergency room and free the Mitchell family—all four of them—from their fearful bodies, once and for all. He planned to work quickly—in and out—while hospital workers continued their noble task of saving lives.

He preferred to use the lidocaine—it was quiet and clean—but, if need be, he would slice their necks starting with Ryan. The uniform should allow him to walk within arm's reach of the weary and concerned husband and father. After Ryan, he would quickly take care of the rest of the family. They should be sleeping, if not in a coma, or already dead.

Samael gathered up his clothes and stored them in the Suburban for safekeeping. He would need to change after saying goodbye to the Mitchell family. He took the pouch and his blade, locked the doors on the Suburban, and marched toward the emergency entrance of the hospital.

CHAPTER 36

Ryan hovered over Keri's motionless body, holding her limp, left hand while he stroked her arm slowly. An intravenous glucose-saline drip fed her body to prevent dehydration and electrolyte imbalances. Supplemental oxygen hissed through the two prongs of the cannula placed in her nostrils. A pulse oximeter was clipped to her right, index finger providing pulse and oxygen saturation levels. Electrodes and sensors attached to her body recorded blood pressure and respiratory rate. The combined information was displayed on a central monitor hanging above her bed.

From where he stood, he could easily see the children in adjacent rooms, separated by glass walls. Every few seconds, he glanced at their corpse-like bodies, searching for any signs of movement. He closed his eyes.

Please God, bring them back to me. You know I can't live without them. Don't let them die. Please...I will never leave their side—ever again.

The sound of footsteps drew his attention. He opened his eyes and turned. A man entered the room. "Mr. Mitchell, I'm Dr. Aulden."

"Doc, are they going to be okay? How long before they wake up?"

"They're going to be fine. The lab results are normal."

"Thank God," Ryan said.

"Yes, we can thank God. However, your wife and children did receive a non-lethal dose of sodium thiopental. Thiopental is basically a rapid-onset, short-acting barbiturate used in general anesthetics. The time it takes for them to wake up will vary, depending on the amount of the drug they each received. Once the drug redistributes to the rest of the body they will wake up. Be thankful, Mr. Mitchell, that you arrived when you did. You saved their lives."

Ryan didn't want to spend the time to correct the fact that it was Rex who saved his family, not him. After all, how could he explain it to the doc when he barely understood it himself.

"Are we talking, one hour…five hours…how long?" Ryan said.

"Considering when the injection was removed, it can be as soon as a few minutes or as long as a few hours. Thiopental would have to be given in large amounts to maintain an anesthetic plane. In that case, due to its 12 to 24 hour half-life, consciousness would take a long time to return. In the case of your family, there's nothing to worry about. Let's give it an hour. I think they'll be fine. I'll check back."

"Thank you, Doc." Ryan felt a weight lifted and his prayers answered. He turned to Keri. She was still sleeping but he wanted her to hear the news. "You're going to be fine, Honey." He leaned down and kissed her forehead. Tears spilled from his eyes and down his cheeks. He contained the urge to burst out crying. "Thank you God," he whispered. His family was safe.

I hope Rex is okay.

Without proof that the same lunatic was responsible for the murder of Emily and the attempted murder of the Mitchell family, Rex would definitely be held as a suspect for both.

Ryan had many more questions concerning Rex: How had he escaped the crash? Where had he been for the last ten months?

Footsteps at the door drew his attention again. He turned, expecting to see Dr. Aulden. Instead, the sight of a large, albino security guard, filling the doorway, startled him.

"Mr. Mitchell?" the guard said.

"Yes, I'm Ryan Mitchell."

"I'm sorry to hear about your family. Are they going to be okay?"

"The doctor said they should be fine. It might take a little while, but they will be fine."

In a soft voice, the guard said, "I'm glad to hear it."

The guard was enormous—at least six-foot-five. From the looks of him, his company must have had trouble finding a shirt large enough to fit. Any sudden movements might rip the shirt off his back, much like the Green Hulk during one of his man-to-monster transitions.

Ryan glanced down at the giant's legs. The material strained against the man's bulging thighs. At least two inches of white sock was visible from where the man's pant leg ended and his black shoe began.

"I was asked to come update you on the situation at your house," the guard said.

Thinking, the man might have information about Rex, Ryan said, "Listen, did they tell you anything about Rex Dean? Is he okay? Where did they take him?"

"Ahhh…." the guard hesitated. "Dean?"

"Yes. Rex Dean was the one who saved my family."

"Ah, yes. Rex Dean. I'm not sure where he was taken."

Something in Ryan's peripheral vision caused him to turn and look toward his son in the adjacent room. David was sitting on the edge of his bed, frantically waving, pointing, and signing. "BAD MAN! KILLER! THAT HIM! SAME MAN! SAME! SAME!" He frantically repeated the sign for "same" by bringing his hands together with extended, index fingers.

Ryan froze. His son was awake, alert—alive! But his panicked mannerisms were confusing. Ryan turned back to the guard. From where the man stood, his view of David was blocked. Ryan's heart raced as he assimilated what his son was trying to tell him. If the guard and the lunatic were one and the same, Ryan needed to act fast.

"Anything wrong, Mr. Mitchell?" the guard said.

That voice...could it be?

As if the freak read Ryan's mind, in a calm—almost hypnotic voice—the guard continued, "Don't worry, Captain Mitchell, I think you can *trust* that Captain Dean will be taken care of. It's all about *trust*, isn't it, Ryan?" A smile formed in the corners of the guard's mouth, obviously aware that his cover had been blown.

It's him!

The lunatic had returned to kill them all. Ryan turned and picked up the lightweight chair to his right and spun around, ramming the four metal legs into the freak's chest. The jolt sent the freak back against the wall, his hat flying off into the hallway.

"Ahhhhhhhhh!" Keri screamed. "That's him! Help! Somebody help!"

Ryan turned toward Keri.

She's awake!

She yelled, "Ryan! He's got a knife!"

Ryan whipped back around just in time to come face to face with the blade of a knife—at least 12 inches, possibly 18 inches long—in the albino's right hand. The blade had no point and was of equal width from top to bottom—shiny, sharp, and scary.

"You see, my dear Keri, fear is in the mind," Samael said, taking a step closer while looking at Keri. "Dear, you would have been better off if you had stayed at the house. I'd hoped it wouldn't end this way." He turned to Ryan. "And *you* cannot be trusted." He gripped the knife firmly. "I think it's time Mrs. Mitchell deals with her fears, but, first, I need to show the captain what happens when you don't trust. Do you remember what I said, Captain Mitchell? You must believe before you can trust, and you obviously do not believe. So now I'm going to make you a believer."

A man's voice called out from the hallway, "Drop the knife or I'll shoot!" The man yelled louder, "Drop it now or I'll shoot!"

Samael slowly turned, still clinching the knife in his hand. The man in the hall had his gun raised, held tightly with both hands, aimed at Samael's chest.

Samael said in a calm voice, "You can kill this body, but you can't kill me. It looks like I'll have to finish this in another life." He raised his head toward the ceiling, closed his eyes, then said something strange: "En ma Fin gît mon Commencement".

In one swift move, the albino sliced the big blade across the left side of his own neck, from back to front, cutting hard and deep through his jugular vein, arteries, trachea, and esophagus. Blood spewed, spurted, and poured from his neck as the white giant crashed to the floor.

Ryan held Keri tight as she sobbed. He removed the wires and tubes constraining her, lifted her from the bed, and carried her out of the room and into the adjacent room where Martha was slowly awakening. With the help of a nurse, David joined them. Ryan wrapped his arms around all three of them as they all cried tears of joy and relief.

"I'm never leaving you guys, ever again," Ryan said, signing as he spoke. "I don't care what we have to do or where we have to live, things are gonna be different."

Martha was the last to wake, but was smiling big. She said, "Mommy, is the big, white man gone?"

"Yes, Darling, he's gone. There's nothing to be afraid of, anymore."

"Well, I really wasn't too afraid. I knew he wouldn't hurt

us. I'll bet he's gone back to where the white monsters live."

"You and David were both very brave," Keri said and signed.

Ryan turned to David. "Son, you are my hero." David's deafness and his ability to communicate with the invisible language of signs had ultimately altered the outcome of a life-threatening situation. If David had not alerted Ryan, Samael would have surely caught him off guard.

For the first time in Ryan's life, he viewed his son in a different light. No longer was his son a mistake; the child that he wished he had never had; the little deaf boy who had no hope or future—but instead, David was perfect. Just as God had used David's deafness to save the lives of their entire family, Ryan was certain God had a wonderful and fulfilling purpose for the rest of David's life.

There is a purpose for every life.

Ryan said, "I almost forgot!"

Keri said. "Forgot what?"

"Rex!"

"Who?"

"Oh, that's right, you don't know—how could you?"

"Know what?"

"Rex is alive! He saved your life."

Keri shook her head. "Am I still dreaming, or did I just hear you say 'Rex is alive'?"

"You heard me right. Rex is alive."

CHAPTER 37

The Mitchell house remained a crime scene for five days while a team of specialists conducted fingerprinting, photography, and trace evidence collection. They gathered liquids, hairs, fibers, shoe tracks, documents with handwriting that could be analyzed, and blood. The evidence was sent to the Orange County Crime Lab for forensic analysis.

Uncertain if the man had been working alone—with the exception of the corpse they'd found in the bathroom—the Orange County Sheriff's Department provided around-the-clock protection for Ryan and his family during their two-day stay in the hospital. At 2:00 a.m. on the morning of the third day, three SUV's with tinted windows pulled up to a side entrance of the hospital. Ryan, Keri, David, and Martha were bundled into one of the SUV's and whisked away to a safe house where they spent the next two weeks under the protection of armed bodyguards.

Before returning home, Ryan had the house thoroughly cleaned, the damaged sheetrock repaired, removing any trace of the freak's visit. He wanted everything to be immaculate, fresh, and clean, hoping to prevent Keri and the kids from having any unnecessary memories of that horrible night.

"Will we ever see Rex, again?" Keri asked as she stirred a

big pot on the stove filled with her homemade spaghetti sauce.

"I've tried to find out where he is, but I can't get the detective or the sheriff's department to tell me anything. Due to the high profile nature of *his* accident, I'm certain they have him tucked away somewhere safe," Ryan said.

"But we told them it was the same guy. The freak told me himself. That's all he talked about. They should let Rex go."

"They're not going to simply take your word that a dead man, who can't speak for himself, killed Emily and was suspected as being responsible for the crash. Not without proof. After all, Rex is your ex-husband and my best friend, and Emily is my ex-wife. Think about it. Rex was convicted of murdering his wife and believed to have possibly committed suicide. The families and friends of all those who died on Rex's flight would love to find justice. Based on the evidence, that person is Rex. And now he is alive."

Keri put the dry noodles into a pot of boiling water and set the timer for seven minutes. "There must be some way to prove it was the same guy, but you said nothing was found at Rex's house."

"No, I said even if they *did* find something, for the sake of satisfying the public and avoiding an expensive investigation, it was too easy to blame it on the "dead" husband. Hopefully, now, they will take a second look at the evidence from Rex's house. I'm hoping there is something—a finger print, a fiber, a footprint, or something—that was saved from Rex's house that can be matched to the evidence found at our house; something that will tie the freak to both places."

"They have to find something. Rex is innocent."

"I just don't understand how Rex managed to remain hidden for almost a year. And why would he magically appear at our house at the perfect time? How could he have known? And where was he all that time?"

"I don't understand why he didn't try to contact you. After all, you were the *one* person he knew he could trust."

"He couldn't chance it. As long as he stayed "dead", he was off the radar. You should have seen him that night. I almost didn't recognize him, even after I looked him in the face."

"Did he tell you anything?"

"He said he would explain it later, and then everything got crazy. SWAT agents burst into the den, yelling, telling us to get down on the floor. The next thing I know, I'm face down on the floor with my hands cuffed behind my back. The minute the detective told me I could leave, I turned and looked at Rex. He told me to go. All I wanted was to be with you and the kids. I ran for the ambulance."

"Rex must have figured out that the man who killed Emily was going to strike again. The freak told me he killed Emily. He kept repeating that if I didn't cooperate with him he would keep killing. Maybe he told Rex the same thing."

Martha skipped into the kitchen with David close behind. "Mommy, are the 'noo-noos' ready?"

Keri pointed to the timer and held up two fingers. "Two minutes."

Ryan signed to David, "You hungry?"

David gave a couple of quick nods of his fist, meaning yes. He wafted the luscious aroma of the spaghetti sauce to his nose with his hand and smiled, indicating he liked it.

Ryan pulled four plates from the cabinet and placed them on the counter, and then signed to David to get the flatware and set the table. Keri drained the cooked spaghetti into a colander in the sink. She then heaped a pile of noodles on each plate, handing them to waiting hands eager to top the noodles with sauce.

Once they were all seated at the table, Ryan said, "Let's pray." Keri and Martha closed their eyes and bowed their heads while David stayed focused on Ryan. Ryan signed while he prayed. "God, we thank you for everything you have done for us and given us. Continue to strengthen us and bring peace, protection, and provision to our family. Make it clear to us what we should do next. Please help our dear friend Rex to be found innocent and freed. Thank you for this meal. In Jesus name, we pray. Amen."

His words, "what we should do next" echoed into an unknown future. He had no idea what was next, where or if they would move, when they would decide, or how he would provide for his family if they did move. He did know that he would never fly again or do anything that required him to travel. For the first time in years, he was sleeping through the night, and the nightmares had not returned. He and Keri had grown inseparable in ways that reminded him of their days as teenagers. His love for her had deepened more than he'd thought possible. He cherished every second they had together.

David and Martha started eating the moment they heard "Amen". Keri looked to Ryan as though she were peering into his soul. She smiled, reaching for his hand. Her smile warmed his heart. The touch of her hand assured him that regardless of where they landed, it didn't matter—they would be together.

The door bell rang. Keri's face tensed. She squeezed his hand. "Should we answer it?" she said.

"I'll take a look," Ryan said.

She pulled on his hand. "Are you sure?"

"It's okay. I'll be sure to see who it is before I open the door. The detective said they were certain the man was acting alone. I don't think they would have taken away our protection if they thought we were in danger." Ryan said what Keri needed to hear, even though he had his reasons to be concerned.

Before flipping on the foyer light, he glanced through the peephole in the door. "I don't believe it!" He turned the light on and opened the door. "Rex!"

CHAPTER 38

Ryan and Rex exchanged a firm handshake and backslapping man hug. Ryan backed away and stared at Rex—clean shaven, fresh haircut, and dressed in casual clothes. "Buddy, I can't tell you how good it is to see you," Ryan said with a big smile. "Where have they been keeping you?"

"Dude, it's over! I'm a free man!"

"What!" Ryan paused, unclear of what he meant by "free". "Everything?"

"Everything! They found the evidence they needed to pin it all on the lunatic. It was the same guy, after all."

"When did this happen? I mean—"

"A couple of hours ago. When the detective told me I was released, I talked him into letting me be the one to tell you."

"This is amazing!"

"Dude, how are Keri and the kids?"

"Great! Come on in." Ryan led the way into the den. "We have a lot of questions."

Keri met Rex as he entered the den, wrapping him up in a hug. "Rex, how will I ever be able to thank you for what you did?" She backed away. "How did you know?"

"I'll tell you everything, but all that matters now is that you and the kids are okay?"

"We're fine," she said.

"Thank God. That was a close one." Rex glanced at the kids, still sitting at the table. "The kids look good," he said. He waved and smiled.

Over the years, Rex had only seen the kids a few times. Emily had insisted he stay away from the Mitchells. He secretly visited Keri and Ryan in the hospital when Martha was born, but had only seen her twice since. On occasions, when he would see Ryan at work—in flight operations before a trip or on a layover—he would get an update on the family, which always included any recent photos.

"Rex, are you hungry?" Keri said. "Can I fix you a plate of spaghetti?"

"I'm good for now, but a glass of water would be great."

"Come sit down," Ryan said. "We need to hear everything."

Rex joined them at the table. Keri got the water and returned.

Martha asked, "Mommy, who is he?"

"Honey, he helped us escape from the big, white man." Martha seemed to be satisfied with the answer, returning to her "noo noos".

"First," Ryan said, "how did they connect the guy to both situations?"

"After you left the house that night, the guy followed you to the hospital, killed a security guard, and took his uniform. They found the dead security guard stripped down to his underwear, stuffed in the backseat of his car. Then they found the lunatic's SUV. Inside the car, they found a satchel with detailed notes of his entire plot to take out the Golden Gate Bridge. It had dates, times, maps—everything. In addition, the crime lab matched the guy's blood with blood they found mixed in the chemicals on the floor at your house. For some reason, the guy had put some of his own blood into one of the IV lines. All of the blood samples matched his DNA."

"I remember," Keri said. "He had some small bottles of dirty water that he poured into one of the tubes. It must have had some of his blood mixed with it."

"What about the evidence from your house?" Ryan said.

"There was absolutely nothing from my house that could directly tie the guy to both places. Or if there had been, it was conveniently lost or destroyed."

"I always wondered if they might have set you up just to appease the media and the public."

Rex took a sip of water. Changing the subject, he said, "Dude, I'm curious. How did you get out of the jet?"

"I used the emergency rope and climbed out the cockpit window."

"I thought so. I did the same thing." Rex chuckled. "It was fresh on my mind after returning from training."

"You mean *she* was fresh on your mind?" Ryan smiled.

"What are you two talking about?" Keri said. "Who is *she*?"

Ryan turned to Rex with a smile. "Go ahead. You tell her."

"I was just having a little fun," Rex said.

Ryan couldn't hold back. "Rex offered to show a cute, young flight attendant how the pilots use the emergency rope to egress from the cockpit. He took her down to one of the trainers and proceeded to help her demo the equipment." Ryan looked at David and Martha. "I think that's all that needs to be said."

Seeing that David and Martha were finished eating, Keri signed and said, "You can go upstairs now. Play or watch TV. I'll be up in a few minutes." They both pushed back from the table, waved goodbye to Rex, and left."

"Anyway," Rex continued, "the idea of using the emergency rope to get out of the cockpit was fresh on my mind." His face turned somber. "Who would have ever thought they would shoot down a commercial airliner?"

"It was not your fault," Ryan said.

"Maybe not, but it haunts me every day."

Ryan attempted to change the tone of the conversation. The last thing Rex needed was to be reminded of the hundreds of lives lost. "So, if there was no evidence at your house, how did they tie the guy to both places?"

"It's funny," Rex said, unable to let go of the tragedy, "it was my copilot's idea to fly the jet solo while I raced home to try and save Emily. Once I told him the situation, he was gung ho. We knew the lunatic would be watching to see if the flight took off, so we decided to at least get the flight airborne. After that, I left it up to him to decide what to do. I just needed time."

"Was the guy tracking you?"

"All he told me, at the time, was that he would be watching me. He said he was like god. He must have had eyes on me."

"What made you think so?"

"Just before I boarded the plane, I attempted to use a payphone in the terminal to call 911. I had pretty much given up on my being able to save Emily, so I decided to let SWAT handle it. Before I could even lift the receiver, my cell rang. When I answered, he told me if I touched the phone, he would kill Emily. I looked around but saw no one suspicious. In hindsight, I should have never let that jet takeoff. He was going to kill Emily, regardless of what I did. At least all those innocent people would not have died."

"Yeah, but like you said, never in a million years would anyone think our military jets would shoot down a commercial airliner so quickly—if at all. It was out over the ocean and nowhere near a building or populated area."

"I guess they were trigger happy; afraid of repeating 9/11."

"Rex, you need to let it go. You did all you could with what you had to deal with. It's over."

"When I returned to the house, the guy was gone, Emily

was dead. I'll never be able to get the image out of my mind. She had been slaughtered like a sheep using an ancient method for killing animals. A knife had been inserted just behind the point of her jaw," Rex put his finger beneath his jaw to demonstrate, "and below the neck bones, then drawn forward quickly severing the trachea, esophagus, the jugular vein, and carotid artery."

"Rex, that's horrible," Keri said, with her face twisted.

Rex continued, appearing numb to the horror in his words. "The method was supposedly a painless death. The immediate hemorrhaging would have induced anoxia in her brain cells, acting as a powerful painkiller. While still conscious, but totally insensitive to pain, her severe bleeding would have disabled her sensory center, with death occurring within a few minutes. However, if not done correctly and with a sharp knife, she would have experienced great pain and suffering."

"Rex, I am so sorry," Ryan said.

"And the crash scene was plastered over every network on TV," Rex said. "Seeing what he had done to Emily, and seeing the debris of the crashed jet floating on the ocean made me crazy. I was sick, scared, and angry at the same time. I knew that if I didn't act fast, the fear would blind me."

Ryan reflected on the morning he flipped on the TV and first saw the news of the crash. He realized that it was the exact same moment when Rex was in his house experiencing the horror of finding Emily. The thought brought back the same, sick feeling he had that morning.

"I had to pull myself together. Get out. Run. I realized they might try to pin Emily's murder on me."

"Which is exactly what they did," Ryan added.

"I panicked. I literally freaked out. I figured as long as they thought I was dead, they wouldn't be looking for me. I could lay low and see how it turned out."

"Rex," Keri said, "do you realize what would have

happened if you had called the cops?"

"Yeah. I would have spent the last ten months with some ape as a prison mate, while I waited for a jury to sentence me."

She said, "More importantly, if you had called the cops, I would not be alive today. And both David and Martha...." she choked up, unable to finish her statement.

Ryan held her hand and said, "Rex, you made the right call."

"The way I saw it, I had nothing to lose by running. Since I was 'dead', I knew they wouldn't be looking for me."

"What did you do for money? Where did you hide?" Ryan said.

"Money was the least of my worries. Emily had enough jewelry—diamonds, pearls, gold—to fund a small army. I gathered up all the good stuff, along with any cash we had laying around the house, drove my car back to LAX, and parked it in the employee lot. That way, it would look like I never returned to my car. I knew I could get just about anywhere in L.A. on public transportation, so I jumped on the bus from LAX to Union Station, and connected to the Metro to Hollywood.

"I hung out in Hollywood, around Melrose. What better place to blend in than in Hollywood. No shortage of freaks and tourists. I had a couple hundred bucks in cash which was enough for a few nights in a seedy motel. I slowly pawned Emily's jewelry and raised over $50,000, with jewelry to spare. I stayed up in the Hollywood area until my beard grew out."

"You still haven't told me how they ended up tying the guy to both places."

"Oh, yeah, the idiot was nice enough to write me a suicide letter."

"So, he *did* want it to look like a murdered/suicide," Keri said.

"Yeah. I left the note after I decided to run, hoping it

would help them pin it on me. I figured that the sooner they closed the case, the sooner I would be forgotten. I later learned that the forensic handwriting specialist at the OC Crime Lab matched the handwriting on the suicide letter to the handwriting on the papers found in the guy's satchel."

"I didn't know they could actually do that," Keri said. "I thought that was something you did at the fair. I once had my handwriting analyzed at the Georgia State Fair."

"I thought the same thing until the detective straightened me out. What you're talking about is graphology. They sometimes use graphology to profile criminals and aid authorities in their investigation, but true handwriting analysis is a totally different animal. It's a science. The purpose is not to profile the writer but to determine if the same hand produced a document known to have been written by the suspect. That's how they found the guy who kidnapped Charles Lindbergh's infant son back in the '30s. The kidnapper had written a bunch of notes to Lindbergh. Handwriting analysis later linked the notes to Bruno Hauptmann. He was convicted and executed."

"I remember studying that while I was at the Academy," Ryan said.

"So with Keri's testimony of the freak telling her he had killed Emily, the detailed information found in the satchel, along with the handwriting match, they had plenty of evidence to let me go."

"I can't believe it's over," Ryan said.

"Dude, you're not alone."

"Do they know if the guy was working alone? Keri said. "You said someone was watching you at the airport."

"The detective said he could have easily paid people to watch me without them ever knowing why. He might have even hired someone to follow me to the airport. My case was low tech compared to Ryan's. After he screwed up with me, I guess the guy decided to get fancy with all the computers and tracking equipment. They determined that the dead guy in the bathroom was his personal geek—until his services were no longer needed."

Keri said, "I still don't understand how you knew he would be at our house."

"From the beginning, he was very clear. He told me if I didn't do what he said, he would kill my wife and then move on to another family until he accomplished his purpose."

"Yeah, he told me the same thing," Keri said.

Rex reached into his right pants pocket. "There *is* something I didn't show the cops. Along with the suicide note, the guy left a wacky poem." Rex pulled out a folded piece of paper. "In this poem are the clues to who he was and what he was after. It was like some kind of psychopathic puzzle. After tons of research, I finally figured it out."

"Why would he leave clues?" Ryan said. "I guess he hoped it would look like you wrote it."

Rex laughed. "Dude, there is no way I could have written this piece of work…you'll see. But I'm glad the lunatic felt differently. This poem is the *only* reason I was at your house that night. From the clues in this poem, I had a good idea of the approximate time of the month he would strike, the time of day, and was pretty sure it would be our airline."

"How?" Ryan said.

Rex unfolded the piece of paper and handed it to Ryan. "Take a look."

Ryan took the poem and held it where Keri could see. They both read silently.

> *Dear Keroessa, hair so golden, skin so white,*
> *Beneath its cover from captor's sight.*
> *I curse my likeness, filled with spite,*
> *One with you is my only delight.*

I told my soul, be still, and wait,
For there is yet but one more gate.
The third lies over the narrow strait,
He named it golden and sealed its fate.

The first I closed, the last conqueror through,
The second I sealed, to stop the Jew.
The third, named wrongly after you,
Will soon no longer be in view.

On Angel wings, I take flight,
My Freedom from this earthly plight.
Under crescent moon, death fills the night,
This journey ends when all is right.

I'll join you soon, the hours thinning,
When past and future cease their spinning.
I leave this world, forever sinning,
My mother's side, forever grinning.
En ma Fin gît mon Commencement...

CHAPTER 39

When Ryan and Keri finished reading the poem, pointing to the last line, Ryan said, "That looks like what the freak said before he sliced his neck. It sounded like French, but I have no idea what it means."

"And the name, *Keroessa*," Keri said, "was tattooed across his chest."

Keri slid the poem across the table to Rex.

"The poem explains it all—that is, after you decode the psychobabble," Rex said.

"Why didn't you show it to the cops?" Keri said.

"I didn't have it. The night they took you to the hospital, they took me to a safe house. The poem was back at my place in Dana Point."

"I thought you were staying in L.A." Keri said.

"I was until I took a closer look at the poem. I remembered how the guy had told me that if I didn't cooperate, he would keep killing—"

"Me too! He told me the same thing," Keri said.

"Being a total nut job, I figured he must have been committed to the cryptic message in his poem. If so, there was a strong probability he would use our airline again." Rex spun the poem around on the table so Ryan and Keri could see, and said, "Look at these lines.

On Angel wings, I take flight,
My Freedom from this earthly plight.

"Angel is the call sign used by Freedom Airlines. I know it sounds like a stretch, but something about the words *Angel* and *Freedom* being in all caps stood out."

"Even if you knew he was going to try it again using one of Freedom Airlines' planes, why would *you* want to be near Dana Point?" Keri said.

Rex looked to Ryan. "I didn't know which flight he would pick next, but based on the poem, I was fairly certain it would be a late night departure out of LAX. And since my bro flies mostly all-nighters, the odds were pretty high it might be one of Ryan's trips. That's when I left Hollywood and came down to Dana Point. From Dana Point, I could be at your house in a matter of minutes."

"What were you thinking?" Keri said. "Were you planning to do this alone?

"No, but I wanted to be close. I planned to call 911 when I was certain something was going on—which is exactly what I did. And as you can see, I was first on the scene—thankfully."

Anger started creeping into Keri's voice. "Why didn't you tell Ryan about all this? Why didn't you contact him? Why didn't you contact somebody—*anybody*?"

"I couldn't chance it. Plus, I couldn't put Ryan in the position of knowing I was alive, and there was no way I was going to trade my life for a few rhymes about the *Man in the Moon* written by some lunatic. Things were too sketchy. I needed time."

"Rex, you did the right thing," Ryan said. "You didn't have a choice. I would have probably played it the same way."

"Rex, I'm sorry for jumping on you," Keri said. "I can't begin to imagine what you were going through."

"No worries."

"While all this was going on, where in Dana Point did you hide out?" Ryan said.

"Interesting how that worked out." He held back a smile. "By then, I had a full beard with my hair over my ears. I looked like an unemployed surf bum. As fate would have it, I met a chick at the beach—"

"Figures," Ryan said with a smirk.

"Dude, she was no betty; in her forties, covered with tats, been rode hard and put away wet, but not a total swamp donkey; nothing a good pair of beer goggles couldn't fix. But I could tell she was still lookin' for love. Definitely ripe for the pickin'. Sorta like a little Georgia peach I once knew." He glanced at Keri and smiled.

Keri shook her head with disgust.

"She lives alone in Dana Point and works as a waitress at one of the harbor restaurants. She was lonely, needy, and didn't have much of a social life. She works in the afternoons till almost midnight. It was the perfect setup. I drove her to work so I would have a car if I needed it. While she was at work, I used her computer to track all the possible departures and crews."

"How did you access the company website without using your employee information?" Ryan said.

"Easy. I used your name and password. That gave me full access to schedules and crews."

Ryan scratched his head. "How did you get my password?"

"Dude, we exchanged passwords back when we were new hires."

"Oh, yeah, I forgot. Okay, let's get back to the poem. I'm dying to unpack this thing and see how you deciphered it."

"Some of it jumped off the page. For example," Rex pointed to a section of the poem.

For there is yet but one more gate.
The third lies over the narrow strait,
He named it golden and sealed its fate.

"Where else could it be other than the Golden Gate Bridge in San Francisco?"

"Yeah, that looks pretty straight forward," Ryan said. "But who was *He*?

"*He* was John C. Fremont. He was the man that named the Golden Gate Strait. Fremont named the strait after the Golden Horn in Istanbul. I think that is what must have ticked off the lunatic the most."

"Interesting," Ryan said.

"I always thought the name was somehow attributed to California's Gold Rush," Keri said.

"That's a common belief," Rex said.

"And I assume you knew it would be at night when you read the part about the moon," Keri said, pointing to the line in the poem she was referring to:

Under crescent moon, death fills the night,

Keri said. "I'll never forget watching the minutes and seconds tick away on the computer screen." She glanced at Ryan and squeezed his hand.

"So you must have narrowed it down to a certain time of the month based on the crescent moon," Ryan said. "The moon only appears as a crescent for two weeks of the month— the week before and the week after the black moon, or the new moon."

"Dude, I didn't know you were into selenology."

"Well, that makes us even. I didn't know you were into two syllable words." Ryan smiled. "I took an astronomy class at the Academy. What's your excuse?"

Keri said, "What the heck is selenology?"

"A word that makes me look smarter than I am," Rex said. "Selenology is the astronomical study of the moon—something I did *way* too much of." There are tons of websites that show the lunar phases for any given month, so that was a no brainer."

"Why was this guy so intent on taking out the bridge under a crescent moon?" Keri said.

"I'm getting to that. First, you have to understand that this guy was living in another world. He could have easily been wearing a tinfoil hat."

"Talk about a 'no brainer'," Keri said.

"I quickly accepted that our guy was not your typical, radical terrorist simply trying to blow up something for a cause. He was more complex than that—possibly a total psycho. There was no doubt he wanted to make a statement. Based on the poem, his underlying motives were based on a delusional belief he was fulfilling some sort of journey into a past life that was totally from mythology."

"Mythology? Wow! I knew this guy was delusional, but *mythology*?" Keri said.

Rex pointed to the last line in the poem:

En ma Fin gît mon Commencement.

"Ryan, you mentioned this earlier, and you were correct, it is French. Translated, it means, *In my beginning my end lies*, or better said, *In my end is my beginning.*"

"You are full of surprises," Ryan said. "First, two syllable words. Now, French?"

"Bonjour Mademoiselle," Rex said in a horrible French accent. "The Rexter must always be prepared."

"Ryan, stop joking around and let him finish," Keri said.

"Merci, Mademoiselle." Rex continued. "Notice, also, where he said" Rex pointed to the poem:

This journey ends when all is right.

"Combined with the last line, it's pretty clear this guy was into reincarnation."

"Reincarnation? That makes perfect sense. He constantly alluded to death like it was irrelevant," Keri said.

"These lines," Rex said, pointing to the poem, "are the puzzle pieces that led me to his two, key past lives." He read:

The first I closed, the last conqueror through,
The second I sealed, to stop the Jew.

"What was he closing and sealing?" Keri said.

"Gates—both golden—just like our Golden Gate in San Francisco. When I googled *gate—conqueror through— crescent moon*, Mehmet the Conqueror popped up. I learned that the lunatic was referring to the imperial entrance gate to the city of Constantinople, present-day Istanbul, Turkey, built by Theodosius the Great to celebrate his victory over Magnus Maximus. It just so happened that it was named the Golden Gate. Our guy was under the delusion that, in a past life, he was Mehmet—*the last conqueror through*. It was on Tuesday, May 29th, 1453, and from what I read, it was a bloody mess."

"Why did Mehmet close the gate in Constantinople?" Keri asked.

"Well, as the story goes, immediately after his victory, Mehmet ordered the Golden Gate sealed, due to a Turkish prophecy that said, *Constantinople will be conquered, the best prince is its prince and the best army is that army.* The prophecy declared that through this gate the next conquerors would enter Constantinople."

"What about the second gate—the one that was sealed?" Ryan asked.

"After I found the first gate, the second one was easy. I

googled *Jew—golden gate—crescent moon*. It took me to the Golden Gate in Jerusalem. Mehmet's great grandson, the Ottoman Sultan Suleyman the Magnificent, bricked up the Golden Gate in Israel in 1541, allegedly believing it would stop, Elijah and the Messiah—both Jews—from passing through. How crazy is that?"

"Freaky," Ryan said.

"Yeah, I couldn't believe it, either. The Bible even prophesied that the Golden Gate in Jerusalem would one day be sealed—long before it happened. It also says that it will be opened at the time of the New Moon—the waning crescent— when the Messiah returns. I'm not sure, but our wacko might have been into opposites—like a yin for a yang or 'For every action, there is an equal and opposite reaction'—that sort of thing. If so, he might have thought that instead of opening gates on the crescent, that it would be the perfect time to close them."

"The more you get into this, the weirder it becomes," Keri said.

"Yeah, trust me; this rabbit hole goes as deep as you care to fall. Everything this guy did was motivated totally by his twisted belief in reincarnation, mythology, metaphysics, prophecy, numerology, astrology...you name it. There came a point, once I had what I needed, I stopped digging."

"That must mean that there was a crescent moon on both July 11, 2002 and May 29, 2003—the dates of our flights," Ryan said.

"You guessed it. July 11th was a crescent new moon and May 29th was three days before the crescent new moon. For the lunatic, it was more about a common purpose he shared with all of his, so-called, past lives. History says Mehmet sealed the Golden Gate to ensure he was the one fulfilling the prophecy, and Suleyman sealed the Golden Gate in Jerusalem to stop the Messiah. Our man thinks that when he was Mehmet and Suleyman, he sealed the Golden Gate in Turkey and Israel for the same reason he wanted the Golden Gate Bridge in San Francisco taken out. To him, it has always been the same motive of his soul, even while in a different body."

"My head is spinning," Keri said.

"I know what you mean. Like a kaleidoscope. But there's a big piece of the puzzle I haven't told you yet. This is where the mythical part comes in, so as our friend, Cipher, said in the movie *The Matrix*, 'Buckle up Dorothy, 'cause Kansas, is going bye-bye'." Rex pointed to the first and last stanzas in the poem and read:

> *Dear Keroessa, hair so golden, skin so white,*
> *Beneath its cover from captor's sight.*
> *I curse my likeness, filled with spite,*
> *One with you is my only delight.*

> *I'll join you soon, the hours thinning,*
> *When past and future cease their spinning.*
> *I leave this world, forever sinning,*
> *My mother's side, forever grinning.*

"Keroessa is the accepted English spelling of the Greek name, Khrysokeras or Chrysoceras. In Greek mythology, Io was a mistress of Zeus that was changed into a white cow in an attempt to hide her from his wife, Hera. The dude should have talked to me before trying such a stupid trick."

Keri laughed.

Rex shot her a glance and continued. "Hera, like most women, picked up on Zeus' little trick, pronto." He looked back at Keri and smirked. She smiled. "Zeus thought he could escape Hera's wrath by offering the white cow to her as a gift. After graciously accepting it, she cursed the cow and sent it wandering the Earth, tortured by a stinging gadfly, driving the poor cow further from home. The cow eventually crossed what is now the Bosphorus Strait in Turkey, giving the strait its name (boos-foros, which is Greek for cow-ford). The white cow settled on the shores of what is now the Golden Horn River where Zeus supposedly reached out and touched the cow, lifting Hera's curse and restoring the cow to her youthful beauty.

"Later impregnated by the divine sperm of Zeus, Io gave birth to a daughter, Keroessa (Chrysoceras: Chryso-gold; ceras-horn). When Keroessa was born, she carried the scars of her mother's transformation: there were two projections on both sides of her forehead, like horns. It was because of her golden hair and the little horns on her forehead that the mythical nymphs along the river named her Keroessa. In Greek mythology, Keroessa later bore a son to Poseidon. This son, in time, became the founder of Byzantium and named the Golden Horn (Chrysoceras) after his mother, Keroessa (Chrysoceras). The freak must have figured he was an albino because of his grandmother, the white cow."

"You've got to be kidding," Keri said.

"Look. It's right here in the poem,

I curse my likeness, filled with spite.

"Must have been something in the gene pool. The last, little tidbit is that Byzas was the founder of Byzantium (later named Constantinople, and then Istanbul). So there we have it—full circle."

"Sounds like Rex and Zeus could have been matched up in a past life," Keri said.

"Keri," Ryan said, "don't rule it out so fast."

She laughed.

"Dude, Zeus couldn't hold a candle to me in my younger days."

"So let me see if I got this right," Ryan said. "This lunatic thinks he, in past lives, sealed the two golden gates as Mehmet and Suleyman and, in his current life, was attempting to take out the Golden Gate Bridge, all for the same reason?"

"Sounds crazy, I know, but, like I said, this guy was *one* messed up dude. When I got inside his head, I figure he considered all three golden gates to be a mockery to someone he loved. For him, Mehmet and Suleyman did what they did for the same reason—not what was told in history."

"Wow. Wow. Wow," Keri said.

"Yeah, the dude was definitely trippin'," Rex said.

"Rex, I must say, I'm impressed," Ryan said. "I will never be able to thank you enough for what you did."

"Thanks, Dude. I've got your back. I'm sure you would have done the same for me."

Keri stood up and hugged Rex. "Thank you."

"Wow. A hug and a thank you from my ex," Rex said. "Looks like my work is done here." They all chuckled.

"So, what are your plans?" Ryan said. "Think you'll go back to the airline?"

"Not so sure the company will want me back."

"That's crazy talk. I'll bet they will give you full back pay and a hero's welcome. I wouldn't be surprised if they made you Chief Pilot."

"Dude. Get real. I'm sure I'll be hearing from them once this hits the news."

Ryan's cell phone rang. He pulled it from his pocket and flipped it open. "Hello."

"Are you watching?" the voice said.

Ryan looked to Keri and Rex and said, "It's Chuck Smith." They both smiled. "Watching what?"

"The news. The story broke tonight."

"Which channel?"

"All of them. Just turn your TV on."

"Chuck says the story is out. All over the news."

Rex jumped up and flipped on the TV. The FOX News Channel came on. "We got it," Ryan told Chuck. "I'll talk to you later." Ryan flipped his cell closed.

While the reporter summarized the events of Ryan's flight, photos of Ryan in his uniform—a much younger Ryan—flashed on the screen.

"Dude, you're a hero," Rex said. "But look at that mug shot. Must've been taken ten years ago."

"Has to be older than that. That was taken back when I first made captain."

The reporter transitioned to the tragedy of Rex's flight. After a few well-spoken words, remembering those that died and the loss that many suffered, the reporter told of the miraculous survival of Captain Rex Dean.

After a brief mention of Emily's death, the reporter followed with how Rex Dean had heroically saved the lives of Ryan's wife and two children. Photos of Rex in his uniform, smiling big, filled the screen.

"Looks like you got your job back if you want it," Ryan said.

"How 'bout you? You going back?"

"I'm done." Ryan looked at Keri. "We still haven't decided what's next, but I'm hangin' it up."

"Dude, I don't blame you. Things have changed a lot since we first started. To be honest, I'm not so sure what I'll do. Maybe I'll write a book, get a movie deal, make millions, and then go surf my life away."

"Yeah, and with that new enhanced two syllable vocabulary of yours, you might even be able to write something other than a children's book."

"Funny," Rex said sarcastically. "I'll be sure to save you a part in the movie."

"Rex, you must be starving. Can I fix you a plate of spaghetti now?" Keri said.

"That would be awesome."

CHAPTER 40

After a plate of spaghetti, Rex headed back to Dana Point to explain his disappearance and real identity to his girlfriend. David and Martha were asleep, and Ryan and Keri were preparing for bed.

"That was pretty amazing," Ryan said after rinsing the toothpaste from his mouth.

"Yeah, a lot to take in. But for the first time, I feel like it is over; a big load off my mind."

"I'm so happy for Rex. Do you think he will continue flying?"

"Depends if he gets his movie deal or not."

"No, seriously."

"I'm more interested in what's next for us. With you not flying, we're going to have to come up with some way to pay the bills."

"If we sell the house, we should clear almost $50,000 in equity, maybe more. The housing market is booming right now. And maybe I can sell my story, or at least get a few networks to pay me for an appearance. Who knows, Oprah might be interested."

"Whatever we decide, we need to be sure that David has the best possible education." Keri slipped out of her clothes and into a nightgown. Ryan caught a glimpse. Even after all the years, he still felt the spark. For the first time in several years, the uncertainty of the future didn't stress him, as it once did. He had Keri, and that was all that mattered.

"I agree." Ryan flipped off the bathroom light and followed Keri into the bedroom. A cool breeze from an open window stirred the air. They climbed into bed.

"It would be nice to sell this house," Keri said. "I really don't want anything to remind me, or the kids, of that night."

"Definitely. That was a nightmare we all want to forget."

"Speaking of nightmares, I'm thankful yours has not returned."

"Yeah, I've been sleeping a lot better."

Keri put her hand on his bare chest and kissed him. "I'm so happy, and I love you so much. I think our dark days are behind us for now."

"I certainly hope so." Ryan took her hand in his and stroked it softly. "As Rex was talking tonight, I had mini-flashbacks of things from my dream."

"Like what?"

"For example, in my dream—the last one I had—do you remember me telling you that Rex was the pilot?"

"Yeah, you said it was the first time you could put a name to one of the pilots in your dream."

"In that dream, he took the emergency rope down and dove out of the window, just like he and I both did—except, not in mid flight."

"It makes you wonder if it was prophetic in ways."

"Yeah. And then there was the time when the copilot looks at me and says, 'Freedom is found in hope. You must not forget that. Everyone is depending on you. If you don't find the answers, we will all die. It's up to you. Everything is up to you. You must find freedom! Time is running out!'"

"You never told me about *that*."

"There were a few things Rex said tonight that made

certain phrases from the dream pop into my mind with unusual clarity. In the dream, I remember Rex saying, 'Act, don't think! Everything you need is here. You'll find the answers in the here. Don't let your fear blind you, get busy!'"

"What does that mean?"

"I'm not sure, but I know I heard Rex say something tonight about fear blinding him. I think it was when he found Emily. Maybe my dream was some sort of subliminal warning of things to come. Perhaps my subconscious was trying to communicate with my mind."

"I didn't know we could dream like that."

"The one thing I can't figure out is the book the copilot in my dream was reading. I remember the copilot say, 'it's inspiring'. Then he marked his place with a two-dollar bill, of all things."

"If he marked his place in the book, it meant he was obviously not finished reading the story. Maybe that has something to do with our future. Oh! I know! It must be the story of our life. The two-dollar bill represents the two of us, and since he marked his place in the novel, he was trying to tell you that there is more to our story. And look at us now. We are all safe, and our life is beginning a new chapter— hopefully one filled with happy days." She kissed him again.

"I think you are right, or at least I'm going to have faith that you are right."

"Did this book have a title, or should we make up our own. Maybe something like *Forever Happy* or *Too Good To Be True*."

"Now that you mention it, I do remember one word on the cover of the book: *Freedom*."

"I've got it! *Finding Freedom*."

"Or how about, *Flight to Freedom*?"

"That's even better. Fantastic! We will 'mount up with wings like eagles', like it says in the Bible, and soar off into a new chapter of our lives."

Having lived through the darkest days in his life, Ryan saw the future through new eyes. The things he once feared no longer shackled him to the demons of anxiety, worry, and fear. His faith was new and strong. He had a renewed sense of hope. The darkness had lifted.

The old adage he often heard his mother call upon when hope seemed to have taken wings and flown away popped into his head, "It's always darkest before the dawn." Again, she had been right.

He and Keri held each other and kissed, rekindling the fires of passion. The love he had for Keri had grown deeper than he had thought humanly possible. He had never loved her more than he did at that moment.

He whispered a prayer of thanks to God for what he had been forced to endure, for it was in those dark hours that he was given new eyes, a new heart, and a renewed faith.

He and Keri were now ready to embark on their *Flight to Freedom*.

THE END

AUTHOR'S NOTE

Times of personal darkness (discouragement, disappointment, sickness, and loss) come in many shades from gray to black: a flat tire, chipped tooth, rebellious child, job loss, financial hardship, marital conflict, natural disaster, family dispute, divorce, act of violence, unfaithful or abusive spouse, health problems, abusive parent, death of a loved one, physical or mental handicap, painful terminal disease, and many, many more examples.

It's one thing when dark episodes in our life are the result of the painful consequences of our own foolish mistakes, but it is quite a different thing when people who love God—who are serving Him faithfully—are ambushed by extremely difficult, dark times. When that happens, it is easy to question whether God really cares or not.

Flight into Darkness was inspired by one man who, in my opinion, experienced three of the darkest days humanly imaginable. Staring at the dark road ahead, he quickly surrendered, trusted, and moved on faith, even though he didn't understand or know how things would turn out. It is a story of love, trust, faith, and obedience. That man's name was Abraham.

Abraham and Isaac: *God said, "Abraham!"*

"Yes?" answered Abraham. "I'm listening."

He said, "Take your dear son Isaac whom you love and go to the land of Moriah. Sacrifice him there as a burnt offering on one of the mountains that I'll point out to you."

Abraham got up early in the morning and saddled his donkey. He took two of his young servants and his son Isaac. He had split wood for the burnt offering. He set out for the place God had directed him.

On the third day he looked up and saw the place in the distance. Abraham told his two young servants, "Stay here with the donkey. The boy and I are going over there to worship; then we'll come back to you."

Abraham took the wood for the burnt offering and gave it to Isaac his son to carry. He carried the flint and the knife. The two of them went off together.

Isaac said to Abraham his father, "Father?"

"Yes, my son."

"We have flint and wood, but where's the sheep for the burnt offering?"

Abraham said, "Son, God will see to it that there's a sheep for the burnt offering."

And they kept on walking together. They arrived at the place to which God had directed him. Abraham built an altar. He laid out the wood. Then he tied up Isaac and laid him on the wood. Abraham reached out and took the knife to kill his son.

Just then an angel of GOD called to him out of Heaven, "Abraham! Abraham!"

"Yes, I'm listening."

"Don't lay a hand on that boy! Don't touch him! Now I know how fearlessly you fear God; you didn't hesitate to place your son, your dear son, on the altar for me."

Abraham looked up. He saw a ram caught by its horns in the thicket. Abraham took the ram and sacrificed it as a burnt offering instead of his son. (Genesis 22:1-13 MSG)

Isaac was in his early teens when he headed out that morning with his father. There was no doubt he trusted and loved his father, just as Abraham loved his son—the heir for who's birth he had waited so long and on who his promises from God depended.

On the third day, loaded down with wood and walking with his father toward *the place in the distance*, Isaac said, "We have flint and wood, but where's the sheep for the burnt offering?"

Putting myself in Abraham's place, my heart sinks in despair as I contemplate how I might have answered my young son. Possibly: "Son, keep your eyes open. I'm sure a sheep will come along soon." Or, "Son, there are times when we must step into the darkness and hope there will be solid ground beneath our foot." Or, "Oh, I didn't tell you? God wants me to use you as the sacrifice instead of a sheep." Or, "No sheep? What was I thinking? I guess we'd better turn around and go home."

But Abraham, without missing a step, continued toward *the place in the distance* as he replied to his son, "Son, God will see to it that there's a sheep for the burnt offering."

I must remind myself that Abraham was just as human as I am today. He was fully aware of what God was asking him to do. To him it was—as it would have been to me—beyond logic and human reason. I know this because he left the house without telling Sarah (his wife) what he intended to do. Obviously, he felt it would be too much for her to understand.

Abraham's unwavering faith was only possible because he believed and trusted that God had a plan, even up until the moment when it appeared that all hope was lost as he *reached out and took the knife to kill his son.*

During the time I was writing *Flight into Darkness* (2006 to 2011), I experienced several dark episodes in my life, similar to those of the character, Ryan Mitchell. While in the midst of my darkness, I often felt like Job, who *hoped for good* but only *evil came*; and for *light*, but found only *darkness*. (Job 30:26, NIV) Or like Isaiah, who uttered: *We look for light but find only darkness. We look for bright skies but walk in gloom. We grope like the blind along a wall, feeling our way like people without eyes. Even at brightest noontime, we stumble as though it were dark. Among the living, we are like the dead.* (Isaiah 59:9-10, NLT)

When I reflect back and read my journal notes during that time—even the chapters in this novel—I see how the trials of my faith were not empty or meaningless. As a result of my dark years, I can now join with Ryan when he acknowledges in the last few lines of the story—*for it was in those dark hours that he was given new eyes, a new heart, and a renewed faith.*

Most of us do not jump for joy at the thought of dark times or the prospect of brokenness, but instead, we naturally run in the opposite direction. However, God loves us so much that He doesn't let us get very far. The darkness is God's way of turning us around and forcing us to allow Him to do whatever is necessary in our lives to purge our souls and spirits so that we can have intimate fellowship with Him—the place of perfect peace—free from all fears and darkness.

Jesus said, *"I am the light of the world, whoever follows me will never walk in darkness, but will have the light of life."* John 8:12

Flight to Freedom
(Flight Trilogy – Book 3)

Three months have passed since *Darkness* traumatized the Mitchell family, May 29, 2003. In hopes of a new beginning—a new life—Ryan Mitchell quits his good-paying airline job, uproots his young family, and moves to Buckhead, Georgia from Southern California.

On moving day, Ryan reflects on the past twenty-nine years of his life—mostly the mistakes he wishes he could erase. He considers the impossible and asks Keri, *"If you could live your life over, what would you do differently?"*

Surprisingly, his far-fetched question is the harbinger of seven, life-altering scenarios that uncover a miracle.

In this unexpected, puzzling, yet satisfying conclusion to the *Flight Trilogy*, readers are warned to buckle up and stay alert. Captain Ryan Mitchell is about to take you on the flight of your life—strange and mysterious, yet full of hope.